THE LOVE KNOT

THE
LOVE KNOT

CATHERINE DARBY

St. Martin's Press
New York

Library of Congress Cataloging-in-Publication Data

Darby, Catherine.
    The love knot.
    1. Chaucer, Geoffrey, d. 1400, in fiction, drama,
poetry, etc.   2. Great Britain—History—Lancaster and
York, 1399–1485—Fiction.   I. Title.
PR6066.E744L68   1991   823'.914   90-15548
ISBN 0-312-04996-X

First published in Great Britain by Robert Hale Limited.

First U.S. Edition: February 1991
10 9 8 7 6 5 4 3 2 1

Prologue

In times to come the poets and the chroniclers will write
about us all. I've no doubt of that. When did they not
write about their betters? Twisting the truth and filling
up the gaps with fantasy. I've not much patience with
them to tell you plainly. I've got a reputation for
speaking plain though there's much I've never spoken
about at all. I've kept my own counsel for years, hidden
my heart. After I'm gone they will probably say that I
never had a heart at all, never felt the pangs of a love
unreturned, nor the joy of a lovesong answered. They
will probably make out that I was plain of face too, the
better to contrast me with my sister. When I look in the
glass I have to admit that I never did possess her
spectacular beauty, but I've always been well favoured.
Small but shapely, with a clear skin that no pockmark
ever disfigured and brown eyes and hair glinted with
amber. Of course when Katherine was by she eclipsed
me as the sun does the moon, but the moon has her own
loveliness when she is allowed to hang alone in the night
sky.

They will probably make out that we were low born
too, which never was so. Our father, Sir Paon de Roet,
was from an ancient and noble Gascon family and he
wed a maid of sound lineage from Picardy. We have
nothing to be ashamed about when it comes to
comparing family trees. He fought bravely, did my
father, and was created Herald Guienne, welcome at

5

Court and respected by King Edward. That was the English Court, though my sister and I were reared during our early years in Picardy. If I close my eyes I can see the manor house now, drowsing in the sunshine, and myself very small just out of leading reins and Katherine at my mother's breast. Three years separated my sister and me, and when she was born I thought of her as a doll to cherish. Even after everything that happened I still cherished her after my fashion. Certainly there was never any open breach to divide us. I couldn't really blame her, you see. As well blame a rose when one is only a daisy. And looking back I cannot even bring myself to blame the one who plucked us both. Now doesn't that show my forgiving nature? That's something my husband will never write about, because he too has been forgiven, and husbands don't like to think of that. 'Busy as usual, wife?' he says, coming into the room where I sit sewing. His voice is indulgent. Once that irritated me, but nowadays I smile with the corners of my mouth tucked in.

Certainly I am busy. I have never been one to sit idly by when there is work to be done. My lady mother was strict about that, teaching us both how to keep house, for when we were married we couldn't hope for the obedience of our servants unless we knew how to perform their tasks as well as they could themselves. So as soon as we could toddle we were set small tasks in house and garden, the growing of plants to be pounded into simples or steeped in wine to yield cordials and tisanes for the relief of illness; we learned also how to preserve meat by smoking it slowly and fruit by covering it with wine and honey; we spent a due portion of time rubbing the furniture with beeswax and taking turns to milk the cows and feed the chickens.

Those tasks have always given me pleasure, though Katherine liked them less. She was one for merriment, singing and dancing and playing upon the lute, but to my mind the most satisfying thing in the world is to beat cream until it be thick and add honey or almond, or to seize a besom and clear a room of stale rushes. When my hands are occupied my mind can roam free, and my husband might be astonished if he could open my skull and look into my brain.

It wasn't all housewifery, of course. Our parents planned to match us well, and so we were given instruction in reading and writing too, and lessons in courtesy and music and fine needlework. At the latter I always excelled. I took great delight in tracing patterns on canvas and silk with glowing colours that captured all the hues of the seasons. Now that I am past my middle years embroidery is my chief occupation. It tires me less than other work and my mind still roams free through all the meadows of my childhood.

They say that as one grows older the past becomes clearer. In one way that's true. I can see the past vividly but when I try to fit myself into it my heart begins to jerk with remembered pain. It is easier for me to stand aside and look at myself and those about me as if they were all separate beings, dolls moving about on the surface of my memory. Two little dolls with the toy manor house behind them and then a storm to sweep the manor house away.

One

(i)

In thirteen forty-nine plague stalked Europe, skull-visaged, gibbering. It had been creeping across the land and sea for nearly three years, but the full flowering of its horror was in that year. In that year a quarter of the population died. Some of them – and they were fortunate – fell down between one breath and the next, twitched and lay still. Others saw the rose-shaped blisters puff upon their flesh and turn black, and suffered cruelly before they lay in their own shit and vomit with jaws clenched in agony. Nobody could find any cure, though there were many to suggest a cause.

It was God's punishment for sin, the preachers said, for He'd no longer ignore the evil that men did in fornicating, killing, stealing, coveting, not to mention downright perversions like the females who put on doublet and hose and competed in the tourney. There were a few to murmur that disease bred in filth, was borne by the black rats that infested the waterfront and bred among the grain, but outward dirt was only a symbol of the dark soul within, and cries for repentance mingled with the lewd songs bawled by drunken revellers who had decided that if Death joined the party they personally intended to be too far gone in drink and lechery to notice.

There was no revelry at the Roet manor, but the Demoiselle de Roet died all the same, thinking it God's mercy that she had time to give instructions regarding her two small daughters. They would go to her cousin in Gascony and thence to England where their father would have to bestir himself on their behalf, and time he did too instead of trailing round after the Plantagenet Court with dreams of advancement in his head.

She had checked her resentful thoughts and given her orders, gasping a little with the pain that griped her bowels, and her steward, cloak wrapped about his mouth and nose as he stood at a prudent distance, had nodded and gone to do her bidding. The children had been excited at the prospect of a ride and not until they were clear of the manor lands did seven-year-old Philippa notice that they carried supplies of food and a change of clothing bursting over the top of a hastily fastened saddle-bag. She started to ask a question but was checked by the steward's frown, and held her peace, only half listening to the prattling of her little sister as she jogged along on her fat pony.

Perhaps they were going to pay a visit to a neighbour's, she thought hopefully, but when they reached the great oak that marked the boundary of their neighbour's land she saw a great red cross flaming upon the gnarled trunk and the first taste of fear soured her mouth. The fear grew and swelled as they came to the village and she beheld the same red cross painted upon the signpost. The steward took a side track that avoided the main street, and from the way he hurried their mounts along she guessed that he too tasted terror. Their father's lands being close to the border they were in Gascony within a couple of hours and Philippa's spirits rose a little. They had visited Cousin Mathilde the year before and stayed for a week. It had been a pleasant week with other children to play with and later bedtimes than usual. Perhaps Mama had planned a treat for them. Philippa, who loved treats, sat up straighter and glared at Katherine who had begun to whine.

But when they came to the timbered house where Cousin Mathilde lived the red cross was scrawled across the front door. Looking at it and then tilting her chin to peer at the steward Philippa felt tears gather in her throat. His face was stern and set and she knew something was very wrong.

'We'd best make for the port,' he said, speaking as if she were an adult and would know exactly what he was talking about.

She nodded her small head gravely, blinking back tears. Whatever was happening would be explained in time and meanwhile she must bear in mind that she was a great girl of seven who must set Katherine an example.

'The little one,' she reminded him now, 'wants to piss.'

'I pissed already,' Katherine said blandly, looking down at a dark trickle that crept from beneath her kirtle.

'Are we to go back?' Philippa said cautiously.

'I told you already – we go to the port,' the steward answered. He sounded cross. Philippa said quickly and placatingly,

'She does not often wet herself. It was the jogging of the pony.'

He nodded curtly, catching at the leading-reins of their ponies and swinging aside from the silent, cross-scrawled house.

She had expected him to find lodging at an inn but he rode on beyond the town and drew to a halt in a cornfield.

'Best we lie here tonight,' he said, dismounting and lifting Katherine down. Philippa stared at him in astonishment. Only vagrants slept out in the fields and were often whipped at the market-place for it. But he was taking out the food and spreading blankets in the shallow ditch as if it were the most natural thing in the world. All was not well in her world. Sensing this she held back her questions, knowing in some deep unchildlike part of herself that she wouldn't want to hear the answers.

Katherine had accepted the situation in her usual lighthearted way and was dancing about amid the corn stooks, having probably wet herself again, her older sister thought critically. At least she wasn't whining and grizzling to go home. Philippa set her own small chin and began to help the steward to drag the blankets into the ditch.

They ate most of the food that had been packed and filled their water bottles up at a little stream that flowed through the lower part of the meadow. Philippa recalled what the steward had said about going to the port, and plucked at his sleeve.

'Are we to go on a ship?' she asked.

'Aye, to England,' he answered, thankful that she hadn't asked anything more difficult. 'I'm to take you to your father on account of the plague.'

Philippa opened her mouth to enquire when her lady mother would be following, and closed it again without uttering a sound. Suddenly, as if someone had shone a bright light into the darkest corner of her mind, she understood what the red crosses meant. She had not looked back at the manor house as they trotted away, but she knew as clearly as if she had seen it there would be a great scarlet cross scrawled upon the door. The tears that had been in her throat gushed into her eyes and rolled silently down her cheeks.

'Now, Mistress Philippa,' the steward said uncomfortably, 'a great girl of seven doesn't cry for nothing. Your sister will be affrighted.'

She wanted to say that she wasn't crying for nothing, but the words wouldn't come, and Katherine was rubbing her eyes sleepily and starting to whine. At seven a child reached the age of reason. Mama had told her that. She wiped her face swiftly with her sleeve and put her arm around Katherine, pinning a crooked little smile to her lips.

Perhaps it would all come right and when they reached the port Mama and the ship would be waiting. Meanwhile she must remember she had reached the age of reason and not cry.

(ii)

The two gentlemen who sat together in the twilight of the summer evening were a contrast in styles. The taller of the two wore a tunic of magpie silk, and a cloak so splendidly trimmed with fur that it would have been impossible to guess that he was actually in mourning had it not been for his grave face, a handsome, high-nosed face that had been winked at by more than one tavern wench. His companion was shorter and stouter, also clad in black, his expression one of interested attention.

'I have sent for word of my wife,' the former was saying, 'but I am already sure that she is dead. She would never have sent the children else.'

'And you are on the point of returning to France.' The other nodded. 'I appreciate your difficulty, Sir Paon.'

'There isn't time to take them to London even if I wished to do so,' the tall knight said.

'The plague still rages there, far more fiercely than even here,' the other said. 'I thank God hourly that I brought my family here to the outskirts of Southampton away from the harbour. Even here we may yet be stricken, though there are rumours the sickness has passed its peak. Perhaps your good lady survived.'

Sir Paon shook his head, his long fingers plucking at the border of his cloak.

'She did not even bid farewell to the children,' he said. 'She would not allow any servant to go near them save my steward who had the plague three years ago and recovered. He tells me that he avoided towns and brought the girls straight here. I have ordered him to return to do whatever is needful for the upkeep of my land until I can travel there.'

'And your children?'

'Her Grace the Queen would take them under her wing but she is still in mourning for the Princess Joanna, and meanwhile –'

His pause was hopeful. His companion pulled thoughtfully at his beard and weighed up possibilities. When he spoke his voice was soothing.

'You have indeed suffered a great loss, Sir Paon. Alas, you are not alone in that. My own half-brother, my uncle and my cousin were victims of the disease too. Certainly your daughters must be lodged until the attention of the Queen can be drawn to them. My own position in life is modest but I shall be glad to take the children under my wing for a short time. My wife, Agnes, will approve my decision.'

'I shall leave sufficient for their board, Master Chaucer,' the knight said gratefully.

'Make yourself easy on that score.' John Chaucer held up his hand. 'Thank God my affairs go well.'

He had in fact just profited from the ill wind that had removed three of his relatives from the world. Their not inconsiderable holdings would revert to him and swell his already bulging coffers. As son and grandson of a merchant, married to the widow of a wealthy vintner, John Chaucer suspected that he could have bought and sold the handsome knight who sat opposite him for all Sir Paon de Roet's proud lineage. Unfortunately the polite world took more account of past ancestry than present prosperity.

'I shall be honoured to undertake the care of your daughters until they can be housed more fittingly,' he insisted. 'They are in the hall still?'

'I didn't care to leave them alone at a tavern,' Sir Paon said.

'My wife will already be making them comfortable,' John Chaucer said.

That was not precisely the word that Philippa would have used. The details of the ride to the port, of the four-day voyage during which Katherine had scarcely stopped vomiting, and the steward had succumbed to the same ailment, were still vivid. When they landed at Southampton she had been terrified by the bustle and noise of the dockside and the sight of her father, rising from the chair in his lodgings, had done nothing to console her for he had taken one look at the steward's face and said heavily,

'The news you bring must be evil.'

Philippa hadn't heard the news since her father had bundled her and Katherine into a corner while the two adults talked for a long time. Then he had gone out and a girl with untidy hair had brought them bread and milk.

Now the two small girls sat side by side on a low settle by the door screen and held hands forlornly. Katherine was still weak after all the vomiting and so was better behaved than usual, but Philippa knew that soon she would start whining again.

The house to which their father had brought them was one in a row of tall, narrow houses, each with a walled garden and a stableyard at the back. A large florid-complexioned man had taken Sir Paon into an inner chamber and a brisk woman had come in and looked at them and gone away again without saying anything.

After what seemed like a very long time the two men

came in again, and Master Chaucer bent down to address Philippa.

'So, Mistress Philippa, you and your sister are to visit with us for a while,' he said. 'I think that we can entertain you until you go to the Queen.'

Philippa wanted to ask about her mother, but she feared the answer too greatly, and her quick eyes had noted that her father had changed into black. He bent in his turn, giving her an awkward hug and lifting Katherine into his arms.

'Be good little wenches for Mistress Chaucer now, and I will see you when I am come back from France,' he said.

'I want to go home,' Katherine said suddenly and opened her pink mouth to roar.

'Leave her to me, Sir Paon.' The brisk woman had appeared again and took the small girl into her own embrace, saying firmly, 'Now, my kitten, we must find you some supper and a nightgown for what you've brought will not suffice.'

Katherine was unmollified by this speech and began to howl lustily whereupon Mistress Chaucer held her more firmly and marched off.

'You are not going to behave so badly, are you?' Sir Paon said anxiously.

'No, Father.' Philippa swallowed hard, reminding herself that she had reached the age of reason, and dropped a neat curtsy. 'I wish you Godspeed.'

'That's my good girl.' Sir Paon patted her head and turned hastily away. There was a look on his face that made Philippa dreadfully afraid that he was going to cry, but he went out instead and Master Chaucer, walking beside him, said,

'Little by little she'll come to realise it.'

They were both fools, she thought achingly, because she had guessed long before that her mother had died, and this might be the last time she ever saw her father since men who went to war frequently got killed. Hastily she crossed herself lest the thought bring him bad luck, and then Mistress Chaucer returned, telling her to make haste since there wasn't all night to get them bedded down. It was a lie because the night had scarcely begun, but Philippa wisely refrained from pointing out the fact. She suffered herself to be given a mess of oatmeal and stripped of her travel-soiled clothes and put into a nightgown that was several sizes too large for her. It was the first nightgown she had ever worn since at home everybody went to bed naked or in their shift. The Chaucers must be very rich, she decided, and then the tears slid gently from beneath her lids and she cried herself silently to sleep.

In the morning things looked brighter because more familiar, but the aching in her chest was still there. In the days that followed it would ease merely because there was little spare time in which to indulge grief, but in the rare moments she was not being chivvied to some occupation by Mistress Chaucer Philippa felt it as painfully as before. She expected that it would always be with her in some measure and it was a long time after it went away before she realised the fact.

The Chaucers were prosperous, respectable folk with plenty of kindly common sense. Not until much later did Philippa appreciate the extent of their kindness since Mistress Chaucer might well have turned away two children brought from a house where there was plague. Instead she lodged them without complaint, only half considering the fact that it might prove an advantage to show kindness to the daughters of a high-born knight. On that first morning Philippa met the two Chaucer children. Mistress Chaucer's oldest son by her first husband was apprenticed in London, but he was expected daily.

'Tom is near sixteen,' Geoffrey said with the light of unmistakable hero-worship in his eyes.

Geoffrey was nine and interested Philippa not at all. He was usually in school but the schools had been closed as a precaution against the spread of infection and he worked with a tutor at home. He was a plump, rosy-cheeked boy who generally greeted his sister Kate by tugging her long plaits, though he tugged gently. Kate was seven, and Mistress Chaucer had said optimistically that the two girls could play together, but she failed to take into account the fact that Kate was wildly jealous of any child who might usurp her place and lost no opportunities that came her way for giving sly nips and digs. Philippa avoided her, performed the small but manifold tasks that her hostess found to keep the Devil at bay, and silently cried herself to sleep at night. Katherine was more fortunate, for though she was often naughty and unreasonable she was only four and was consequently more indulged. Even Kate made a fuss of her.

Tom Heron was due to travel to Southampton within a week or so, and Mistress Chaucer was fully occupied in preparing fatted calves all over the place.

'For it's close on a year since we've seen my brother,' Geoffrey explained, 'and as he is the first-born it's natural my mother should value him more.'

Philippa didn't regard it as particularly natural. In her own limited experience it was the younger who was indulged and petted, but he spoke as loftily as if he were already in his teens, so she held her peace.

What frightened her was that after only a few weeks her mother had begun to fade in her mind, to be crowded out by other matters. Whole hours went by when she didn't yearn for her, and one day she even found herself laughing at a cat's cradle that Katherine had got into a tangle. So it was a kind of relief when a messenger arrived with word of Tom's death from plague on the eve of his starting south. It gave her freedom to remember again and to join the rest of the family in weeping, ostensibly for a lad she'd never seen, but in reality for a gentle figure whose face became more blurred as day followed day.

But the grip of the plague was slackening as the colder weather came. The schools opened again and Geoffrey went off importantly every morning with his satchel on his back. He was learning grammar and rhetoric and astronomy, he informed the uncomprehending Philippa, but he didn't want to be a cleric. He wanted to be a man of affairs like his father. Philippa, who was having difficulty enough learning to speak English all the time, wished him joy of his studies. When the Chaucers spoke French their accents made her want to giggle, and fearing that her English accent would have the same effect on them she took pains to improve it. From now on their lives would be in England until Sir Paon returned to his lands. Without being told Philippa guessed they would be in England for a long time.

But not, however, in Southampton. In the New Year – a dismal one since the Chaucers had little heart for merriment since Tom's death – word came from the Court that Mistress Philippa and Mistress Katherine de Roet were to proceed to the castle of Woodstock in Oxfordshire where numerous high-born children were being reared, many of them at the Queen's expense.

'You will be a fine lady when we meet again,' Geoffrey said solemnly when he bade her farewell. 'Married to a prince probably.'

Philippa didn't think it very likely. High-born wasn't always the same as rich, and as far as she had gathered from scraps of conversation let fall by adults princes wed for money as often as not.

'You will not forget us, my dear?' Mistress Chaucer said.

It was the first time she had used an endearment, and Philippa felt a rush of affection, but it was checked when John Chaucer said,

'She will be sure to mention our kindness in the right quarters.'

'I will tell my father of your kindness, Mistress,' Philippa said in a small, cold voice. Part of the coldness was due to a sudden effort she was forced to make not to cry. She was growing accustomed to the bustling routine of the merchant's family, and now she would have to get accustomed to a different life in a castle, which would be vastly larger than a house.

A burly man with the lilies and leopards emblazoned on his surcoat had come to escort the two children. Katherine was to ride pillion with him and Philippa was to ride with his companion who was younger and had a merry face. Philippa wished she could ride her own pony, but it had been left behind in France and she knew that the journey would be a long one, more than seventy miles which was a longer distance than she could measure in her mind.

The details of that journey blurred in her mind like the features of her mother as the little party slowly ate up the miles. Later she would recall silent villages with ungathered crops rotting in the fields and houses with fading red crosses painted on the doors. She would retain a vague picture of a tonsured head, bending to trace the sign of blessing on her forehead and of spiced bread served with a mug of milk in one of the hospices where they broke their journey along the way. And she would remember the pointing fingers of the Oxford spires as they came down the long slope into the plain. For the rest it was a muddle of scenes that were changing even as she saw them, of the thick voices of their escort, of a mangy dog barking after them as they rode through a deserted village.

Woodstock seemed very large to her, though she learned later it was one of the more modest royal properties, once a hunting-lodge but later extended to provide a kind of nursery for sundry royal children.

Part of it was timbered with a thatched roof, and there were woods all about it, mossy oaks encroaching on the gardens where black and bare rose bushes waved twig fingers against the wintry sky.

Lifted from their places the two children were bustled across a series of courtyards and delivered, with unmistakable sighs of relief from their escorts, into the hands of a broad-faced young woman who surveyed them in silence for a moment before commenting,

'More evidence of Her Grace's charity, I see.'

Colour flamed Philippa's small face but she kept her eyes lowered. Answering back was rude, and she wasn't at all sure whether they were charity cases or not. She had often heard her father grumble that his estate yielded small profits and if he didn't bring back booty from the wars he didn't know where they'd be.

'The Roet children,' the thick-set man said.

The woman nodded, her voice not unkind as she said, 'They'll settle. Come with me.'

That command was to the sisters, their escort having been waved in the direction of the kitchens. Philippa took firm hold of Katherine's hand and trotted obediently after her into a long, tapestried apartment where what looked like an inordinate number of little girls were seated at embroidery frames.

'Oh, the dear little souls!'

A woman older than the children with red-gold hair and a lively, laughing face rose from a stool by the fire and swooped upon them like a plump and kindly bird in her trailing robe of green and gold.

'They are the Roet children, my lady,' the woman said. Her tone was respectful, but Philippa had the distinct impression that she didn't like the pretty lady.

'Philippa and Katherine,' the other nodded. 'You must bring them some food, Griselle, and see that their beds are ready. They will be worn out after the journey.'

'Yes, Lady Joan,' Griselle said, sounding sulky.

The pretty lady didn't appear to notice. She had taken Katherine on her knee and with her other arm encircled Philippa.

'I am Lady Joan, wife to Sir Thomas Holland,' she said. 'I am staying here while my lord is at the wars. Later on you shall meet the other children. They are not always as good and quiet as this, I fear.'

She laughed as she spoke, her green eyes glinting with mischief. She reminded Philippa of a rather large but naughtily charming child herself, her full breasts almost spilling over the low neckline of her tight bodice. Though she looked at least twenty she also looked as if she had not forgotten the fun of climbing trees or stirring the Yuletide pudding.

She swept them off into a smaller room where the sulky Griselle brought them some food, though Philippa was too weary and confused to do more than pick at it. The Lady Joan coaxed her to taste a little, and then rang a little silver bell and handed them over to a maidservant who looked more agreeable than Griselle, but hurried them along a narrow corridor into another long room with rows of beds in it.

Katherine, sitting down on the nearest one, said unexpectedly,

'I want to go home.'

Her mouth was square as if she were planning to roar. Philippa said quickly,

'Lady Joan might come back in a minute. You like her, don't you?'

'Flaysome wight,' Griselle said, coming in and catching the sentence. 'Wed secretly at twelve, married bigamously at fourteen, and now allowed to divorce and wed her common-law man. No shame.'

Philippa had no idea what half the words meant, but she knew that the Lady Joan was unpopular with women like Griselle, and she made up her mind to like her the better for it.

In the days that followed she saw little of the pretty laughing young woman. Joan's husband, the one she had secretly wed who had come back from the wars to claim her, whisked her off for days at a time, and when she was gone the castle seemed a dull place, though it was full of people. The little girls Philippa had seen at their needlework were all wards of the Queen, their fathers away at the wars or dead, their mothers serving at Court. They came from good families but were not of royal blood. The royal children came to Woodstock for part of each summer, Philippa was told, and sometimes the Queen came with them. Meanwhile the ones who were there were educated and taught courtesy, and the long winter dragged into spring. Katherine was soon a general favourite. She was often quick-tempered and mischievous but she had a way of slanting a smile and giving an impulsive hug that saved her many a scolding. Philippa who strained every nerve to be good found that, after a while, goodness was expected of her and not much praised. When the priest told them that more joy was felt in heaven over one black sheep than ninety-nine others, Philippa knew exactly what he meant.

(iii)

Summer came gently to Woodstock, the bare rose bushes swelling into green shoots, the trees in the orchards shedding drifts of white blossom, the river leaping higher over the flat shining pebbles. There had been a grand sweetening in the castle itself, the old rushes swept up and fresh ones cut, the tapestries brushed and shaken, the linen washed and hung to dry between the apple trees. Kirtles had to be let down and let out to accommodate growing girls, and new shoes

cobbled, and baths taken in wooden tubs fragrant with
sprigs of rosemary and bay floating on the steaming
water. The royal children were coming to visit and
everything and everyone must sparkle.

Lady Joan wasn't there. She had retired to her own
home to bear her first child, so there was nobody for
Griselle to grumble about.

The arrival of the royal party threw Philippa into a
state of quiet but intense excitement. The cavalcade
wound like a serpent, glittering with colour, flanked by
outriders carrying pikes, carts piled high with baggage,
ponies laden with saddlebags. There was a great bustle
of dismounting and greeting and much craning of
necks as the Queen was helped down from her litter.
Philippa stood on tiptoe and craned her neck with the
rest.

Her Grace was swathed in fur-trimmed robes, but her
face was plump and kindly, and she waved her
bejewelled hand to her waiting household before
vanishing in the direction of the royal apartments. The
royal children, escorted by nurses, governesses, tutors
and guards followed her. Philippa had the impression
there were a great many of them.

Not until the evening did she get the opportunity to
see them more closely. With the other children she was
seated on a bench below the high table and as the meal
progressed she was able to separate one of the heirs of
England from another. Not all the royal family had
come. Edward, the Prince of Wales, was with his father
in France and Princess Isabella had remained at
Windsor, but the two princes, Lionel and John, had
come with their mother. They were tall lads of twelve
and ten with golden hair and haughty expressions.
They sat together, daggers thrust into their belts, not
deigning to talk to the younger children. Of these
Edmund sat near the Queen, as blond as his brothers
and already tall for five. The two youngest girls,

Blanche and Margaret, were perched on high chairs and regarded the rest of the company with the same haughty indifference as their siblings.

It must be wonderful to be of royal blood, Philippa thought with a pang of envy. It must be wonderful still to have a mother. She drew a little sobbing breath and bent her head, fiddling with a wing of chicken on her plate.

The next day the Queen came to inspect the work her charges had done. Griselle had scolded them into their places by their embroidery frames and the Queen walked slowly and somewhat heavily down the room, pausing at each one to admire and question. She was near forty and had never been pretty, but there was a calmness in her face that lent it sweetness. When she reached Philippa she frowned slightly and whispered to the lady-in-waiting at her side. Clearly she was asking who this child was. Hearing the answer her brow cleared and she nodded.

'The children of Herald Guienne. Of course. My namesake, is it not?'

'Yes, Your Grace.' Philippa rose and made the curtsy they had all practised.

'Your mother died of the plague, did she not?' The voice held pity.

Philippa nodded because her throat had tightened up painfully.

'We hear that your father has acquitted himself most bravely,' the Queen said kindly. 'I shall have good report of you sent to him. Is this your work? It is most neatly done.' She smiled approvingly and passed by, followed by her attendants. Now she had reached the younger children and accepted a chair in their midst. Katherine's eager voice rose.

'I spoilt my work but 'tis because I am little, Griselle says.'

Katherine's needlework was a tangle of knotted silk,

but the Queen was laughing and telling her that as she grew older her fingers would become more nimble. It was always thus, Philippa thought. Katherine's youth and prettiness excused her.

'Later we shall place you in one of our households,' the Queen said, giving the lamentable bit of sewing back to Katherine and glancing in Philippa's direction. 'We shall consult with your father in due course.'

So she would be in royal service after all. Philippa's heart lifted. She was determined to work hard and grow up quickly. Then she remembered with a pang of guilt that she had not kept her promise to Mistress Chaucer.

As the Queen prepared to leave she took her courage in both hands and spoke out loudly.

'Madam, I was bidden to give you loyal greeting from Mistress Chaucer.'

The plucked eyebrows of the lady-in-waiting had shot up, but the Queen paused, looking at her kindly.

'Who is Mistress Chaucer, child?' she enquired.

'I stayed with her when I came first to England,' Philippa said. 'She is Master Chaucer's wife and lives in Southampton.'

'Then we must find a way to repay her kindness,' the Queen said, and moved on.

Sinking into a curtsy with the rest, Philippa wondered if she would remember.

Two

(i)

Philippa's first sight of London was in the snow-crisp afternoon of a December day, with a pale sun gilding the towers and turrets. The journey from Woodstock had taken four days with the roads slippery as glass under their coating of ice and the attendants cursing in the bitter wind as they tugged the baggage carts out of drifts. They were going to Westminster for Yuletide, and the prospect of that brought a glow to her cheeks that owed nothing to the weather. To be sure her own position would be a modest one, as maid of honour to the Lady Elizabeth de Burgh who had just been married to Prince Lionel, but she would be close to the heart of events, near the glitter of royalty. Their visits to Oxfordshire had failed to dim the aura of enchantment her fancy wove around them.

Westminster was less like a palace than a town, acres of buildings built of wood and stone, joined by courtyards and staircases and covered passages, with the river running past unheeding and the ancient abbey seeming to look with scorn from its dignified cloisters to the crowded and bustling antechambers and corridors of its neighbour.

'Freezing as usual,' Griselle pronounced gloomily when they had been shepherded to their quarters. 'In twenty years they've never found a way to get rid of the draughts.'

The chambers given to the demoiselles were certainly
bleak, Philippa thought, looking with some dismay at
the cramped space between the beds, the inadequate
garde-robe, the faded tapestry screen that blocked the
unglazed windows.

Then she cheered up, reminding herself that she had
two new gowns and would be paid a small salary for her
duties. At sixteen she was in a situation that many girls
would envy. Katherine had certainly worn a long face
when she had bidden her sister farewell.

'I wish I were coming with you,' she had said wistfully.

When Katherine looked wistful she looked even
prettier than usual, her grey eyes brimming with
unshed tears, her full red mouth trembling a little.

'When you are sixteen you will likely be given a place
too,' Philippa had consoled. She was sorry for Katherine
and would miss her, but the truth was that alone she had
more chance of being noticed.

Philippa had grown into a pretty girl, her small figure
slender and graceful, her skin clear, her features neat,
her hair a rich golden brown, but when her sister ran in,
her chestnut hair in disarray, her legs as long as a colt's,
Philippa shrank into the background.

She wasn't in the least envious of Katherine but she
knew that without the younger girl her own chances of
making a good marriage were improved. By a good
marriage Philippa meant a prosperous and respectable
one with a knight of good family. There were always
such at Court and if she didn't attract the attention of at
least one of them then she would be surprised. Without
being immodest Philippa knew her own value.

'Mistress de Roet?' A squire put his head in at the
door, occasioning squeals of mock outrage from a few
of the more light-minded damsels.

'Yes?' Philippa hurried to the door.

'Your father's here, Mistress, and waits for speech
with you,' the squire told her.

'My father here? Where?' She had given no thought to the possibility of Sir Paon even being in England.

'In the south hall,' the squire said, turning to lead the way.

It was as well that he did since otherwise she would have been hopelessly lost within a few minutes. Corridors twisted past tiny, windowless rooms, and staircases turned back on themselves to her inexperienced eyes and it was with immense relief that she heard the squire announce as he strode through an archway,

'This is the south hall, Mistress.'

It was not to be compared with the great hall where she would later dine but it was larger than any of the halls at Woodstock, its floor paved and swept clean of rushes, its windows glassed in and fires blazing at each end. There were a great number of people there, and she stood in confusion for a moment wondering which one was her father. Then a tall man detached himself from a group of others and stepped forward with his hand outstretched.

'Philippa?' He sounded uncertain for an instant, and then he said on a firmer note, 'Philippa,' and she remembered his deep voice and the way he bent his head a little to the side to look at her. Had she been a child like Katherine she would have leapt into his arms but she had never been a child like Katherine, and she merely curtsied, her eyes shining and a flush shading her cheeks.

'So, Philippa, you have grown,' Sir Paon said stupidly.

'It is nine years since you saw me,' Philippa said, adding hastily lest he construe her remarks as impertinent, 'but I am indeed grown.'

'And happy to be at Court, I'll be bound?'

'Yes, Father.'

'Good, good.' Sir Paon rocked slightly on his heels as he looked down at her. He would have preferred to see Katherine whom he remembered as a monkey of a child always making him laugh. Philippa was the gentler one, her round sweet face too much like his dead wife's for him to feel at ease with her.

'Are you here for Yuletide?' she asked.

'Until the New Year and then I return to France.'

'Have you been –?' She hesitated, unwilling to cause pain.

'The estate is well maintained, but not prosperous,' he said. 'I shall however make provision for you according to your rank.'

But he had been saying that even when her mother had been alive, she thought. He was always on the verge of making a lot of money, but somehow or other it slipped through his fingers and he had to go to war again to make more.

'If you were on the estate –' she began, and saw colour quickly flush his face.

'God's death, daughter, I'm a vowed knight, not a pesky yeoman,' he said irritably. His smile had faded. The small figure looking up at him reminded him of his wife whom he had loved very much when he was absent from her and found difficult when they were together.

'Yes, of course,' Philippa said. Her voice was sweet and clear, but it was her mother's voice. He was torn between sorrow at the loss of the woman he had married for love and a steely determination never to allow a woman to nag him again.

'Be a good maid,' he said awkwardly. 'Perform your duties well and you will doubtless find favour.'

'I hope so, Father,' she said meekly, and curtsied again before he could pat her on the head and tell her to run along. He patted her shoulder instead and turned back to his companions. They were fighting some battle or other all over again and she knew as she moved away that, having greeted her, he would promptly forget all about her again.

The squire who had shown her to the south hall had

vanished. She made her way back into the corridor and started to retrace her steps, wishing she had taken more notice of the direction in which she had come.

It was of no avail. The staircase she mounted brought her into a long gallery she was sure she had never seen before and she paused, her eyes sweeping its length of tiled floor on which rectangles of scarlet were cast by the setting sun.

In contrast to the hall below this gallery was deserted and she felt the chill of silence ripple through her. It was a sad gallery, she thought, and closed off the little hurt that pricked her at the cool reception she had received from her father. No doubt he was a busy and important man with little to say to a daughter he could scarcely recall.

'Are you lost?'

The youth running up the stairs behind her stopped short as he drew level, his eyes on her face. At that moment, with her brown eyes bright with unshed tears and her mouth trembling, she might have rivalled Katherine for wistfulness.

'I believe that I have taken the wrong stairs,' she said and abruptly dipped into a flustered curtsy, realising that it was Prince John who had overtaken her. It was three years since he had visited Woodstock with his younger brother and sister, but she remembered his handsome, arrogant features and brilliant gaze.

'You are one of the demoiselles?' He asked the question carelessly, not much interested in the answer, but she replied at once, with a certain quaint dignity that insisted she was to be considered as an individual.

'I am Mistress Philippa de Roet, my lord.'

'Oh?' John gave her a politely uncomprehending smile.

'Sir Paon de Roet's daughter,' she said.

'Sir Paon – to be sure. A brave and valiant knight.'

'Yes, sir.' She dimpled suddenly and said, her voice

quivering with laughter, 'You really don't know him, do you?'

'There are so many knights at Court,' he said, chuckling himself, 'but I am sure that your father is brave and valiant.'

'He goes to France again at the New Year,' Philippa said.

'As do we all.' The prince looked excited and eager. 'My brothers and I will campaign with our father. Now that I am eighteen I am to have my own command.'

'I am pleased for you,' Philippa said, wondering why boys took such delight in the prospect of fighting.

'You wanted to return to your quarters?' He recalled her straying thoughts.

'If you know the way.' She gave him a doubtful glance.

'Westminster is the most confusing of places, but I believe I know every inch of it,' he told her. 'Come.'

Without warning he took her hand and went with her along the gallery, turning off into a low doorway half-way along and showing her a connecting corridor that led to a staircase she recognised by the carved lamp that hung at its foot.

'Turn right and then left at the top and you will find yourself in your own quarters again,' he informed her.

'I am greatly obliged to you, my lord,' she said a trifle breathlessly. He had walked fast and his legs were much longer than her own.

'My pleasure, Mistress de Roet.' He loosed her hand, gave a little bow and strode off, his fair head bright in the last rays of the sun that slanted down from a window high in the wall.

Philippa stood for a moment, looking after him. It was the first time she had spoken directly to one of the royal children — not that the King's sons could be regarded as babes. John, called of Gaunt, since he had been born in that province, was at least eighteen, she reckoned. He was the fourth son in that large family, his elder brothers Edward and Lionel being men grown. William had died in his infancy and there were two younger brothers, Edmund who was thirteen and the latest child, Thomas, who was three. It was said they were all very loving with one another. She thought that it must feel splendid to be part of a large and affectionate family with both parents still alive.

'Mistress Philippa, will you hurry up?'

Griselle had appeared at the head of the shorter corridor and was beckoning her impatiently.

'I beg your pardon.' Philippa hastily flitted towards her.

'We have to be in our places in hall before His Grace and Her Grace arrive,' Griselle said crossly. ''Tis not like you to be wool gathering.'

'I met with my father,' Philippa excused herself.

Her small face bore a look that was suddenly bleak. Her father had not troubled to keep her very long at his side, she thought.

'Come along, Mistress,' Griselle repeated. She had not missed the look, and she had a shrewd idea what had occasioned it, but her task was to ensure that the demoiselles were in their places on time and sentiment had no place in that.

The great hall with its decorated stone columns, its blazing fires, its attendant guards ranged round the walls beneath the fluttering banners proclaiming the highest names in the land might well have overwhelmed a more sophisticated person than the girl who took her seat at the table reserved for the demoiselles. To her right the high table, set on its dais, glittered with gold and silver plate and fine crystal. The family was already filing in to the blare of trumpets in a gallery somewhere. It was the first time she had seen them in state, and all together, and her brown eyes widened at their magnificence.

His Grace King Edward the Third might be in his mid-forties but his beard was not yet streaked with grey and his hair was as thick and tawny-yellow as his older sons. The Prince of Wales overtopped his father by half a head and was as handsome with a drooping moustache covering his upper lip. At his side Lionel and John were as richly clad as he in robes of dark velvet with miniver banding the hems. Edmund was already rivalling his elders in height and breadth and his blue eyes ranged boldly over the upturned faces of the maids of honour. The Queen looked as kind and comfortable as when she examined samples of needlework at Woodstock, her plain, good-natured face unpainted above robes embroidered in silver. At her side the Princess Isabella looked sulky, as well she might, Philippa thought, since she was nearly twenty-five years old and still unwed. The three youngest children were clustered at the end of the table, with their nurses hovering. Blanche and Margaret were fair as the rest, but Thomas was a dark, narrow-faced little boy who looked as if he had been born into the family by mistake.

There were more courses served than Philippa had ever seen at Woodstock. She forgot the splendour of the royal party as the roasted meats, the creamed vegetables, the pies and pastries were placed upon the tables, servants scurrying up and down to refill the wine jugs and replenish the sauce boats.

She had looked for her father and seen him among a group of other gentlemen at the far side of the hall, his head tilted as he drank wine from the neck of a jug with much applause from his companions. He had not returned her look and she helped herself to an extra slice of goose and ate it with conscious enjoyment.

The meal lasted a long time and she was almost asleep before the final grace was said and the King and Queen withdrew. Their departure with the younger children trailing after was the signal for the rest to relax, for the

young men to wander over in search of their
sweethearts, for more wine to be poured and for the
side tables to be cleared away, and a space created for
dancing.

Those who had duties about the Court went to
perform them, but Philippa who had no idea when her
work would commence, squeezed herself into a space
between door and firescreen and watched the swirling
skirts and flying cloaks of those who had chosen to
dance.

'You don't remember me, Mistress Philippa?' a voice
questioned.

Philippa turned her head and smiled politely at the
pleasant-faced boy who stood at her elbow. He was clad
in parti-coloured hose of red and black and a short
black tunic, and there was something vaguely familiar
about him.

'My mother will be pleased to hear that we have met
again,' he continued.

'Your moth –? Oh, but you are Geoffrey Chaucer!'
Philippa's face lit up. She had not felt any particular
interest in him during the weeks she had spent at the
house in Southampton, but it was good to see someone
who was so obviously pleased to see her.

'My thanks are due to you, Mistress,' he said, 'for Her
Grace took the trouble to enquire into the hospitality my
parents extended to you and as a result I am appointed
to serve among Prince Lionel's train. I heard that you
too are appointed to the royal household.'

'As demoiselle,' she nodded, 'but they have not told
me my duties yet.'

'That depends on which of the family you serve,' he
said, taking a seat next to her on the narrow bench. 'Her
Grace is very kind and undemanding to her ladies, the
Princess Isabella less so.'

'Oh hush!' Philippa begged nervously, but he grinned
cheerfully at her.

'Nobody listens to gossip here,' he assured her. 'They are all too busy inventing their own. Or whispering love nonsense in a wench's ear.'

He put on such a comical face as he spoke that she found herself laughing outright.

'And have you whispered thus?' she demanded.

'More fervently than I dare to tell,' he said mournfully. 'There are but two topics of conversation in the Court. One is war and the other is love, and often it is impossible to distinguish between the two.'

'I would prefer to learn who all the people are,' Philippa said. 'There are so many.'

'Like fleas – of which you will also find a goodly number in this palace. My mother would have a fit.'

'Is she well?' She remembered the brisk, lively woman.

'She and my father are in good health and prospering,' he told her. 'My sister is also well, as I hope yours is. Katherine, wasn't it?'

'She is at Woodstock still,' Philippa said.

'I hope you will send her my regards when you write to her,' he said. 'She was a noisy child, but she probably grew up quiet.'

'On occasion,' Philippa said drily.

'You asked about the people at Court. Surely you have seen most of them at Woodstock?'

'Only now and then and never all together.'

'When they are together the Plantagenets are formidable indeed,' he said, his eyes twinkling. His eyes were the same brown as her own, she noticed, but had a quiet amusement lurking in them that made him seem older than his eighteen years.

'They are very splendid,' she said wistfully.

'Descended from the Devil – or so their family traditions maintain,' he nodded. 'I am bound to say that the younger children give proof of it from time to time. They are most horribly indulged.'

'Don't you like children, Master Geoffrey?' she asked.

'Very much, especially when they are asleep.' His smile told her that he was teasing.

'The older princes are not children,' she said, and was pleased at the enthusiasm in his face as he turned to her.

'His Grace has cause to be proud of them,' he said. 'What man would not feel pride in such sons? Duke John –'

'I know him – personally,' she interposed.

'I too,' Geoffrey said with equal pride. 'I have lent him books, for he is a great reader as well as a brave fighter.'

'I can read,' Philippa said, adding, 'but not yet perfectly. I like to sew better than strain my eyes over manuscripts.'

'Reading is a particular pleasure,' Geoffrey insisted, 'but until books are less expensive it is a pleasure that will be denied to many.'

He sounded serious and the thought crossed her mind that he had grown into a rather dull young man after all, but then a young couple went by, the girl's arm tucked into her partner's, her serene face turned up to his arrogant one.

'The Lady Blanche of Lancaster,' Geoffrey said to Philippa's questioning look. 'She is cousin to the royal family and betrothed to John.'

'Betrothed?' Philippa felt a sudden sinking in the region of her heart. 'I didn't know.'

'Since they were children,' Geoffrey said. There was a shadow on his own face. 'She is the loveliest girl at Court.'

'Then they match well,' Philippa said brightly.

'Aye.' Geoffrey uttered a sigh that seemed to arise from his shoes. 'They have been reared to fall in love, and being dutiful, have done so.'

The Lady Blanche was as blonde as her partner, but whereas his features were already stamped with the haughtiness of his lineage hers were cast in a gentler mould, her blue eyes mild and adoring under a broad white brow, her long hair gathered into a ribbon that seemed less gold than its shining strands. Neither she nor the prince appeared to notice anyone else as they walked arm in arm, her eyes on his face.

'There's more than duty there,' Philippa said sharply, as much to prick herself as Geoffrey.

'He is a fortunate being,' Geoffrey said and sighed again.

The Lady Blanche was certainly lovely, Philippa thought with a spasm of irritation, but Geoffrey Chaucer seemed to have grown into a rather foolish young man.

(ii)

She had been assigned as demoiselle to Lady Elizabeth de Burgh, the betrothed of Prince Lionel. Lady Elizabeth was a tiny, delicate creature, whose fair head scarcely reached the prince's waist. Of all the family Lionel was the tallest and the slowest of mind, but he was invariably good-humoured and openly adored the girl chosen as his bride.

Philippa's duties were light, to supervise the maids when they laid out Lady Elizabeth's garments, to accompany her on her walks in the gardens when the weather allowed it, and to amuse her when the weather was unkind. She was only one of half a dozen maids, all daughters of knights and four of them wards of the Queen.

Griselle had returned to Woodstock to continue her dour supervision of the younger wards, taking with her a letter that Philippa had painstakingly penned for Katherine.

'My dear sister,

'I am well and serve the Lady Elizabeth. I have spoken with Prince John and met Master Geoffrey Chaucer again. It is cold here but there is good food and music. The palace is very large. I have seen our father who is in good health.

'Your loving sister,

'Philippa de Roet.'

It was the first letter that she had ever written and she was proud of the fact that she had made no spelling mistakes.

Yuletide was very gay, with great sheaves of holly and mistletoe, and pies shaped like mangers and filled with minced meat, roast goose and piglets spitted on long staves and basted with honey. She would have liked to spend time in the kitchens, helping to stir the puddings of oatmeal and raisins or watching the chief cook as he built up spun sugar and white of egg into subtleties representing castles and dragons and angels, but her duties precluded it. In this huge household tasks were clearly defined and when one had leisure it was expected that one would spend it in amusements like dancing, singing and gossip, not in cooking.

The French campaign was to be resumed before the New Year and a few quiet tears were shed by various ladies whose sweethearts were due to sail. The grief had to be private since in public one had to behave as if having one's lover leave for the war was an honour. Philippa was both glad and sorry that she had no lover for whom to dampen her pillow. She had spoken with her father again, but their second meeting had been as brief and unsatisfactory as the first one.

'I expect to bring back considerable booty from this campaign.'

Thus Sir Paon, rocking slightly on his heels as he

looked down at his daughter. She was a neat little body, he thought, with her hair combed beneath a tiny cap and her eyes huge in her round face. She resembled her mother and that made him vaguely uncomfortable, since he had wed for love but never been the most attentive of husbands.

Philippa, looking up at him, thought that his words had an all too familiar ring. They had echoed through her childhood, repeated every time he came home. 'Next time I shall be rich.' And her mother had smiled and tried to interest him in the profits from the harvest.

'When I return I shall take steps to arrange a marriage for you,' he said kindly. 'As a Roet you must be well matched.'

'Yes, Father.' She smiled, wondering if he realised that high birth meant little in a palace where nearly everybody was high-born. It was more useful to have money. Perhaps he did realise it, for he turned from her almost petulantly, reaching for the wine jug as he said,

'Run along now. It will not do to neglect your duties.'

That was something of which she could never be accused. Of all the demoiselles Philippa de Roet was the most reliable and painstaking, always on time, always neat and cheerful, never having to be chivvied out of some corner where she was locked in the arms of some lovelorn squire.

'You are the kind of maiden that men marry,' Geoffrey informed her. 'They sport with other girls, but in the end they choose wisely.'

They were walking together in the alley that led to the tiltyard. The snow was still thick but the paths had been swept clear and from the tiltyard came the sound of shouting and laughter as the men practised their swordsmanship. It was important to practise since the day of embarkation was drawing nearer.

Philippa frowned slightly, not certain that it was very flattering to be regarded as a 'wise choice'. She would have given much to be light and flirtatious, but her natural seriousness held her back.

'You are also pretty,' Geoffrey added, but the flattery came slightly too late. It meant nothing anyway since Master Chaucer was one of the liveliest young men at the Court, forever in pursuit of some demoiselle or other, though he reserved his highest admiration for the Lady Blanche who never saw any man except Prince John.

They had almost reached the tiltyard, and the shouting was louder but it sounded angry and the laughter had ceased. As Geoffrey and Philippa glanced at each other Prince John strode into the alley, his face scarlet with exertion and temper.

'What's amiss, my lord?' Geoffrey hurried to him.

'The French,' John said wrathfully, 'have attacked Dover and Folkestone, doing great damage to the ships mustering there. The campaign must be postponed until repairs can be effected. We must swing our heels until the autumn because of French treachery. To sneak into our harbours and attack without warning, if you please! Against all code of chivalry.'

Philippa thought privately that such conduct showed intelligence, but had the sense not to voice her opinion. The two young men were eagerly discussing the latest news, while others poured out of the tiltyard, vociferous in their disapproval of such unchivalrous behaviour. The talk was all of revenge and war.

She pulled her cloak more tightly about her and slipped away, unnoticed. When war was the subject women became invisible. It had always been so, and she doubted if it would change.

Now the campaign would begin in the autumn and would be a punitive expedition. Those who had secretly welcomed the delay and hoped for more time with their men were disappointed, for the men had little on their minds except the prospect of fighting.

After New Year the royal household dispersed so that the enormous palace of Westminster could be sweetened. For the first but not the last time in her life, Philippa joined the cavalcade of royalty as it moved from one castle to the next, carrying with it everything portable that would serve to make habitable the next dwelling. Carts piled with beds, pallets, stools, folding tables, rolls of carpet and tapestry, chests of crockery and cutlery and garments were dispatched ahead of the travellers so that upon arrival they would find furniture set in place and bare walls hung with arras.

This first journey was to Windsor while the King and Queen travelled further south to inspect the damage to the ports and to raise money for the new and vastly larger campaign. The Prince of Wales had gone with his parents but Prince Lionel and Prince John were in Lincolnshire rallying troops.

Within the walls of Windsor the company was largely feminine, the talk of lovers and husbands, pregnancies, new dresses and the celebrations of St George's Day which were to be held with more magnificence than usual to make clear to the French that England had an inexhaustible supply of money. The King of France who had been a prisoner in England for several years was to be guest of honour, since nobody held him responsible for the death of chivalry in his own country.

Spring came in a flutter of green and gold, the chill wind warming, the trees sporting blossom again. This was the season of the year to which the whole world looked forward, with the dark days of winter gone, and the thin cattle released to graze on the new pasture.

'Windsor is my favourite home,' Lady Elizabeth confided to her ladies as they dressed her hair in preparation for the Festival. 'One feels safe here.'

It was an odd thing for the pampered girl to say and Philippa looked at her sharply. Her mistress caught the look and said, her voice suddenly low, 'Since I was a

child I have often felt as if something waited for me –
out there somewhere beyond the walls. I have dreamed
of it but never seen its face. Is that not foolish?'

Philippa was inclined to think it very foolish. Lady
Elizabeth de Burgh was one of the favourites of
Fortune, the daughter of the Earl of Ulster and heiress
to half Ireland, not yet seventeen and already bride to
Prince Lionel who adored her. She had less to fear than
almost anybody whom Philippa knew, but she was
constantly jumping at shadows and her tiny hands
shook when she lifted a wine cup.

'A dose of rhubarb usually banishes night terrors,'
Philippa said sensibly, and the tiny Countess giggled
suddenly, the shadow leaving her eyes.

'You do me good, Philippa de Roet,' she declared, 'for
when my foolish fears overwhelm me you always have a
practical weapon to send them scurrying away. Of all
the demoiselles you are as sensible as – as a pan! I shall
call you so. My Philippa Pan.'

It was a nickname that others took up, and though
Philippa would have preferred something more
romantic the nickname distinguished her from the
other demoiselles. Among the groups of lively, smiling
girls who waited upon the royal ladies competition,
though unadmitted, was keen. Since Philippa could not
compete with beauty or wit it was fortunate that she was
known for her good sense.

For St George's Day the castle was crammed to
bursting. It was a gauntlet flung down to taunt the
French, to show the world that England would move in
her own good time to avenge the attacks on Dover and
Folkestone. The masques were more elaborate than
they had ever been, with fire-breathing dragons and the
King himself as a splendid St George, flanked by his
four elder sons in the scarlet and gold of England. The
hint to their distinguished guest and prisoner, King
John, was clear. England had a family of heroes ready to

kill as many dragons as the French could send against them. King John, smiling tightly, acknowledged the hit with an elegant inclination of his head.

Philippa herself was overwhelmed by the excitement of it all. The sight of the lake on which a fleet of tiny wooden ships bearing the banners of France were set alight, the day-long tournament when the King beat all comers including his own sons and kissed his Queen full on the mouth as she gave him his prize, the lengthy banquets where modest as her place was it was still close to the royal dais, the candlelit evenings where those who danced wore their gayest clothes and those who watched stamped their feet in time to the music – every moment brought its own enchantment.

Lady Elizabeth had given presents to her demoiselles, and Philippa had gasped with delight at the fur cloak that swirled to her ankles and framed her face with its high collar.

'It is very practical, my dear Pan,' the tiny Countess dimpled. 'In cold weather you can mock the frost.'

'It is most kind of you, my lady,' Philippa said.

The cloak was so luxurious that she feared the other girls might be envious, but she was too well liked for envy to show its face. Philippa was not beautiful enough to inspire jealousy, and her brisk, sensible ways were no threat to more romantic maidens.

The festivities were brought to a climax by the marriage of Prince John to the Lady Blanche and the marriage of Prince Lionel to the Lady Elizabeth.

'With all the princes save the younger boys going to France it is needful that heirs are conceived,' Geoffrey told her.

He was going to France too, and his face was gloomy, not on that account but because his adored Lady Blanche was finally to be wed.

'That makes good sense to me,' Philippa said.

'Aye, it's good sense.' Geoffrey sighed deeply. 'The

Lady Blanche will be lost to me for ever.'

'Oh, that is ridiculous and you know it,' Philippa scoffed. 'The Lady Blanche hardly knows that you exist.'

'Alas!' He sighed again, casting his eyes heavenward. 'If she once took her eyes from Milord of Gaunt she would fall fathoms deep in love with me and abandon her royal rank.'

'Geoffrey, you are such a fool!' Philippa said, chuckling. 'Because it is the fashion to be in love you must choose the one person who is madly in love with her bridegroom.'

'Which makes the lady very safe and eminently suitable to be loved,' he retorted. 'There is not the least danger of my being landed with her for life. You should fall in love too, Mistress Philippa, for it does wonders for the figure.'

'How? And what's wrong with my figure?' she asked crossly.

'Nothing in the world,' he said hastily, 'but the style now is to be slim as a reed, and when one falls in love one loses all appetite.'

'I hadn't noticed,' Philippa said, surveying his stocky frame.

'I am the exception that proves the rule,' he informed her.

Philippa burst out laughing and, after a moment, he laughed with her, tucking her hand into her arm and strolling on in a companionship that pleased both of them.

Nevertheless she surveyed herself anxiously as soon as she was in the demoiselles' quarters. There was no denying that the excellent food at Court had imparted a certain plumpness to her figure. A little was flattering but too much was ugly. She resolved to keep her fingers out of the sugared almonds dish in future.

The two royal weddings were duly celebrated,

functions in which she had little part to play. Of the two brides the Lady Blanche was held to be the more dignified, almost as tall as her handsome husband. Lady Elizabeth looked as if Lionel could pick her up in one hand. What was very clear was that both couples were in love. Squashed into the back of the chapel with her companions, Philippa prayed under her breath for their happiness, and wondered if her father would remember his promise to find her a husband when the campaign was over.

Preparations for the expedition to France now occupied every minute. The Court returned to Westminster which rang with the clash of steel as daily practice in the lists was increased from one hour to several, and the whinnying of horses bought at markets and fairs all over England to be shipped across the Channel. There were thirty thousand men preparing to sail, with five thousand of them fully equipped fighting warriors. From every village and town in the country money and supplies were pouring in. War-fever was higher than love-longing in that hot summer of thirteen fifty-nine.

Philippa couldn't avoid getting caught up in the excitement though she sometimes suspected they would all have been much better off staying quietly at home. Geoffrey didn't agree with her. He had laid aside his foolish play-acting at unrequited love and was practising as hard as anyone else with sword and axe. As a commoner he would fight on foot, and his enthusiasm for the adventure ahead was only faintly tempered by the possibility of getting killed. Her father was to travel with the advance guard and though he had taken little notice of her since her arrival at Court she was proud of the handsome figure he cut when he bade her farewell. It was a pity that his horse was a borrowed one and that he had not yet paid his tailor for the fine suit he was wearing, but perhaps this time he would really make his

fortune. Philippa wished him Godspeed and watched
him ride away with a distinct feeling of relief. Her
childish belief that Sir Paon de Roet was a very important
man had given way to the realisation that, though his
rank was high, his fortune was small and his head usually
in the clouds. It had also been a disappointment to find
out that the demoiselles received no salary except bed
and board and two new gowns every year. Anything else
was given only at the whim of whichever of the royal
ladies they served. The fur cloak became more precious
in Philippa's eyes and she welcomed cold days that gave
her the excuse for wearing it.

(iii)

They had wintered in Hatfield House which was one of
the pleasantest royal residences. Both the Lady Blanche
and the Lady Elizabeth were with child and the Queen
fussed between the two of them like a jewelled and
amiable hen.

'For until Prince Edward marries these babes will be
heirs to the throne,' Mistress Alice said as the
demoiselles sat at their needlework.

Outside rain beat against the small panes of the
windows but in the winter parlour a bright fire burned
and heavy curtains repelled the draught.

'He will wait for Lady Joan to accept him,' another
said.

The twice-married Joan was a widow now, her
husband having been killed during the campaign, and
the prince's devotion to his beautiful cousin of Kent was
well known, though she was two years older than him
and the mother of four children.

'Her Grace will not be happy about such a match,'
Alice said. 'She believes Lady Joan is too light-minded.'

'Also the loveliest woman in England,' Mistress Joanna put in. 'Beauty is a potent weapon.'

'Intelligence is more potent,' Alice said, flicking her tapestry frame with a narrow nail.

'Is that what your husband says?' someone asked, and there was a ripple of amusement, for Alice's husband was generally considered to be an idiot, deeply in love with her and never realising that she continually mocked him behind his back.

Philippa rose and went over to the window, leaning her head against the rain-swept pane and gazing out into the rose arbour where the first buds were being tossed by the wind. Sometimes she grew weary of the gossip and backbiting, and longed for the summer when it would be possible to be alone sometimes.

She heard her own name spoken and scowled at her faint reflection in the glass. Alice was talking in the sweetly sympathetic voice that hid claws.

'If this wretched campaign lasts much longer Mistress Philippa will have to seek a husband for herself. And there are so few suitable men.'

What she meant was that Philippa was close on eighteen and still not betrothed.

'Her Grace wants to speak to Mistress de Roet.' A page put his hand round the door and made the announcement without ceremony.

'Master Chaucer has been ransomed perhaps?' Alice said and giggled.

Geoffrey's capture at Rheims had been a signal for teasing since their friendship was regarded as a jest, the Chaucers being of low degree and his devotion to the Lady Blanche being well known.

Philippa ignored the gibe and hurried to the Queen's apartments. Her royal namesake spent much of the day in her own chamber, dictating endless letters to her beloved husband and sons while she sewed patiently at garments for the new babies.

'Madam.' The younger woman curtsied and stood, hands folded at her waist.

'Philippa, dear.' The Queen's broad face was distressed. 'A despatch has come from Calais, with evil news. Your father has been killed in a battle on the outskirts of Rouen. He was pierced by an arrow and died almost instantly. I am truly most sorry.'

Philippa swallowed hard, forcing back sudden and unexpected tears. Her father meant little to her as a person. Their brief interviews had been cool and unsatisfying, but he had been her father and his intentions had been good even though he had never done very much for her. Now he never would.

'He had property in Picardy, did he not?' the Queen was asking kindly.

'A small estate,' Philippa said 'It was never very prosperous.'

'When the war is over I shall make enquiries on your behalf concerning the profits,' the other said.

She too meant well, but the campaigns in France went on and on with no sign of truce. The steward could not be expected to manage the Roet affairs for ever. Philippa drew a deep breath.

'Meanwhile your home is here with us,' Queen Philippa said. 'My Lady Elizabeth tells me she could not manage without her dear Philippa Pan. Your father's soul will be prayed for at my own expense.'

'You are very kind, Madam,' Philippa said gratefully.

'Your sister is at Woodstock still? A charming child.'

'She is near fifteen,' Philippa hinted.

'And in due course will take her place among the demoiselles,' the Queen said comfortably.

'Thank you, Your Grace.' Philippa curtsied again.

'There is happier news.' The Queen smiled. 'Master Chaucer is to be ransomed. My son, John, has made the necessary arrangements. So you will see your friend again when the men return.'

'That was most generous of the Duke.' Philippa flushed with pleasure.

'Master Geoffrey's verses amuse John,' the Queen said, smiling slightly. 'He is a pleasant young man. You are excused from your duties for the rest of the day. You will wish to mourn for your father. A brave and gallant gentleman.'

'With a head full of dreams and no money in his pouch,' the girl thought, bowing her head as she kissed the fat, beringed hand.

Three

(i)

The Lady Elizabeth had borne a daughter, named after
the Queen, and Lady Blanche had borne a son named
after his father. The girl child was thriving but the little
boy was not, a fact that put fresh lines in the Queen's
plain face. She was as devoted a grandmother as she was
a mother, constantly visiting her daughters-in-law with
advice and gifts.

'Some women are born to be mothers,' Mistress Alice
said, curling her lip slightly.

She herself showed no sign of ever quickening, but it
was whispered that her husband was impotent. Perhaps
it was better so, Philippa thought, for Alice with her
sharp tongue and cleverness lacked the softness that
marked a woman who loved children. Yet she was
attractive to men. Even the King would linger to listen
when Alice was talking. So did Geoffrey Chaucer, a
circumstance that irritated Philippa intensely.

Geoffrey often irritated her these days, for since his
return from captivity in France he had spared no pains
to become a fashionable young man. He was frequently
absent, studying at the Temple, visiting his family,
supping with one lord or another, and when he was at
Court he spent his time in flirtation, reading his current
fancy his latest verses, making it clear that of all women
he idolised the Lady Blanche above them. Yet his
friendship with Philippa continued. He was like the

brother she had never had, she thought, and though
they often wrangled on the whole they were comfortable together.

They wrangled now as he came to the end of a verse
he had translated and she shook her head.

'It is too lewd for my tastes,' she objected.

'Your tastes are too particular. Alice laughed at the
jest.'

'Alice would,' she said crossly.

'She is not popular with the other demoiselles,'
Geoffrey said, 'but I am sorry to see you follow the
common opinion. She may need friends one day.'

'Champions you mean, and the men will provide
those,' Philippa said. 'None of us can tell where her
attraction lies. She is not pretty.'

'She has wit and a good brain.'

'Wit is foam on the wave and her brain is bent upon
self-advancement.'

'A good line. Let me make a note of it.'

'So now you steal your verses from me?' Philippa
grinned for it was hard to remain at outs with him for
long.

'Did you know,' said Geoffrey, looking at her more
closely, 'that you have a little space between your front
teeth?'

'Must you remind me?'

'It is a sign of a passionate nature. I have often
wondered what lies behind that calm, pretty face.'

'A common-sense mind,' she retorted and gave him a
little push. Compliments from Master Chaucer were
duplicated to too many ladies to have much value.

'And a cold heart?'

'You just called me passionate.'

'Which is it?' he asked. 'You are marvellously
self-sufficient.'

'Girls have to be.'

But she stifled a sigh because she was past twenty and

not yet betrothed. The lands in Picardy had never
yielded much in the way of profits and her poverty
outweighed her charms.

'You will be married,' Geoffrey said comfortably. 'I
have told you before that you are the kind of maid that
men marry.'

'When they are so old that no other woman will have
them,' Philippa said wryly.

'You're in a gloomy mood today. What's amiss?'

'Nothing – everything! My Lady Elizabeth is not well
again.'

'They whisper it is the lung disease.' His cheerful face
sobered.

'God forbid.' She spoke softly, crossing herself. 'Since
the child was born she has ailed. She told me once that
she had always felt something waiting for her,
something that was a threat. It frightens her.'

'Aye, there's much in life to frighten us all.' He was
still grave and then his whimsical gaze fell upon her and
he chuckled. 'For my own part I dread the bondage of
wedlock and will hold off for as long as I can.'

But it was no disgrace for a young man to postpone
marrying until he had made his mark upon the world,
Philippa thought irritably as she went back to her duties.

At least she had proved herself useful to the Lady
Elizabeth. Prince Lionel's delicate little wife had made a
confidante of the pleasant-faced Roet demoiselle, telling
her of her childhood when she had known she was to
wed the King's son and had spent much time standing
on tiptoe in the hope she might grow taller and so match
him more nearly.

'It was to no avail, of course,' she said, 'for my lady
mother was very small too, and my father loved her just
the same. Lionel loves me too – after his mother. Of all
her sons he is the most devoted.'

'A loving son makes a loving husband,' Philippa said.

'And my lord is most loving.' Lady Elizabeth sighed.

'There is a possibility that I am with child again. It will be born in Ireland for His Grace wishes us go there. My own estates are in Ulster though I have never seen them. You will come with me to Ireland?'

'Yes, of course,' Philippa said, but her heart sank. Ireland was a wild place where the savage tribesmen were constantly feuding. She had never been adventurous, and the dangers and discomforts of the journey worried her.

When the Lady Elizabeth had dismissed her she delayed her return to the chamber where the other demoiselles were embroidering and gossiping and wandered out into the rose arbour. The bushes sprayed blossom and perfume against the greensward and the sky was blue over the ancient walls of Westminster. She could find her way round now if she marked certain items of furniture or noticed who stood guard, but the sprawling palace had never felt like home. And soon she would be on the sea bound for Ireland.

She wasn't alone in the rose arbour. The sound of a soft laugh roused her from her pensive thoughts and she looked up, blinking at two figures who stood with their backs to her. The girl was one of the demoiselles, Marie St Hilaire, who had joined the household recently. She was a plump, dark-haired wench of seventeen with a tinkling laugh and a good-natured, incurably lazy personality. She had bow and arrow in her hands and was trying without much success to draw back the strings while the man who held the long curve of yew kept his free arm tightly about her.

Philippa took a step back and turned to flee. Whatever sport Prince John was engaged in needed no third person. She had stepped unwarily, however, and a twig snapped beneath her heel just as the arrow twanged and went wide.

'Almost there, Marie,' John said. 'No more than a league off target. Mistress Philippa, do you often creep up in order to spoil the marksman's aim?'

He was smiling but she sensed he was not overjoyed at the interruption.

'I beg your pardon, my lord.' Philippa dropped a placating curtsy. 'I thought myself alone.'

'And sought company?' He dropped his arm from Marie's waist and let his vivid blue eyes roam over Philippa's blushing face.

'No, sir.' She blushed more hotly.

'I will see you later, Marie.' He lifted his hand casually to the girl and fell into step beside Philippa. 'How is it that you crave solitude?' he enquired after a moment or two.

'Doesn't everyone, sometimes?' she countered.

'Not in my experience. You are more serious than the others though. I have noticed how you avoid gossip and tend to your duties.'

'You need not fear that I am a gossip, my lord,' she said pointedly.

'Marie?' He smiled again with a touch of embarrassment. 'She means no more than the pleasing of an hour. My wife knows about her.'

'You need not explain –' Philippa was now deeply embarrassed.

'Of course not, but you were looking at me with the self-same expression my nurse used to wear when I had ripped my tunic climbing a tree.' His rueful look made her smile despite her disapproval.

'Now you look charming,' he said. 'You have pretty teeth, Mistress Philippa. With a gap between the front ones – has anyone ever told you that?'

'Master Chaucer,' she told him.

'Geoffrey has sharp eyes and a flattering tongue.' He took her hand suddenly, holding it in his own with a casual friendliness that seemed genuine. But he had seemed to be in love with his wife, Philippa reminded herself, and drew her hand away.

'You dislike me?' he said, and there was surprise in his voice as if he had never met anyone who might do that before.

'No, my lord. I never think about you at all,' she said, and knew as she spoke that it was not altogether true. She had always been conscious of him, of his thick fair hair that waved over his well shaped head, the long lashes tipped with gold that shielded his blue eyes. At twenty-two he had attained his prime, his lean frame hard and graceful, his smile softening his hawk features.

'I love my lady wife deeply,' he said, and she jumped for it was as if he had read her thoughts.

'The Lady Blanche is a beautiful woman,' she said.

'Beautiful and gentle and virtuous. But the child in me needs to amuse himself from time to time. Most men are like that.'

'Which doesn't make it right,' she said.

'Prim little Philippa Pan,' he said and laughed, though she sensed that her criticism hadn't pleased him.

'It is not only duchesses who can be virtuous,' she flashed.

'And I don't paddle my fingers in unwilling bodices.' He sounded haughty now, his smile withdrawn. 'You need not fear me, demoiselle. Between my wife and Mistress Marie I am well served.'

'I didn't mean to offend.' She had lost her blush and her voice was distressed.

'And none was taken. Good day, Mistress Roet.'

But she had offended him, she thought, staring after him as he walked back to his companion. The Plantagenets loved their wives, but they loved other women too, and helped themselves like greedy children. Women were flowers to be plucked and loyalty was not considered their due. And women were as greatly to blame because they accepted that state of affairs, holding themselves cheaply. Geoffrey was right when he mocked lovers.

'Mistress Philippa!' Agnes Archer was running towards her, her skirts tucked up, her cap awry. 'Oh, do make haste.'

'What's amiss?' Philippa hurried to join the other.

'My Lady Elizabeth is taken bad – not five minutes after you left her. She began to cough, and then to spit blood. The physicians have been summoned and her confessor, but she is awfully sick.'

Philippa caught her breath on a little sob. Somehow she already knew that the dark threat for which Prince Lionel's wife had waited all her short life was come.

(ii)

The Lady Elizabeth de Burgh had lived twenty-two years. John of Gaunt's son had lived less than two years. Prince Lionel, all his good nature hardened by grief into ferocity, stormed off to Ireland to harry the chieftains there, and Philippa was appointed as one of the Lady Blanche's demoiselles.

'Lady Elizabeth, God rest her soul, was always very fond of you, my dear,' the Queen said. 'If you serve the Lady Blanche as well she will be most satisfied.'

Philippa curtsied meekly. She longed to ask if Her Grace had given any thought to the choice of a husband for her, but this was not the time. The Queen's face was drawn with grief for she had lost a beloved daughter-in-law and an even more beloved grandson. The Lady Blanche was pregnant again but the shock of her child's death might have harmed the unborn babe. Queen Philippa was sometimes glad that her own days of childbearing were at an end. Twelve confinements had robbed her of any beauty she had ever had, and of her children none of the older ones was, as yet, proving prolific.

Philippa guessed what was passing through the older woman's mind. It was common gossip among the household.

'Since Prince Edward wed the Lady Joan nothing has gone well,' Agnes Archer said.

'He would look at no other woman.' Alice gave a mock sigh, rolling her long eyes heavenward. 'She has four children by her Holland husband, so let us hope she provides the Prince of Wales with an heir. She is past thirty already.'

'But still most comely,' Philippa said loyally.

Alice shrugged and returned to the examination of her complexion in the hand mirror she was holding. For a girl who had so little beauty she spent an inordinate amount of time looking at herself.

A few days later Geoffrey Chaucer came to bid her farewell. He was going to Oxford to study law and could talk of nothing but the generosity of Prince John who was paying the fees.

'A wonderful opportunity for me,' he said happily. 'I shall have the chance to study and meet with some of our finest minds. Milord of Gaunt sees a diplomatic career ahead of me.'

'You will have no time to write verse or court ladies,' Philippa teased.

'I shall make time,' he vowed. 'Not all my hours will be spent poring over dusty manuscripts. I am making a translation of *La Roman de la Rose* and I have other ideas for future work, all in English.'

'Nobody will bother to read it,' she objected.

'I shall recite it,' he told her. 'In a short time English will be as popular as French or Latin. You will see.'

'Perhaps.' Philippa changed the subject. 'Will you be able to visit Woodstock? I am worried about Katherine. She is still there with no present prospect of coming to Court, for I don't like to trouble Her Grace when she has so many other problems.'

'I shall make a point of visiting her,' he promised. 'She must be quite a young lady now.'

'Seventeen. I find it hard to believe myself,' she admitted. 'But she is all the family I have now and I want her to be well settled.'

'You have a good heart, Mistress,' he said, and kissed her hand with an approving look in his brown eyes.

It would be lonelier for her when he had gone, she realised. Their friendship, despite its moments of acrimony, was based on mutual liking. She could talk with him about matters that concerned her without any fears of having them repeated in the wrong quarters. Her anxiety over her unwedded state could be construed as discontent with her position at Court in the wrong mouth, but for all his light-hearted teasing Geoffrey was discreet.

'So you are to be demoiselle to Lady Blanche,' he said as they continued their stroll. 'I believe you will be happy in her service. The Savoy Palace is the last word in luxury.'

'You have been there?'

'To give my condolences on the death of the babe. The Duchess has taken her loss with great courage. And she has the next child due very soon. That will be some comfort to her.'

When he spoke of Blanche of Lancaster his teasing manner vanished and there was something akin to worship in his eyes. For him Gaunt's wife was the ideal woman.

'I pity the maiden you decide to wed,' Philippa said impulsively. 'She will never match the picture of Milady Blanche that you carry in your heart.'

'She is unique. I'd not expect to find her like,' he replied, 'and as for wedlock – I shall delay that until my studies are completed and my career more firmly established. For all the favour shown to me I must remember that I'm neither wealthy nor titled.'

Beneath his amiable cheerfulness then ambition ran strongly. She didn't blame him for it. In a land where men rose and fell according to royal favour ambition was laudable.

'You will convey my respects to the Duke and Duchess?' Geoffrey said as he took his leave. 'The friendship of them both means much to me. Milord had the kindness to tell me that he was certain I have a brilliant future.'

It seemed unlikely, Philippa thought, flicking a glance at his stocky frame and pleasant face. He lacked the dash and glamour that characterised the favoured of fortune, but if he paid due attention to his law studies and didn't waste all his time trying to compose verses in English he might rise high enough.

For herself the move to the Savoy Palace was only one more short journey between royal households. What was different was the palace itself. It had been built a century before as a home for younger members of the royal family, but the King had given it outright to his son of Gaunt and John had enlarged and redecorated it to suit his own extravagant tastes. Now it occupied more than a hundred acres, its gilded battlements rising above terraces and lawns and pleasaunce gardens with which no other royal dwelling could compare.

Here were no draughty corridors that made winter a purgatory in Westminster, but covered passages, warmed by braziers, hung with rich tapestries, and mosaic floors with fine Byzantine carpets laid in the private apartments. The quarters to which Philippa was conducted were much more comfortable than any provided for the demoiselles elsewhere, and her spirits rose as she wiped the dust from her face with a damp cloth and smoothed her hair beneath its lace cap.

The Duchess was reclining on a daybed when Philippa was announced. Her swollen figure was concealed beneath a loose robe of white silk and only

her black veil and the slight puffiness of her long eyelids
hinted at the tears she must have shed for her babe.

'Mistress Roet.' She bowed her pale golden head as
the other made her curtsy. 'I am pleased that you could
join my household. Her Grace tells me that you served
the late Duchess with devotion until her most unhappy
death.'

'My Lady Elizabeth was good enough to show me
favour,' Philippa said.

'She was a most sweet lady.' Tears suddenly brimmed
in Blanche's calm blue eyes. 'We were cousins as well as
sisters-in-law so for me it is a double loss. She called you
Philippa Pan, did she not?'

'It was a jest, because she told me that I was as
practical and useful as a pan,' Philippa explained.

The Duchess smiled, but there was a vagueness in the
smile that demonstrated a certain bewilderment. Clearly
Blanche for all her goodness and beauty lacked
humour.

'Your duties will be the same as in her household,' she
was saying. 'You have dresses?'

'Two, my lady.'

Despite herself Philippa couldn't restrain a pang of
irritation. The dresses that were replaced every year
were given to the poor, though they were still in
excellent condition, thus ensuring that the demoiselles
never increased their wardrobes.

'When my child has been safely born,' Blanche said, 'I
intend to give each of my ladies an extra dress to mark
the event.'

'You are generous, my lady,' Philippa said gratefully.
An extra gown would make a difference.

'Say rather my dear husband is generous,' Blanche
returned, her tears drying as her smile beamed forth.
'He suggested it, as he advised that I employ you in my
train.'

Philippa's mouth opened and closed again. That

Prince John had recommended her to his wife seemed incredible. She recalled their curt dialogue in the rose arbour on the day that the little duchess had died, and the coldness in his face and voice when he had left her.

'I was not aware,' she said cautiously, 'that Milord Duke had ever noticed me.'

'John always notices the pretty demoiselles,' Blanche said. Her voice held an almost maternal tenderness. 'It is the greater compliment to me that he remains so devoted.' If she knew about Marie St Hilaire the knowledge lay lightly on her. She was secure in her wealth and beauty and her lord's love.

'I hope you will be contented here with us,' she was saying now, her sweet smile breaking out again to light up her face. 'And here is John, to welcome you himself.'

He had entered without realising that anyone else was there and, for a moment, the look on his face as he saw Philippa reminded her of a small boy caught stealing marchpane. Then he bowed slightly, the mask of indifferent arrogance covering his features.

'Mistress Roet? I had not expected you so soon.' His voice was as cool as his face.

'She came at your lady mother's bidding as soon as arrangements could be made,' Blanche said serenely. 'Her Grace is always so kind.'

'I hope to serve my Lady Blanche as well as I served Lady Elizabeth,' Philippa said, nervous under his vivid blue gaze.

'My brother's wife was fond of you, I understand,' John said carelessly. 'As my own wife requires another attendant your name came to mind.'

But that wasn't the reason he had mentioned her name, Philippa thought. It was because she had seen him with Marie St Hilaire and thought it safer to keep a potential gossip in his own employ. A flash of anger shot through her that he should think her capable of causing trouble.

'She will be a great help to me,' Blanche said. 'Begin your duties tomorrow, Mistress. I know that you will want to find your way about first.'

'If she is left to do that she will be commencing her duties in about a year's time,' the Duke said, laughing. 'Come with me, Mistress Roet, and I shall give you the grand tour.'

Philippa threw an anguished glance towards the Duchess but Blanche said placidly, 'How good of you, John. You will be able to explain everything so neatly. My dear husband designed much of the interior himself.'

There was nothing for it but to make her curtsy and follow him meekly out of the room. He lingered for an instant to kiss his wife and then strode out into the passage beyond with Philippa trotting at his heels.

'My lord?' As they reached the antechamber beyond she stopped short, gathering all her courage.

'Yes?' He too paused and looked at her.

'There was no need,' Philippa said breathlessly, 'to recommend me to your lady wife, though I am most grateful. I would not have spoken.'

'About what?' he enquired.

Scarlet dyed her cheeks and she unconsciously plucked at her skirt.

'I thought – I would never willingly give pain to the Duchess by gossiping,' she stammered.

'How could you? Ah, now I understand.' To her bewilderment he put back his head and gave vent to a hearty laugh in which there was no sign of strain or embarrassment. 'You are thinking of Madam Marie. You will not tittle-tattle about her. Is that what you are trying to say?'

Philippa nodded.

'My dear girl, I told Blanche all about Marie,' he said impatiently. 'She forgave me before I had finished the sorry tale. Marie is to be married and given a handsome pension, and my days of dalliance are over. Did you imagine that I hoped to bribe you into silence?'

Of course he had not. She was too unimportant for him to regard as any kind of threat to the happiness he enjoyed with his wife. Tears of shame sprang to her eyes and she hung her head miserably.

'Why, what's this?' His voice had gentled and he took a step towards her, putting his hand beneath her round chin, forcing up her head. 'I had no desire to make you weep. I am apt to speak sharply sometimes, but it means nothing.'

'I feared that you might have a bad opinion of me,' Philippa said, blinking rapidly. It would be too humiliating if she broke down completely.

'Nonsense!' He smiled at her, the haughty arrogance completely gone.

'But that was foolish of me,' she floundered on, 'for I am sure you have no opinion of me at all.'

'I have never yet met a girl and held no opinions about her,' he said, still holding her chin. 'I have always considered you to be an honest and useful person. My lady mother has mentioned how conscientiously you carry out your duties. That was why I gave your name to Blanche. Since we lost our babe she is often prey to nervous fears about the one she carries, and I want her to have demoiselles about her who have more in their heads than lovers.'

'I shall do my best,' Philippa said, and the Duke released her chin and took her hand instead, talking as they traversed the anteroom.

'Now I shall show you how to find your way about the Savoy. I was at pains to keep the kitchens as near to the great hall as possible so that our meat is not lukewarm when it arrives at the table and the stables as far as is practicable from the living-quarters to mitigate the smells. Had I not been a king's son I do believe I might have made a splendid architect. I wish my lord father would allow me to make some improvements at Westminster and Windsor, but he declares the budget won't stand it. The crystal is from Venice. I had it specially designed and shipped here. Can you read?'

'And write,' Philippa said proudly.

'I intend to collect books,' he told her. 'My protégé, Master Chaucer, has promised to write tales for me – in English, for he swears that the common tongue is now more and more fashionable.'

'Master Geoffrey is a friend of mine,' Philippa said.

'So he is. I had forgotten. A young man of great promise. Do you not agree?'

'He talks a lot,' Philippa said doubtfully.

The Duke laughed, dropping her hand and pushing open another door.

'I'm laying out money on the hope of his doing more,' he said. 'He was prisoner in France, and spent his time while waiting to be ransomed in making careful notes of the scale of French manpower and defences. He was able to give us most useful information when he came home.'

'He said he was going to study law,' Philippa said.

'And then undertake certain diplomatic missions,' John nodded. 'He is not much of a soldier, though he was brave enough, but his talents lie elsewhere. We are of an age, he and I, and it pleases me to advance him. This fountain will spout wine when the child is born. I am hoping for a son, but a daughter will be equally loved. I like children.'

For an instant there was the shadow of pain in his eyes and then he smiled again, inviting her to tilt her head and admire the gold-painted ceiling.

He was not so formidable, she decided. His enthusiasm was like a boy's, and his flashes of temper brief. The affair with Marie St Hilaire had meant little. She sensed that nothing would ever spoil the bond between himself and his lovely Blanche. All the

Plantagenets fell in love with their wives, it seemed, and had little left over for other women. It was something she would be wise to remember.

(iii)

The Lady Blanche bore a daughter without any trouble at all and the baby was named Philippa after her grandmother the Queen. She was a tiny version of Blanche with paler eyes and hair and after the first disappointment over her sex most tenderly beloved.

Life in the Savoy Palace was pleasant. The unaccustomed luxury of a spacious room for the demoiselles and carpets instead of straw on the floors of the private apartments quickly became familiar. Philippa hoped they would remain there for a long time. Her duties were light and the Duchess a gentle taskmistress. She had a serenity that made it difficult to remember that she was only a couple of years older than Philippa herself. Perhaps the serenity came from her happy marriage or perhaps from the grief she had fought and conquered when her son had died. Occasionally Philippa, catching sight of her own smooth young face in a mirror, wondered if she was destined always to wear that untouched and inexperienced look, if having made herself indispensable to the Lady Blanche she was fated to remain unwed. The thought depressed her and she thrust it to the back of her mind and turned again to the letter that Geoffrey Chaucer had sent her.

'My dear Mistress Philippa,
'For a long time now I have promised myself the pleasure of writing to you, but one thing after another arises to delay me. There are my studies,

of course, but of them I can only say that not until this time did I realise how deficient I am in scholarship and how fascinating it is to acquire it.

'My lodgings are comfortable, and I have made several friends including a few who, like myself, seek a betrothal with Lady Poesy, though she is a quicksilver maiden who eludes us much of the time, twisting away just when we believe her seduced. But I shall tame the lady one day.

'The company here is not always prim, for I must confess that after a day bent over my books I often wander down to the tavern to sing wassail. Recently some of us, my friend Gower and others, fell into disputation with a scurvy friar who insisted that females had no souls. Of course we could not let such an insult to our mothers pass, and from words passed to blows with the friar screaming he was being murdered and the rest of us ordering him to admit the goodness of women. The friar got the best of it in the end, for the proctors came running and we were fined two shillings apiece for causing an affray.

'You will be happy to hear that I went to Woodstock to give your greetings to your sister. She can no longer be called your little sister save in years being taller than yourself with hair more red than brown. She wishes very much to see you again, or to obtain a post at Court. It is long since the Queen visited her palace there and the household feels the lack of her keenly. It would be a kindness in you to mention the fact when you next get the opportunity of a word with Her Grace.

'For her part Mistress Katherine sends you her best love and begs that you do not forget her. She wishes now for a wider world than the one she has known.

'Now, with regrets, I must cut my pleasure short

since I have a lecture to attend. Please convey my
loyal greetings to the Duke and Duchess and if time
permits send me a reply to this brief missive.

'Written by the hand of your affectionate
friend,

'Geoffrey Chaucer.'

She had not yet answered the note, but she had read it
several times. His remarks about Katherine pricked her
conscience slightly. In the years since she had left
Woodstock she had given her sister little serious
thought. In Philippa's mind the younger girl had
remained a lively, chattering child, but Katherine was
eighteen now and some provision ought to be made for
her future. Tall with hair more red than brown.
Geoffrey had not said whether she was fair or plain, nor
given her any information about Katherine's tastes or
talents. A husband would have to be found for her
sooner or later, as soon as Philippa herself was settled.

She must have heaved an unconscious sigh because
the Duke, entering, said, 'What ails you, Mistress?'

'My lord.' She rose hastily to dip into a curtsy. 'I was
reading a letter from Master Chaucer.'

'It must have contained gloomy news to cause such a
look on your face,' he said.

'Oh no indeed!' She shook her head. 'He is well and
conveys his loyal greetings. It is my sister –.'

'She is ill?'

'No, only still at Woodstock with no prospect of
leaving. She is my responsibility and I can do little for
her.'

'She is my lady mother's ward, isn't she?' he asked.

'Yes, my lord.'

'Provision will doubtless be made in due course,' he
said easily. 'You are not hankering to rush into
Oxfordshire, are you?'

'No, sir.' She hesitated, then said shyly, 'I like it well here.'

'I would be loth to bid you farewell,' he said, and held her gaze with his own blue one before he turned aside and went out again.

He had said 'I' and not 'we'. Philippa clasped her hands tightly around the tube she had made of the letter. No arrangements for her marriage had been made. She had wondered why, but now she was beginning to grope her way towards an answer. It was not the answer she approved but she feared greatly it was the answer she was beginning to desire.

Four

(i)

The marriage of the Princess Isabella to the Sieur de Coucy was the main event in that summer of thirteen sixty-four. There was a distinct note of relief among the congratulations for the King's eldest and sole surviving daughter was an old maid of thirty who had already been jilted by one suitor.

'And they say this one is guarded wherever he goes for fear he too tries to run away,' Alice joked.

There were a few stifled giggles but most of the demoiselles pretended not to hear. Alice, with her narrow black eyes and sharp tongue, was not popular with her own sex though the men, for reasons her own sex couldn't understand, always sought her as a partner in the dance. The King himself was frequently seen in conversation with her, another mark to set against her.

Philippa smiled faintly and concentrated more closely on the lengths of gold and silver thread she was weaving into a plait. She wished she were back at the Savoy and not at Westminster, but the Lady Blanche had insisted that she come.

'A royal wedding is a joyous event and it would be a shame for you to miss the festivities just because I cannot be there. Her Grace will appreciate your help too, for though she makes light of it she is far from well.'

The Duchess was within a week or two of another confinement, and everybody was hoping that it would be a brother for two-year-old Philippa. Pregnancy suited Blanche, imparting a rose flush to her alabaster skin and a sheen to the pale gold hair looped in braids at each side of her perfect face.

So Philippa had come to Westminster and after a day felt as if she had never known the comforts of the Savoy. Fortunately the hot weather eliminated draughts, but the stink from stables and latrines was as odoriferous as ever. She had been crammed into an extra bed put up in the demoiselles' quarters, and was engaged in doing what she could to refurbish her plain blue gown and make it festive enough for the ceremony.

The braid finished to her satisfaction she wound it about the long tail of brown hair that hung to her waist and smoothed her surcoat. She couldn't hope to compete with the more important ladies who would attend the ceremony but she would pass muster.

She had already made her curtsy to the Queen and been shocked by the rapidity with which the older woman had aged. Always plump and homely she now was swollen, her wrists and fingers bulging over the rings and bracelets she wore, and in her puffy face her eyes were dark shadowed.

'It is a pleasure to see you again, my dear.' The Queen's voice held all its old sweetness. 'I hear excellent reports of you from the Duchess. She tells me that you are quite invaluable to her.'

Philippa murmured her gratitude, though the well meant words struck a tiny chill through her. At twenty-two a young woman hoped to be more than an invaluable servant. She wanted to be a wife and mother with a husband who treated her with affection.

'I have arranged for your sister to spend some time at Sheppey Convent,' the Queen was continuing. 'My son John reminded me that I have not yet made full provision for you both, but of late I tire easily and neglect my responsibilities.'

'Your Grace, I have never complained,' Philippa said in alarm.

'It was Master Chaucer who mentioned the matter to John. You have a good friend in that young man. Both the King and John think most highly of his abilities.'

'Is Katherine to take the veil?' Philippa asked.

'No indeed,' the Queen said. 'She must decide that for herself, though I suspect she will prefer to take a husband. When I am feeling better I shall stir myself to the task.'

No word of a husband for Philippa though she surely knew that the elder sister should be matched before the younger. The interview had ended there with the arrival of Monsieur Froissart who came every day to read to Her Grace from the chronicle he was writing of her husband's reign. Philippa had bowed herself out and, deciding her garments were too plain for the occasion, hurried to find ornament.

Whatever she or anyone else wore would never rival the magnificence with which the bride was clad. Princess Isabella was too much like her mother ever to have been regarded as a beauty, and she looked every month of her thirty years, but her robes were stiff with gold embroidery and the coronet on her faded fair hair dazzled the eye with its wealth of diamonds, emeralds and pearls. Her broad freckled face had been thickly painted and her brisk step as she walked to the door of the Abbey was in contrast to her bridegroom's more laggard stroll.

Seated among the other demoiselles Philippa watched the ceremony with a curious mixture of pleasure and pain. She was glad for Isabella's sake that this marriage was taking place, though she had always thought the eldest Plantagenet devoid of charm, but there was pain in seeing another go smiling to her wedding.

The Queen was beaming, wiping away happy tears as she watched. Her other daughters, Joanna, Mary,

Blanche and Margaret had all died, the two latter only eighteen months before, and in her fond maternal eyes Isabella was beautiful.

The Prince of Wales and his wife, Joan, were not present, having travelled into the realm of Aquitaine where Joan was reported to be expecting the first child of this third marriage. Prince Lionel was still in Ireland where report had it that since his wife's death he had lost his amiable temper and become ferocious, and John had remained at the Savoy near his adored Blanche, so it was Prince Edmund, as blond and tall as his older brothers, who led his sister to the canopied dais where the bridegroom, eight years her junior, waited with an expression on his face that suggested the rumours of his reluctance were not inaccurate. The youngest prince, Thomas, escorted his mother, his thin features and lank, dark hair a contrast to the rest of the family.

Not only the Queen had aged, Philippa thought. The King had grey plentifully sprinkled through his beard and hair and his face was more lined than she recalled it, but he was in excellent spirits, nodding vigorously as his daughter made her vows, leaning to tuck a fold of her robe more snugly round the Queen with a tenderness that brought the moisture to Philippa's eyes.

The ceremony over and the Mass offered the company streamed back into the great hall. The banquet had been set out upon trestle tables covered with white cloths and swathes of rose branches and ivy decorated the cornices. With the ring firmly on her finger, the Princess Isabella sat smiling round at everybody while, at her side, her French husband drank wine as if it were vinegar. Among the demoiselles Philippa felt curiously out of place, as if she had grown beyond the giggling and the gossip. The sound of her own name recalled her straying attention and she lifted her head, staring across the table at Alice.

'I was just saying,' the latter said, bridling slightly,

'that you are wise not to tie yourself down in matrimony. One never gets the husband one wants.'

'And some of us don't get a husband at all.' A thin-faced girl, anxious to curry favour, made the remark in a sniggering little voice.

Philippa flushed indignantly. They were mocking her maidenhood, she thought, and wished she had wit to meet it.

'Mistress Roet is wise enough to know where her comfort lies,' Alice said. 'Is is true that Milord of Gaunt personally engaged you to wait upon his wife?'

'No, I was recommended by Her Grace also,' Philippa said. Her bright colour had faded and she answered with a quiet dignity that caused Alice to toss her black head.

'Her Grace is not well,' Eliza Persson said, changing the subject. 'The physicians cannot tell what ails her, but to my eye it looks like dropsy.'

'Yourself being an expert?' Alice made the gibe, and Philippa felt shame-faced relief that she was no longer the object of attention.

There was jealousy in it, no doubt, since positions at the Savoy were eagerly sought, but there had been truth in it too. She was without husband or sweetheart, and suddenly Princess Isabella with her painted face and elaborate robes looked not comical but pathetic.

As soon as possible she slipped away and found a corner of the immense chamber where she could watch the entertainments that followed the banquet without having to keep company with Alice. The entertainments themselves were brilliant. She had never outgrown her childish delight in the splendidly costumed masques that were presented at festival-time at Court.

The climax of this was particularly exciting as a dozen masked knights, among them the King and the bridegroom, trotted into the hall on caparisoned steeds and seized the ladies of their choice, the King first approaching the Queen who laughed and shook her head. He mimed despair at the rejection and circled the hall again, leaning suddenly to grip Alice about her narrow waist and seat her before him.

'So that's the way the wind blows,' a voice murmured almost in Philippa's ear.

'Geoffrey! What are you doing here?' She turned to him with surprise and pleasure.

'Paying my respects to the wedded pair. Why are you hiding like a mouse in the corner?'

'For fear of the Alice cat,' she answered.

'There is no real malice in her,' he said tolerantly. 'She wishes to rise in the world, as we all do, that's all.'

'Into the King's saddle?'

'The Queen is rumoured to approve. She is older than her years and unable these days to act the wife, so she chooses a girl who will amuse him but not capture his heart.'

'The Queen is a good woman,' Philippa said, and wondered if she could have scaled such heights of un-selfishness.

'As keeper of his heart she cares not who rides on his saddle,' Geoffrey said. 'How goes life with you, Mistress? You look exceedingly pretty. Life at the Savoy must agree with you.'

'I am happy in the life,' she informed him. 'The Duchess is as gentle a mistress as the Lady Elizabeth was.'

'I too am to serve the Lancasters when my studies are done.'

'And you have finished beating up friars.' She tilted her head at him.

'One lapse and I was in my cups at the time,' Geoffrey said. 'But I have met a friar of a different stamp – a man called Wycliff, who has revolutionary notions. He believes with me that English is the coming tongue and declares that the Scriptures themselves ought to be trans-lated into the vernacular.'

'But that's dreadful!' Philippa gave a disapproving shake of the head. 'Why, the common folk might learn to read them then, and how could they possibly understand?'

'No doubt you have an excellent point,' he said peaceably, and broke off as another knight, masked and armoured, rode towards them, bending at the last moment to snatch up Philippa. She had no time for more than a stifled squeal before she was perched on the saddle and her abductor was trotting out of the hall into the courtyard where he slid from the saddle, lifting her down and pulling off his mask.

'Oh, good heavens,' Philippa said weakly, staring up at the Duke. 'I thought you at the Savoy.'

'I rode over with my good news.' He looked happy and flushed.

'You have a son? Oh, I ought to have been with the Duchess.'

'Another daughter.' For an instant his face lost its brightness, and then he smiled. 'But she will be company for little Philippa, and we shall make a boy next time. This one came earlier than was expected, but is strong and healthy. We shall call her Elizabeth.'

'I must get back to the Savoy,' Philippa said.

'And miss the rest of the celebrations? I rode over to tell my family the news, but I could not resist taking part.' He handed her the mask with a little bow. 'I shall claim it later, but now I must speak to my parents. Was that Geoffrey you were talking to?'

'He came to pay his respects to the bride,' Philippa said.

'I shall take a glass of wine with him later.'

He patted her shoulder and went on into the hall, moving easily in the light armour, his fair head catching the last gleams of sunlight. Philippa stood for a few moments, gazing after him. The wife whom he dearly loved had safely borne a child, and he had come first to

let Philippa de Roet know. He might talk of impulsively
deciding to join in the masque, but she was the lady he
had chosen.

Inside her a voice mocked, 'Just like Alice', but she
pushed the thought away. She was not like Alice, not at
all.

(ii)

The royal family was increasing, with the Princess of
Wales finally producing a son. 'Edward for his
grandfather and father,' the Duchess said. 'They must
be delighted.' But the delight faded when word came
that the baby was not progressing as he should. At four
months he lay supine, not crying much nor seeming to
recognise his wet-nurse. Joan had written from the
Court in Aquitaine to tell the family that her baby had
slanted eyes and a tongue too big for his mouth.

'I have seen such children,' Philippa told Geoffrey.
'They never grow up in mind and they seldom live long.
Many call them idiots and hide them away.'

'Poor mite.' He shook his head. 'A king who never
grows up is no true monarch. We must pray she is
mistaken.'

'Princess Joan has had four children already,'
Philippa said. 'She is not likely to be mistaken.'

'Then let us hope for improvement at least,' he said.
'England needs a strong king.'

'And has one,' she said loyally, but she could not help
remembering how the king had chosen Alice and
danced with her afterwards while Queen Philippa sat,
her swollen feet tapping, a brave smile on her face.

The Duke had not returned to claim the mask, but
had been swallowed up by his relatives, accepting
congratulations on the birth of his new daughter.

Philippa had returned to her seat and found that
Geoffrey had led another demoiselle on to the floor and
was dancing with her. Alice's husband, William
Windsor, had offered his arm but he couldn't keep in
time with the music and Philippa had been glad when
the evening came to an end and she could retire. She
had feared teasing from the others because the Duke
had swept her up to the saddle, but nobody seemed to
have noticed and the talk had been all of the jewels worn
by the bride and the hang-dog looks of the bridegroom.

The next day, escorted by a squire, she had returned
to the Savoy where she had found Lady Blanche
recovering rapidly from the ordeal of childbirth.

'Nothing would suit my dear John but to rush to
Westminster and announce the birth himself,' she said,
laughing. 'We had prayed for a boy, but now we would
not change her.'

The new baby was fair and blue-eyed, a miniature
version of the Duchess. Her two-year-old sister trotted
round importantly with a doll in her arms, pretending
to be a mother also. When Philippa looked at them both
something ached in her heart. She liked children. Her
own she would love, but first there must be a father for
them. Looking in her glass, she stroked her smooth skin
and peered closely for signs of crow's feet. Had it been
thus for Princess Isabella, watching the years pass in
waiting, desperate for the embrace of a husband?

Turning from the glass she took up her needlework
and forced herself to concentrate on the choice between
a design of peacocks or butterflies for the cushion she
was making. It was an Easter gift for the Duchess and
neither butterflies nor peacocks seemed appropriate.
Blanche was more like a cool white lily, Philippa
thought, always serene and gentle. It was impossible to
imagine her in a temper. Nothing ever ruffled her
lovely serenity, nor brought more than a passing
shadow to her face. It was no wonder that the Duke

loved her so deeply. Philippa put down the square of velvet gently and sighed.

'The Duke wants to speak to you, Mistress.' A servant, entering, was panting slightly. John of Gaunt was a man frequently in a hurry, and his servants were accustomed to obeying orders on the run.

'Where is the Duke?' To her annoyance Philippa found herself blushing.

'In the library, Mistress,' the servant told her.

The library was the most highly prized by the Duke of all the rooms in his palace. He was the owner of sixty books, each one most beautifully illuminated and bound, with fine gold chains to attach them to the carved reading-lecterns. The lecterns were set in windowed alcoves that trapped the light, and there were high-backed chairs for the greater comfort of the reader.

As she entered John of Gaunt closed the pages of a volume he was perusing and rose.

'You came in good time, Mistress Philippa,' he said, his smile faintly teasing.

'I have learned that my lord Duke is generally in a hurry,' Philippa said demurely.

'It is no bad thing to keep one's household on its toes,' he said. 'But you need not have run so fast as to lose your breath. You may sit down.'

'Is it evil news?' Philippa sank on to the stool he indicated and raised anxious eyes to his face.

'Not in the least,' he reassured her. 'I have had enquiries made into the state of your late father's property in Picardy.'

'That was very thoughtful of you, sir,' she said gratefully.

'I wish I could give you happier news concerning the estate, but the recent wars have wrought havoc upon the farmlands of France, and though your steward is honest, he has had poor harvests and few workers. It will be many years before the place even begins to show a profit.'

'My father always said that he was a knight and not a farmer,' Philippa said. She spoke lightly to hide her disappointment, for without realising it she had always hoped that her inheritance would be larger than she expected.

'As I said I wish it were more cheering news,' he repeated. 'However, as wards of the Queen both you and your sister will always be well provided for. You need have no fears on that score.'

'My sister –' Philippa hesitated.

'Katherine, is it not? She is in a convent somewhere. It is of Katherine I wish to speak.'

'Forgive me, but from what I remember of her,' Philippa said, 'she would not be contented as a professed nun.'

'My own views, though my judgement derives from no personal knowledge of her. She is – twenty?'

'Yes, my lord.'

'Sir Hugh Swynford has asked me to provide him with a wife,' John said. 'His father recently died and he has come into his inheritance in Lincolnshire. Sir Hugh is not known to you?'

'No, sir.' Philippa shook her head.

'He has spent most of the past several years fighting and has paid little heed to the demands of Venus,' John said, smiling slightly, 'but he is still in his mid-twenties and fairly wealthy. It struck me as an excellent scheme to give Mistress Katherine to him as wife.'

This was a worse disappointment than learning that her inheritance was worth nothing. She stared at him speechlessly for a moment and then said, her voice shaking, 'My lord, Katherine is younger than I am.'

'Three years younger. I had not forgotten.'

'Then don't you think –?' She bit her lip.

'Philippa Pan,' he said softly, 'do you think that I

could willingly let you go into the wilds of Lincolnshire
to become Hugh Swynford's wife? Oh, one day you will
marry, but not yet. We don't wish to lose you just yet.'
'The Duchess and yourself?'
'The Duchess finds you one of the most reliable and
charming of her attendants,' he said, 'but I find you
maddening.'
'How so?' Startled, she gaped at him.
'Because you hide your heart,' he said. 'You hide it so
well that some swear you have none.'
'That's not true, my lord.' She spoke quietly, but her
face had flushed.
'Of all the demoiselles you are the one who holds
aloof,' he continued. 'Apart from our good friend,
Geoffrey Chaucer, you have no masculine companions.
Yet you are certainly comely, with a sweetness in your
aspect that's like young apples in spring. Do you have a
heart, Philippa Pan?'
'Yes, my lord.' She had paled again, and her hands
were trembling.
'If I asked you to give it into my keeping, what would
your answer be?'
'That you have a wife whom you love and that my
name is not Alice,' she flashed.
'My wife is an angel and I would never hurt her,' he
said, 'but she has nothing to do with you and me and
you have nothing to do with Alice.'
'And you and I,' Philippa said, 'can have nothing to
do with each other.'
'I have never forced a lady,' he said slowly, 'and I have
never penalised one for honesty. Can you tell me
honestly that you feel no desire?'
She shook her head, her heart beating unevenly
beneath her bodice. At that moment a door was opening
in her mind, showing a glimpse of something bright and
forbidden and sweet.
'Philippa, will you trust me when I tell you that no

hurt will ever come to you through any friendship between you and me?' he said.

'I do trust you,' she protested, 'but I know that when a woman has no fortune she is a fool to fling away respect as well.'

'My respect would not alter.'

'The Duchess –?'

'Blanche sees only what her goodness allows her to see. Philippa, I told you that I would claim the mask I wore at my sister's wedding ball. Have you lost it?'

'I laid it in lavender,' she admitted.

'I shall claim it tonight,' said the Duke.

Five

(i)

There were days when she was so happy that the rain was soft as thistledown, falling on her upturned face, and days when she was so unhappy that the sun was dim even on the brightest afternoon. Since that night, months before, when the Duke had come to her room to claim the mask he had donned at Princess Isabella's wedding.

She had never known the embrace of a man and when John of Gaunt held her in his arms she prayed silently that she would never know another. He was both tender and masterful, his magnificent body stirring her to heights of passion she had never dreamed lay within her. Those stolen hours in her chamber, the door barred lest any of the other demoiselles decided to retire early, had been repeated albeit at infrequent intervals in other rooms tucked away in the vast and luxurious Savoy.

'There is no need for you to feel guilt,' John told her when she murmured of the Duchess.

'But I serve her still,' Philippa said. 'Every day I help her to comb her hair and lay out her jewels. One day she will look up, meet my eyes in the mirror, and know.'

'Blanche is above such petty suspicion,' John said. 'Oh, she knows that now and then, if I am long absent from her or she is not well, then I stray, but the occasions are rare.'

'And of no importance?'

'I have never taken any woman lightly,' he told her. 'In my eyes all your sex are deserving of respect and affection, even Alice whom I know you despise. She makes my father happy and my lady mother gazes in the other direction. As does Blanche.'

The rules had been spelled out. She must continue to serve the Duchess and when the mood was upon him the Duke visited her, always sending a discreet message with the excuse that she was required to discuss the affairs of her Picardy estate or help him to plan some entertainment for his wife. If others in the household guessed they kept silent.

Philippa had made her own private rules. She confided in nobody and was glad for the first time that she had no bosom friend among the other demoiselles. In public she seldom spoke to the Duke and she was careful never to allow herself to gaze at him with affection. When he sent for her she went calmly, hiding the trembling that gripped her, dropping a demure curtsy until the door was barred and he stepped forward to take her in his arms and bury his face in the hollow of her neck.

'I never imagined,' she said to him one day, 'that I would be pleased to be unwed.'

'Why so?' He arched an eyebrow in the way that made him look like a mischievous boy.

'Because I cannot imagine giving to any other man what I give to you,' she answered simply.

'You're a pretty thing.' He drew her closer, running his fingers through her hair. 'So you will stay a spinster for love of me? I shall remind you of that when you come to tell me that you are wild for love of some squire or other. And speaking of marriage –'

'Which I can live without,' she said, truly believing it at that instant.

'Sir Hugh Swynford is back at Westminster and eager

to meet his affianced bride. Have you written to your sister?'

'Some months since. She sent back word that she would be happy to be wed but worries that her dowry will be so small.'

'He'll take her without dowry. The Swynfords are rich and Hugh is shy with women. I shall send someone to bring her to Court.'

'To the Savoy?'

'To Windsor. We go there for the celebration of St George's Day. Had you forgotten?'

She had not forgotten, but she had pushed it out of her mind. Away from the Savoy there would be no private place where she and John might spend an hour without fear of discovery. Unlike Alice who gloried openly in the relationship she enjoyed with the King, Philippa saw her love for the Duke as something that belonged to themselves alone, too precious to be sullied by gossip and sidelong glances.

'It will be splendid to see Katherine again,' she said with determined cheerfulness. The truth was that her sister had grown shadowy in her memory. She had remained the lively, untidy child who always got her embroidery silks in a tangle. Philippa did a quick mental calculation, realising that Katherine was now past twenty-one, and probably bored to death with the tedium of convent life.

Apart from the Prince and Princess of Wales who were still in Aquitaine the entire royal family were going to Windsor for the St George's Day celebrations. Philippa had a new gown of pale lemon that emphasised the golden streaks in her brown hair, and though she knew that John would have no leisure to spend with her the prospect of the gaieties planned was exciting.

She had hoped to see Geoffrey but he, having completed his studies at Oxford, had gone to Italy on his first minor diplomatic mission for the King. Philippa knew she would miss his company, but on the other hand she would not have to conceal her interest in the Duke. Geoffrey had sharp eyes, and she was anxious to keep the affair a secret.

The Queen was ill. Making her curtsy Philippa was shocked by the grossly swollen body, the heavy eyes and labouring breath of the kindly lady. Of course the Queen was old, in her mid-fifties, and worn out with frequent childbearing, but it seemed unfair that she, who had been such a loving helpmate to the King, must lie for most of the day in a darkened room while the King attended the festivities with Alice at his side.

Katherine was to be escorted from the convent on the day of the main tournament, and Philippa found herself unaccountably nervous as she obeyed the summons from a page to go down to the courtyard where her sister waited. The younger Roet girl had never been to Court, and would have to learn the delicate and elaborate etiquette that separated life in the main palaces from the more informal existence at Woodstock and Sheppey.

For a moment she stood, bewildered, looking round, and then a tall, thin girl with a cloud of red hair floating about her face stepped forward, flinging her arms about her.

'Oh, Philippa, you are grown so pretty. I would have known you anywhere by your neatness.'

Katherine had not grown pretty, Philippa thought, returning the embrace. She was too slender, her skin browned by the sun and her hair too vivid a red. Though Philippa knew that it was impossible the shade looked unnatural.

'Welcome, my dear sister.' Suddenly relieved that Katherine had not, after all, grown into a beauty, Philippa hugged her, the years slipping away. 'I am truly glad to see you.'

'And I to be out of the convent,' Katherine said,

making a comical little grimace. 'The nuns were very kind but they kept hinting how happy they would be if I took the veil. I was never so pleased in my life as when I received word that Sir Hugh Swynford had offered for me. Is he handsome? When shall I meet him? Am I to make my curtsy to the Queen? She will not recall me, I daresay, from –'

'Gently, gently,' Philippa said, laughing. 'You cannot bridge all our time apart in five minutes. Come with me and I'll show you the demoiselles' quarters. Then we shall see if Her Grace is well enough to receive you.'

First she must find a more fitting gown than the shabby kirtle that Katherine was wearing. Elizabeth Persson was about her height and good-natured enough to lend one.

'This is a beautiful castle, isn't it?' Katherine was chattering as Philippa hurried her along. 'Much larger than Woodstock and I always thought that very fine. The nuns made me promise to write and tell them all about everything. Do those gentlemen know you?'

She glanced towards a small group of squires who had paused in their game of dice to stare as the sisters went by. An approving murmur reached Philippa's ears. Her sister had already attracted favourable notice, it seemed. Philippa wondered why, for the girl lacked the small features and braided hair so greatly admired.

Elizabeth Persson was obliging enough to present Katherine with a discarded gown of her own and Philippa used a length of green silk to tie back her sister's unruly hair, but the thick, curly strands escaped from the silk and clung to her broad, sun-tanned brow.

'My hair never will lie flat,' Katherine said cheerfully. 'The nuns used to tease me about it.'

'It will have to suffice,' Philippa said, giving up the attempt. 'Come. We shall wait upon Her Grace if she is well enough to receive visitors.'

The Queen lay, as so often she lay these days, on a

couch in a dim corner of her chamber, for the bright
sunlight hurt her eyes and puffed the already swollen
lids. She held out her hand with all her old kindliness of
manner as Katherine dropped her curtsy, her smile as
sweet in her weary face.

'Katherine de Roet. I remember you, my dear, from
my visits to Woodstock. When I am stronger I shall go
there again. It used to afford me great pleasure to see
my wards and note their progress.'

'I fear I made very little, Your Grace,' Katherine said.

'But now you are to be married.' The Queen smiled
faintly. Perhaps she recalled her own love-affair when
as a girl of fourteen in Hainault she had met the future
king of England.

'To Sir Hugh Swynford,' Katherine said.

'A most admirable young man from a fine old family,'
the Queen approved. 'I wish you every happiness. Your
sister will show you the way of things here until your
wedding takes you from us for you will reside in
Lincolnshire. The Swynfords have lived there for many
centuries.'

'They must all be exceedingly old, Your Grace,'
Katherine said with a twinkle.

Philippa held her breath for despite her kindly ways
the Queen possessed little humour, but the other
chuckled.

'Your little sister has a pretty wit,' she said to Philippa.
'Sir Hugh will be the better for it. He is apt to be too
solemn for a young man.'

Her voice sounded weary suddenly, and the physician
who hovered watchfully in the corner rose, shooting a
warning look towards the two girls.

'I am very happy to be at Court and near to Your
Grace again,' Katherine said, and the Queen's face
broke into a smile again as she looked at the girl's keen
grey eyes and eager smile.

'She is very ill, is she not?' Katherine whispered as

they went down the stairs again. 'I am sorry, but one can understand why the King takes Alice Perrers to his bed.'

'Katherine, where in the world do you think of such tales?' Philippa said in fright.

'It is common knowledge in the convent at Sheppey,' Katherine said innocently. 'Is it not generally known?'

'It is not spoken about,' Philippa said hurriedly. 'Certain matters are seen, but not spoken about openly. You must understand that.'

'I know when to hold my peace.' Katherine looked faintly hurt. 'I may speak openly to you, my sister?' Her voice trailed into wistfulness and Philippa felt the tug of their old affection mingled with uneasiness.

'Of what else do they gossip at the convent?' she enquired.

'Of the Prince and Princess of Wales being in hopes of a second child and of Prince Lionel going to marry the Lady Violante of Milan though he mourns still for his first wife.'

Philippa controlled a sigh of relief. From Katherine's artless reply it was obvious that no gossip about herself and John of Gaunt was current. Their affair was too discreet to become the subject of scandal.

'When am I to meet Sir Hugh?' Katherine was enquiring eagerly.

Philippa was about to reply that Sir Hugh would doubtless pay his respects in due course when the gentleman in question rounded the corner and almost ran full tilt into them. He opened his mouth to apologise and remained, looking from Philippa to Katherine with such surprise in his rather dull face that the former's heart sank. Katherine in her borrowed dress with her red hair already escaping from its confining filet looked sadly countrified.

'My sister Katherine is only just arrived –' she began nervously, but he interrupted.

'But I was not told she was so fair. She lights up the

Court.'

'Does she?' Philippa surveyed her sister doubtfully, then belatedly remembered her manners. 'Katherine, this is —'

'My betrothed,' Katherine said. 'I had guessed it. I am happy to meet you, sir. All this is very strange to me so you must pardon me if I gape at everything like a zany.'

Sir Hugh, who looked as if he would have pardoned her anything including murder, gaped wider than Katherine claimed for herself and bowed, reddening to the ears.

'We shall see you in Hall,' Philippa said, and he mumbled something and backed away, his eyes still devouring her sister.

'He is not as handsome as I pictured,' Katherine murmured, when he was out of earshot.

'He is a brave and valiant knight from an old and greatly respected family,' Philippa said severely. 'Though our father was a knight he never became rich so you are a most fortunate girl to be marrying him.'

'Oh, I am sure that I shall accustom myself to it,' Katherine said cheerfully. 'But I shall enjoy myself for a week or two with you, my sister, before I settle into wedlock.'

Philippa, hurrying her sister past a group of archers who had paused to stare admiringly, decided that the wedding ought to be hastened as much as possible. Her sister seemed to be attracting far too much attention from every male who laid eyes on her.

(ii)

Had it not been for Alice the marriage of Katherine de Roet and Sir Hugh Swynford might not have taken place as speedily as it did. Katherine took to the gaieties of the Court with all the enthusiasm of a young woman who has spent her life in obscurity, and there was no mistaking the effect her tall, graceful figure, her vivid hair and her ringing laughter had upon those who met her. She had charm, Philippa was forced to admit, and it was the more potent because it was unself-conscious. To do Katherine justice she seemed not to notice the glances and whispers of admiration that followed her. Alice did notice, and lost no time in seeking out Philippa.

'If Sir Hugh is not to be cut out by a more daring suitor,' she began, slipping her arm through the other's with unusual friendliness, 'you and I must speed on the wedding.'

'It is not for me but for Her Grace to make the arrangements,' Philippa said stiffly.

'Her Grace is not well,' Alice said. 'If your poor sister waits for her to recover she will stay unwed for a very long time. Let me see what plans can be hatched to make your sister a married lady with the pomp behoving her state.'

What Alice meant, Philippa thought, was that the King himself had noticed the newcomer and sent a compliment down from the high table. Alice was jealous of her position and would brook no fancied rivals.

'I am sure,' said Philippa aloud, 'that Katherine is most anxious to be wed.'

'I shall arrange everything.' Alice smiled her cat-like smile and glided away.

Within the week a priest had been engaged and the necessary papers signed. Sir Hugh, looking as if he found it impossible to believe his good fortune, led Katherine, her hair streaming loose from beneath a chaplet of white flowers, to the church door where Philippa waited to watch her sister joined in marriage. Alice had shown uncharacteristic generosity, giving the bride a robe of white silk and a sash that was heavy with silver beads, and Philippa as she heard Katherine's sweet young voice making the vows was seized by a sudden thankfulness.

Her sister was safely married and would soon be living on the Swynford estate in Lincolnshire. There would be no further need to fret lest her head be turned by all the admiring looks and remarks shot in her direction. Katherine was safe and Milord of Gaunt had not even noticed her.

'You will visit me one day?' At the last moment Katherine clung to the elder girl, tears in her eyes. 'We have been apart for so many years and now I must lose you again.'

'I shall be godmother to your first child,' Philippa promised, kissing her. 'Sir Hugh, you will take good care of my sister, for she is very dear to me.'

It was true. At that moment Katherine seemed infinitely precious, a link to a life that had vanished for ever.

He mumbled something. Philippa hoped that he would learn to be more articulate or Katherine would find his company tedious, and helped his bride to the saddle of the horse that waited. Waving her hand as they rode away, Philippa blinked back her own tears. She loved her sister very deeply and she was ashamed of the relief she felt at her leaving.

A few days later they returned to the Savoy, Lady Blanche travelling in a litter since there was reason to believe she was pregnant again.

'This time I am sure it will be a little boy,' she informed her demoiselles. 'My prayers have never been more fervent. It would please the Duke so greatly if we had another son in place of the one we lost. Not that one child can ever replace another, but a man craves a son.'

Her pleasure in her pregnancy gave Philippa a little pang, not of envy but of sadness. Though she herself was the Duke's mistress she knew that his deepest and most abiding love was reserved for his beautiful wife. His eyes, when they rested upon her, glowed softly and his voice was tender. Yet since Blanche had discovered her pregnancy and they had returned to the Savoy he sought out Philippa with increasing frequency.

As chief demoiselle she now had a tiny chamber to herself, a perquisite which she guessed the Duke had arranged. It was a slip of a room overlooking an inner courtyard with a narrow staircase giving egress to the outside, perfect for the Duke who could slip unnoticed away when he left her bed.

'One day,' Philippa thought sometimes, 'I shall regret my foolishness, but for this summer I shall put my conscience to bed.'

Summer was at the height of her loveliness when Philippa found that Blanche was not the only one expecting the Duke's child.

'It cannot be.' Philippa spoke aloud, sitting on her bed, counting frantically on her fingers. 'I must have noticed other symptoms.'

But she had brushed aside her loss of appetite, her frequent trips to the privy as symptoms of some malaise caused by the hot weather. Now she must face the truth. She was carrying the Duke's child and for a few moments she was filled with panic. She was twenty-four years old and no man had yet offered marriage. Now no man ever would.

If her calculations were right the baby would be born in seven months. A February babe.

'In time for Candlemas,' she said aloud and jumped nervously as the door opened and John, entering, said,

'What will be in time for Candlemas?'

'My baby,' Philippa said starkly and burst into tears.

'You are with child?' John's face was a study in conflicting emotions, natural pride fighting with consternation. 'Are you sure?'

'Yes.' Philippa sniffed and wiped her damp eyelids on

her wide sleeve. She had never been a person who spilled her emotions all over the place, and she despised herself for her weakness now. Her charm for John of Gaunt lay, she instinctively knew, in her neat and pretty manners, in her discretion and unfailing good humour.

'You make me laugh,' he always said when they talked together. He was a man who needed gaiety, and there was no gaiety in her now.

'In February?' he said.

Philippa nodded.

'I wouldn't want Blanche to know,' he said, and she wanted to cry again at hearing his first thoughts which were for his wife's peace of mind.

'I shall leave, of course.' She drew the rags of her dignity about her and sat up a little straighter. 'I will not bring shame –'

'It is not of shame that I think,' he said quickly, flushing slightly. 'It is only that I made a promise to Blanche that Marie St Hilaire would be the last. She was also the first, even before Blanche and I were wed, and I did promise –'

'It is then of your own shame that you think,' Philippa said. Her eyes had begun to sparkle with temper but she kept her voice low. 'You don't want your wife to find out that you are forsworn. You need not fear, my lord. When this began I wasn't a silly child, but a young woman prepared to take the consequences. We are equally to blame.'

'We must find you a husband,' John said.

'A splendid idea,' she said levelly. 'Shall we have it cried through the Court? Mistress Philippa de Roet is with child by the Duke of Lancaster, and seeks a husband who is willing to father another man's child?'

'Bitterness solves nothing.' His eyes flashed a warning. 'You cannot possibly run away without a word. Blanche is fond of you and would be terribly anxious.'

His wife again, but he had never pretended to love

anyone more than Blanche. According to his own lights he had been honest and there had been no force involved.

'Then what am I to do?' she asked, trying to maintain the calmness of her tone though her heart was hammering. 'I have no dowry, John. You have told me often enough there are no profits from the farm my father left.'

'Do you trust me so little that you believe me capable of turning you off without a groat?'

He looked so indignant that she suddenly wanted to laugh.

'I have had no thoughts in my head,' she replied, 'save that I love both you and the Duchess, and would not allow myself to realise that one love makes mockery of the other.'

'Not in the least,' he said quickly. 'We are bonded more near because of our love for Blanche, and that makes it impossible for either of us to hurt her. Our mutual affection —'

'Must cease,' she interrupted. 'You must see that the situation would be quite intolerable were I to stay here. I was never more than a light-of-love for you.'

'We must find you a husband,' he repeated, and bent to kiss her cheek. 'Give me a few days and this will be happily resolved. I give you my word.'

(iii)

'Master Chaucer, when did you return from Italy?'

Philippa's face was rosy with pleasure as she greeted him. Geoffrey looked prosperous in a handsome tunic with high collar and hanging sleeves trimmed with gold braid, and a velvet liripipe with a gold tassel. It was a pity he was not taller, she thought, for he was a well set-up man with a skin free of pockmarks and good teeth.

'Two months since but I had business for my father to transact in Southampton. You know that he died?'

'No, I didn't hear. I have been so preoccupied with my own affairs,' she said remorsefully. 'I am sorry indeed to hear it, for I recall how kind he was to my sister and myself when we were brought from France.'

'Your sister is wed, I hear.'

'To Sir Hugh Swynford and gone into Lincolnshire to live. I have not heard from her yet, but neither of us writes many letters.'

'I am writing constantly,' he told her. 'My translation of the Romance of the Rose has found favour at Court. I have recited it for Their Graces.'

'I am happy for you,' she said politely, and wondered if the poem had been very long and tedious.

'You look very pretty today,' he said, so abruptly that she stared at him. Compliments were not part of the currency in their friendship.

'It's last year's dress,' she told him. 'You have seen it many times before.'

'I was looking at the face,' he corrected. 'I take little interest in women's gowns, but faces I always see. Yours has a bloom upon it.'

She knew from her glass that he was not flattering. Her complexion was peaches and her hair was thick and luxuriant. It was ironic that at the time she was most insecure she should be looking her best.

'You learned gallantry in Italy,' she countered lightly.

'I met some fascinating people,' he told her, his face lighting up. 'No, not ladies, though the southern ones are often beautiful, but a poet called Boccaccio who tells tales that make you laugh and weep and then do both at once. We shared many a glass of wine together and the land of Italy itself is full of colour and light and shifting shadows. Mistress Philippa, will you marry me?'

For a moment the sense of his question failed to penetrate her mind and then she understood the meaning and at the same time understood more. It was all there in his sudden arrival, in the kindness of his brown eyes, in his voice.

'Milord Duke has told you,' she said flatly.

'And explained the predicament in which you find yourself. I hurried here before some other offered for you.'

'You hurried here to oblige the Duke,' she said. 'I have never known you to lie before, Geoffrey. I wish you would not start now.'

'It is no lie.' He took her hand. 'Philippa, my dear, we have been excellent friends since our youth, and friendship is a rare and precious thing between men and women. I never thought to offer for you because you are the daughter of a knight and I am the son of a vintner, but the Duke told me that you carry his child and he wishes to make provision for you. It is true that he spoke of the necessity of finding you a husband and I said at once that I wished I were the one chosen for I never met any woman I like as well as you.'

'Like is not love,' she said very low.

'And love cannot always lead to marriage. Women have little choice.'

'I was not seduced,' she said with painful honesty. 'I went into the affair with my eyes open knowing it was wrong and could never last. It is ended now. We cannot hurt the Duchess.'

'Whom I also love,' Geoffrey said softly.

'You would be willing to father another man's baby?' Philippa asked harshly.

'It will be your child, and mine.'

'And not a bastard.' Philippa was silent for a space, turning over possibilities in her mind. She could leave the Savoy and bear the child without wedlock, or travel to Lincolnshire and let Katherine, so auspiciously mated, know her shame, or she could wed Geoffrey Chaucer who offered out of kindness and to oblige his patron. Women, she thought sadly, had very little choice at all.

Six

(i)

The Duchess was as pleased about the wedding as if she had arranged it herself.

'Master Chaucer is a most excellent and accomplished person,' she said. 'You need not fear his being of lower rank than yourself, for he is a man who would shine in any company.' Which was nonsense, Philippa thought even as she smiled and nodded, for Geoffrey, though he was pleasant and good-natured, lacked the glitter and sparkle of more sophisticated men. He was ambitious and hard-working to be sure, but he was more apt to listen than to talk and his poetry occupied far too large a share of his attention.

Geoffrey behaved as if he were also delighted at the impending marriage. He took her to his mother's house near Cheapside and Mistress Chaucer greeted her with the brisk kindness that Philippa remembered from her childhood.

'Such a long time since we met and so much has happened since then. Come and sit down. You know that Kate is wed? To Simon Mannington. A love-match if you please, like yourself and Geoffrey I'll be bound. She is with child and very content.'

'Like yourself' was in her glance. Doubtless she imagined her son had anticipated the wedding night and doubtless she considered him the better man for it.

The Chaucer house was a handsome one with a strip

99

of garden at the back but it was still cheek by jowl with
its neighbours and the constant bustle and rumble of
traffic past the windows made it a far cry from the
elegance of the Savoy.

For the time they would remain at the Savoy.
Geoffrey had no dwelling of his own as yet, and
expected to be often absent on diplomatic business for
the King, so it made good sense for his wife to continue
in attendance on the Duchess.

'Our children will grow up to play together,' Blanche
said in happy innocence, and Philippa felt guilt strike
through her like a needle. Blanche was a good and
gentle mistress, and it was useless to seek to excuse her
own conduct with the knowledge that the other knew
nothing. A thief was not less culpable because the one
robbed had no idea of it.

The wedding would take place in the chapel of the
Savoy and the Duke would meet the costs. 'It is our gift
to you and Geoffrey,' Blanche said smilingly.

But not the only gift. Philippa, walking in the grounds
on the day before the marriage, was overtaken by the
Duke. He looked handsome in a furred cloak to keep at
bay the winds of early autumn and she felt her heart
miss a beat and then race on as he fell into step beside
her.

'We have not talked for some time,' he said.

'There is nothing to say,' Philippa rejoined. At that
instant she felt something close to hatred for this man
who used his power and charm to snare.

'There is much to say,' he corrected gravely. 'Philippa,
you must not imagine that my regard and affection are
less for you because you are to be wed or because our
loving is done. I am not a man to neglect old friends.'

Like Marie St Hilaire, she thought, clenching her
hands under the folds of the gown she wore. Friendship
was his name for it. Love he reserved for his wife.

'I am,' she said with a touch of defiance, 'content to

become Master Chaucer's wife. He is one of my oldest friends.'

'He is a man who will go far in life. It has been my pleasure to help him a little.'

Even to a wife, she reflected ironically, but held her peace.

'I hope that you will accept a gift from me,' John said.

'My Lady has told me that you have granted me a yearly allowance of ten marks,' she said. 'I am most grateful to you both.'

'This gift is from myself alone.' He stopped in their walking, drawing something from his sleeve. 'It is a measure of my own gratitude, my dear.'

The brooch sparkled against the palm of his hand, each trembling twig of gold topped by a tiny flower, the petals of gold, the hearts of precious stones. Philippa gazed at it silently, seeing the diamond, the topaz, the garnet, the ruby and the pearl centring each blossom.

'It is very lovely,' she said at last. 'It is fit for a fine lady.'

'Which is why I bought it for you,' he said. 'The five flowers are like the decades of a rosary, for each has five petals – you see? I want you to remember what lay between us as something very precious.'

The very act of adultery had to be turned into something gallant, she thought, not sure whether to laugh or cry. She smiled instead, thinking that the five flowers were like herself and Geoffrey, John and Blanche. The diamond for the Duke and the spotless pearl for his innocent wife, the topaz for Geoffrey and the ruby for herself. The garnet was for the child she was carrying. Even as that fancy entered her mind it was displaced by a premonitory chill that rippled through her without warning. The garnet was for someone who had not yet appeared and it was no child.

'Is something wrong?' John was asking.

Philippa shut out the fear that threatened to paralyse

her. She was fanciful due to her condition, she reasoned. No stone could threaten as the garnet had seemed to do.

'I shall wear it with pride,' she said at last, 'but not on my wedding day. It would not be fitting to marry Geoffrey with another man's jewel against my heart. He deserves better.'

'You will be a good wife for him,' John said, looking pleased. 'I like to see those whom I love made happy.'

He liked to put people into neat boxes and tie them securely with ribbon too, she realised. As the wife of his friend she ceased to be a threat to his own good opinion of himself. He was a child as all men were children. In that moment she had never been more irritated with him nor loved him so much.

'Thank you for your kindness to me, my lord Duke,' she said, the words putting distance between them. 'Excuse me, but I have preparations to make for tomorrow.'

She dipped into a swift curtsy and was gone, walking quickly back to the room which after this night she would share with Geoffrey when he was home.

It was a modest ceremony, with only a brief ill-spelled note from Katherine in Lincolnshire to wish her joy, and only the Duke and Duchess there to witness the vows. Making them, Philippa promised herself silently that she would be a faithful wife. She would cease to think of John or to turn over in her mind the memory of the hours they had spent together. She was full of conscious resolution, and the kiss that John dropped upon her cheek when the plain gold ring was on her finger burned scarcely at all.

For her own part she felt herself to be in a kind of dream. Though her dress was loosely cut, a sideless surcoat of velvet covering the bodice and kirtle, she could feel the child within kicking fiercely as if it sought to remind her that it existed even though her shape was so cunningly disguised. She kept her eyes lowered modestly, not raising them until she was safely wed, and then the relief on the Duke's face struck her like a blow. He was grateful to his protégé for taking a discarded and pregnant mistress off his hands.

'You must not fret that I shall make love to you against your desire,' Geoffrey whispered as they sat at table later. 'There will be no forcing.'

Philippa felt a gratitude towards him that rivalled the Duke's. The prospect of lying with him under the same roof, in the same bed, where she had received John's caresses, had been a dark threat and was now removed. She pressed his hand fervently beneath the tablecloth, whispering back,

'In truth I would prefer to wait until after the child is born, for women at these times feel little desire, you know.'

Geoffrey smiled and nodded, hiding the disappointment in his eyes. That he should have wed a knight's daughter who was the favourite companion of his adored Duchess and would bear the child of his admired patron must suffice for the present.

'We begin our marriage under fortunate auspices,' he said cheerfully. 'The Duke has granted me an annuity of twenty marks in addition to your own ten, so when we set up our own household we shall be able to furnish it well. I take it that you don't wish to live with my mother?'

'She is a most amiable lady –' Philippa began hesitantly.

'But no kitchen was ever big enough for two women.' He smiled at her. 'And my mother plans to take a new husband herself. A man somewhat younger than herself but a good fellow, called Bartholomew Chapel. He will make her life less lonely for with my father dead and my sister married, she lacks someone to fuss over.'

'I shall visit her often,' Philippa said.

'She looks forward to the birth of her grandchild,' Geoffrey said.

But it would be true grandchild, albeit unacknowledged, of Queen Philippa who lay, bloated with dropsy, at Westminster, seldom fit to receive visitors, while her husband sought comfort with Alice Perrers. 'My child,' Philippa thought, 'will have royal blood.'

The thought that it might resemble the Duke so closely as to prove a disaster occurred to her. Quickly she said,

'I would like it well if the child could be born in your mother's house. I would feel more secure in the presence of a mother-in-law.'

'She would not have it otherwise,' Geoffrey said, and his smile reassured her.

(ii)

That the child should not resemble the Duke became her constant prayer in the months that followed. She superstitiously avoided looking too often at him when he was present in the company and tried, when his image crept into her mind, to replace it by a picture of Geoffrey's pleasant countenance, but she was not proof against the invasion of her dreams. Night after night John strode through them, golden and beautiful, and when she moaned herself into wakefulness again she felt sharp resentment that it was Geoffrey's hand that pressed her shoulder, his voice that said,

'You are but riding the nightmare, love.'

It was after one such nightmare that she afterwards failed to remember that her husband's comforting hand became more urgent, the gentleness in his voice charged with desire. He had promised not to force her, and he did not, for in that moment with the edges of the dream hanging like cobwebs across the surface of her mind she turned and clung to him, and let herself be loved.

He was gentle and skilful, even though her body had become unwieldy, and she was glad of his warmth and the clean scent of him, but afterwards she turned her face into the pillow and silently wept, feeling as if she had betrayed something precious that had been hers and the Duke's.

In the last week of January she moved to the Chaucer house, over the innocent protests of the Duchess.

'I planned for my own physician to attend you, my dear Philippa, and now you run off to Cheapside. Your mother-in-law is welcome to come here, you know. The Savoy could contain twice as many people.'

'She would not be at her ease here, Madam,' Philippa said truthfully.

'Then I must not be selfish.' Blanche gave her an affectionate glance. 'But you will return when I have need of you. No other demoiselle can soothe a backache as you can or amuse me out of a melancholy mood.'

Philippa had given her word, avoided the Duke's eye, and been escorted by Geoffrey to the handsome but cramped dwelling in Cheapside where his mother had set aside Kate's old room for them.

'You must tell me if you find it chilly though I've had it aired and sweetened and a daily fire lit against any damp or draught,' she said. 'Geoffrey may amuse himself with his poems, but we women have more important matters to occupy our time.'

At that she was at one with Dame Agnes who regarded reading and writing as the last refuge of a person with nothing more important to occupy his mind. That her son was educated was a matter of great pride to her, since learning enabled one to get on faster in business, but to use one's learning for the purpose of scribbling verses struck her as ridiculous. The time passed pleasantly enough, in sewing and gossiping about other confinements.

'Such a time I had with Geoffrey,' the older woman confided, 'I would not like to tell you. Twenty-five hours in labour and then the cord was about his neck. I feared that neither of us would survive, but I had an excellent midwife. I wish she were still alive but the plague took her. However Dame Felicitas will do as well. She has considerable experience, and will see you safely through it.'

She was a good woman, Philippa reminded herself, shifting herself into a position more comfortable for her aching back. She had made no sly remarks about the child being due only five months after the wedding. Perhaps in her eyes it proved her son to have more in him than the wish to write poetry. Philippa tried not to think of John's brilliant blue eyes, so different from the brown ones of herself and Geoffrey. If perchance the babe – but all babies had blue eyes.

The first pains were so slight that she might have mistaken them for cramp had not her linen been spotted with blood. That was the signal for the control of her body to be taken from her and given into the capable hands of Dame Felicitas and Dame Agnes. Obediently she followed their instructions to bear down, to desist bearing down, to sip the hot posset that would ease her thirst and her pains, to fix her mind on the child now struggling into the world instead of weeping for the mother who had died so long ago.

'Six hours,' the midwife declared with satisfaction as the head emerged. 'An easy labour, thanks be to Our Lady.'

Philippa wondered what a hard labour was like and then the lusty cry of the child made the pain worth while, and she heard her own weaker crow of triumph.

'A bonny little girl,' Agnes Chaucer said. 'Oh, but she is a beauty. The image of Geoffrey when he was born.'

Which must surely prove that all babies looked alike! When the baby was finally placed in her arms Philippa could see no resemblance save to a monkey that the King had owned, its eyes wise and sad, its little face screwed up.

'Have you chosen a name? The priest must be informed at once that the baptism may be arranged,' her mother-in-law said. 'The sooner the devil is driven out the better.'

'Elizabeth,' Philippa said.

Geoffrey would have preferred Blanche, but with the sensitivity that she was learning was a part of him he had suggested the name of Prince Lionel's delicate first wife.

'For we both served in her household first and it is fitting she should be remembered.'

'Elizabeth Chaucer,' Geoffrey's mother repeated. ' 'Tis a pretty name.'

By the end of the first month she had grown into a pretty child, her eyes less blue than grey, her tiny fists flailing the air whenever she was released from her swaddling bands.

'She will grow up into a fighter,' Geoffrey said, holding her gingerly while his mother hovered anxiously near, convinced that he might drop her.

'As long as she does not grow up and write poetry,' Philippa said. She had meant it as a jest but the words came out sharply and Geoffrey shot her a glance as he laid the child in the cradle.

'She will probably grow up to resemble you, my dear,' he said mildly, and did not again offer to hold Elizabeth until he was asked. It was as if her words reminded him that her true father was at the Savoy, celebrating the birth of his son, Henry. Blanche had prayed to good purpose, it seemed.

'A sturdy red-haired lad with his father's eyes, they say,' Agnes said. 'He is heir after the Prince of Wales, and poor little Prince Edward who they whisper is not

all in his wits, and the baby Lady Joan has just borne –
whether boy or girl I know not.'

'A boy,' Geoffrey told her. 'He's to be named Richard
after the Lionheart.'

'My son knows all the Court gossip,' Agnes said, half
proud, half exasperated. 'So the new Lancaster babe is
fourth in line, though for my own part I think it matters
little who sits upon the throne provided there be neither
plague nor famine.'

'Elizabeth has a less important destiny,' Philippa said
lightly. 'She will be wed, I dare say, and make us
grandparents.'

'Listen to the silly wight,' Agnes scolded. 'Chattering
of grandchildren when Elizabeth will have many
brothers and sisters yet, please God and Our Lady.'

It was her clear duty, Philippa thought. Geoffrey
deserved a child of his own blood, but not yet.

The thought of having him make love to her when
she had just begun to feel her body was her own again
was unwelcome. She was feeding Elizabeth herself
though the midwife had advised a wet nurse in
deference to Philippa's position as one of the Duchess of
Lancaster's attendants.

'Which is nonsense,' Philippa told Geoffrey, 'for a
child thrives best on its own mother's milk.'

It also delayed the moment when Geoffrey would ask
for his rights again. Philippa had not found his
attentions unpleasant but she had illogically felt as if she
were being unfaithful to her true love. Illogical, because
the Duke was now the father of a legitimate son, and
more deeply in love with his wife than ever.

She had recovered quickly from the birth. Her
mother-in-law declared that never in her life had she
known a woman suffer less, especially a woman who
bore her first child at the age of twenty-five. A quarter
of a century, Philippa thought. I have lived a quarter of
a century. She ran her fingers lightly over the smooth

skin of her face and smiled at herself in the little hand mirror on the table.

'Motherhood suits you well,' said a voice from the door.

'My lord Duke!' Startled, she began to rise but he prevented her, his eyes kind.

'Nobody was about so I took the liberty of walking up. Are you usually left neglected?'

'No indeed, but Dame Chaucer was called to a neighbour's house – an argument with the butcher and she was required to give opinion as to who was correct in the dispute, and Geoffrey is in the city on some business or other, but the servant should have opened the door.'

'I desired her to spare herself the trouble,' John said. 'I hoped to find you alone. The first time a man looks at his child he should be alone.'

'Her name is Elizabeth Chaucer and Geoffrey is her father,' Philippa said. 'It was agreed so.'

'I will not break silence,' he said, 'but I wish to see her.'

Philippa indicated the cradle and he stepped to it, bending over it, his face hidden by the slouched liripipe he wore. She heard a little indrawing of breath and then he stood straight again, looking at her.

'She is very pretty like you,' he said gravely. 'And her colouring is such that she can pass as Geoffrey's daughter. He will grow to regard her as such, I've no doubt.'

'He is fond of children,' she said defensively.

'As I am. Now I have four daughters and a son.'

'Four daughters?' Philippa stared at him. 'There are your legitimate ones, Philippa and Elizabeth, and my own Elizabeth but I don't –'

'Marie St Hilaire gave me a daughter before my marriage,' he told her. 'Marie also.'

'I see.' Her voice was flat and dull. No doubt he had visited Marie and her baby too.

'I would have come before,' he said, 'but Blanche has not recovered as quickly as I could wish from Henry's birth —'

'It were better had you not come at all,' she interrupted sadly. 'You have no reason to visit.'

'You fear my coming will cause scandal?' He cocked an eyebrow, smiling at her. 'You ought to be named Prudence instead of Philippa. What is more natural than that I should call upon my wife's demoiselle who is also the wife of my good friend and pay honour to their first-born? And if it flouts convention who will stand up and criticise John of Gaunt?'

He spoke with all the arrogance of a king's son. She sighed inwardly, knowing him to be right. His conduct would not be remarked upon save as an example of extraordinary kindness. It was only in her own head and heart that the conflict still raged.

'Will you take a cup of something?' she asked formally.

'Nothing, thank you.' He looked about him, not with contempt but with a kind of wonderment.

'So, this is where Dame Chaucer lives? It is a pretty little house, and well appointed. She is to be married again, I believe. To a younger man.'

'Cheapside gossip travels far,' Philippa said wryly.

'From Geoffrey's mouth to my ear. She must be close on fifty.'

'She wouldn't thank you for reminding her.'

'Then I shall not. Philippa, when are you coming back to the Savoy? Blanche charged me with the task of persuading you to return. She misses you sorely. The babe will like to grow up in a palace, I think?'

'You have no claim upon her,' Philippa warned.

'That needs no saying,' he protested, 'but the advantages of the Savoy must be apparent to you. She will have an education —'

'She will have what Geoffrey can provide.'

'Of course.' He bowed slightly, accepting the rebuke.
Softening despite herself, Philippa said,
'You have been more than generous to Geoffrey and to
me, my lord. We are both grateful.'
'If you ever require aught for Elizabeth – after Lionel's
little wife? She was a sweet thing, and he loves her still
though he must make an Italian marriage. Will you call
her Beth, to please me?'
'Are you afraid of getting her muddled with your
true-born daughter?' she asked sharply.
'I wanted her to have a pet name,' he said. 'Something
that belongs to her alone. She is not, as you remind me,
my true-born daughter, but she was conceived in love,
my dear. And in giving you to Geoffrey I acted as I
thought best for all.'
She opened her mouth upon a furious retort and
closed it again. There was no point in being angry, in
trying to make him understand that people were not
pieces on a chessboard to be moved about at the whim of
the player. A king's son could not be expected to
understand.
'In a week or two I shall wait upon the Duchess again,'
she said.
'Blanche will be pleased. She looks forward to seeing
your baby.'
And the Duchess would never guess that it was her
husband's child. She had a mind above suspicion and that
made her formidable.
'You are happy in your marriage?' he asked abruptly.
'Very happy,' she said, adding to prick him a little, 'and
Geoffrey is a most tender lover.'
Unpricked, he beamed at her, clasping her hand in
both his own.
'So all ends well,' he said. 'I am pleased for you, my
dear.'
In a moment he would be thanking her for the
pleasure of having bedded her. She drew her hand away

hastily and said,

'Your arrival has been broadcast throughout the district, my lord. Here comes my mother-in-law in a fine ferment.'

But in that she did Dame Agnes an injustice. The older woman might be flattered by the visit of a great lord but not for the world would she show consternation.

'This is an honour, my lord Duke.' Entering the chamber, she knelt briefly, and relieved her excitement by scolding.

The servant was scolded for not having brought refreshment and Philippa for not having ordered it. The Duke was scolded, though mildly, for giving no warning of the honour he paid them. She even scolded the baby for having wet herself and not given notice of it by crying. And all the time she beamed at the sight of a Duke actually seated in her house and taking two of the cakes she had most fortunately baked the previous day. It was a shame that Philippa did not seem very appreciative of the honour, but she was accustomed to the society of the nobility, as was Geoffrey of whom John of Gaunt spoke so warmly that Dame Agnes fell to scolding all over again.

Seven

(i)

The Queen was dying. No longer could her physicians drain the fluids that bloated her body and choked her lungs. The last rites had been given and the King sat now by the bed, holding his wife's swollen hand as she gasped out messages for those children who had survived her. Of them only fifteen-year-old Thomas was present, his thin dark face solemn, his eyes red. This youngest boy was the odd one out in that fair and brilliant family, his nature studious, his personality lacking any touch of charm.

Philippa, waiting in the anteroom beyond with the other demoiselles, stifled a yawn. She had been in attendance for nearly twelve hours without a break and her natural distress was overcome by sheer weariness. Westminster was as draughty and inconvenient as she recalled and she couldn't avoid wishing that Her Grace would take a little less time about breathing her last.

'It will not be long now,' Alice Perrers whispered, leaning towards her. 'I had an aunt once died of the dropsy and at the last she went fast. She was the same age as Her Grace.' Philippa nodded, moving aside slightly. She had never liked Alice who flaunted her affair with the King, apparently with the tacit consent of the Queen. Well, Her Grace had always been a tolerant soul.

'It is a pity that the other princes are not here,' Agnes Archer said.

The Prince of Wales was in France with his wife and two little sons, Lionel and Edmund had gone to Italy for the former's marriage to Violante Visconti. John of Gaunt was raising troops at Dover in preparation for a new campaign.

'They will be grieved,' Alice said. 'The family is most loving.'

'The King fell in love with Her Grace when both were fourteen,' Philippa said. It was a small dig at Alice who merely answered with undiminished good humour,

'Aye, His Grace has told me the story more times than I can count. Tell me, Mistress Chaucer, how goes your own marriage? That too was a love-match, was it not?'

'Geoffrey is with the Duke of Lancaster,' Philippa said, refusing to blush. 'I have been with the Duchess this past year, so as we both serve in the same household our ways are pleasant.'

'You have a daughter, don't you?' Agnes enquired.

'Beth. She is not yet three. My mother-in-law takes care of her when I am on duty at the Savoy.'

It had been contrary to the wishes of the Duke and Duchess who, for their separate reasons, had wanted the little girl to be reared at the Savoy. Blanche had seen a playmate for her own small Harry and John had craved frequent sight of Beth, but Philippa had stood firm. Beth would benefit more from a steady routine without the continual travelling from one place to another which would be her lot if she accompanied her mother on Philippa's long spells of attendance on Blanche and the Queen. She was happier in the Chaucer house where Dame Agnes cheerfully took over the rearing of the child when Philippa was absent.

'So you are contented?' Alice said, with a sideways glance that warned of teasing.

'Yes,' said Philippa firmly, believing it.

After nearly three years of marriage she had made peace with her own dreaming heart. Her friendship with Geoffrey had not been diminished by the infrequent occasions on which they made love, and as the Duke was generally absent when she was in attendance at the Savoy she believed herself cured of the midsummer madness that had led to their affair.

From within the bedchamber came a cry of anguish, telling them that the King was now a widower. Philippa dropped to her knees with the others, bowing her head as the chanting began. At her side Alice uttered a short, dry sob. It sounded sincere and unwillingly Philippa remembered that even when she had lain in John's arms she had not felt less affection for his wife.

A week later she dropped a curtsy to that same wife and was rewarded with Blanche's gentle smile.

'There is word from our husbands,' she said. 'They are at Dover, waiting to embark, and express a desire for our company. The Duke has taken his mother's death hard, and needs comfort. He is anxious too about the increasing numbers of plague cases that are being reported in London. Will you come with me, Philippa? Of all my demoiselles you are the one whom I wish to take more than any others. Your good sense will make light of the voyage.'

'The voyage?' Philippa echoed.

'We are to go as far as Calais,' Blanche said. 'You have not crossed the sea since you were a child, have you?'

'No, Madam.' Despite herself Philippa's heart gave a tiny leap of excitement.

'Then you will come? To please me and your husband?'

'I am yours to command,' Philippa said, 'but is there truly danger from plague? I was thinking of my child.'

'As I think of mine,' Blanche said. 'I have a scheme as to that. John has property in Lincoln and I propose to send my children there into the country until we return from Calais. Will you not allow your Beth to join them? I am sure Dame Agnes cares for her grandchild with all the skill she possesses but the plague strikes hardest at children in cities.'

'That is most kind of you,' Philippa said gratefully. 'I would feel more at ease in my mind if I knew she was safe in the country – and my sister would welcome an opportunity to see her for the first time.'

'I will have all arrangements made,' Blanche promised.

Seeing her niece might jolt Katherine out of the depression into which she seemed to have sunk if her recent letter was anything to go by. With her usual disregard for spelling she had written,

> 'My dere sister and bruther in law,
> 'I send word that my 2nd child is now cum. A boy who is to be named Tom. My dorter Blanche is well. My husband gose to France and I am gladde of the quiett time that cums when he gose. Nuthing ever happens here. Only rain and poor croppes and nuthing to lift the sperrits. I hope so much you will cum and see me one day. Sir Hugh is well. I also, but low in mood,
> > 'Yore loving sister,
> > 'Katherine Swynford.'

She would have liked to see Katherine herself, to check on her sister's reasons for being miserable. Sir Hugh Swynford had struck her as a lumpish young man whom Katherine might have swiftly grown bored with. A word from her elder sister regarding her duties would not have come amiss, Philippa thought, momentarily forgetting that the little sister was now in her mid-twenties with two children and an estate to manage.

Philippa's mother-in-law made less fuss over Beth's going into Lincolnshire than she had expected. Dame Agnes had wed her third husband within a year of her son's own marriage, and had her hands full ever since with the care of her grandchild. Though she loved Beth dearly the chance of having time to devote to her husband was not to be sniffed at, and she contented herself with only a little scolding before she hurried to pack for her.

Beth was a tiny version of her mother, her eyes more hazel than brown, but her round face and soft brown hair were Philippa in miniature. She was a docile child, with no trace of the brilliance that her true father displayed. On the rare occasions that her mother had taken her to the Savoy John had been absent.

She was to travel with the Lancaster children, grave seven-year-old Philippa, five-year-old Elizabeth, and the baby Henry.

'This is the first time I was away from them for more than a few days,' Blanche said softly. 'I wish there were some way of splitting myself into two so that I could be with John and my children at the same time, but there, we are foolish to imagine the impossible. You must feel the same way.'

'Yes,' Philippa said and wondered uneasily if that were quite true. She loved Beth very much, but every time she looked at her she was reminded of her own transgression. As for Geoffrey, though they fadged well together when he was at home she seldom missed him save in a vague and general way when he was absent.

The cavalcade of the Duchess of Lancaster wound its way south-east through an October that was unseasonably warm. As mourning for the late Queen was still in force it was a sombre-hued procession, though as they rode through villages where many doors were marked with the vivid red cross that brought sad memories to Philippa the colour seemed right. Long before they reached Dover it was clear that the plague was spreading its tentacles into the countryside and Philippa tried not to think of her tiny daughter jogging into

Lincolnshire with the Lancaster children. Pray God and
Our Lady that the sickness would not have spread there.

The high-masted ships rode at anchor in the bay and
every wharf was crammed with men bustling themselves
and their weapons up the swaying gangplanks. There
was no plague here yet, but the speed with which
embarkation was taking place betrayed unease.

The Duke, garbed in black, his fair head bare, rode to
welcome his wife, his face lighting up at the sight of her
in a way that gave Philippa a pang she immediately
stifled. What had been between herself and John of
Gaunt had meant nothing to him and must therefore
mean nothing to her.

Instead she must smile and accept Geoffrey's embrace
with all the eagerness of a wife who is pleased to see her
man again.

'A ship has been set aside for the Duke and Duchess,'
he told her. 'You and I will sail in it – in her, I ought to
say since vessels are female.'

'Because they are the only things that keep men from
perishing, I suppose,' Philippa said, and Geoffrey
laughed, drawing her arm through his own.

'I have missed your quick tongue,' he confessed.
'Preparing for campaign is a tedious business. The
death of Her Grace has not helped, for the Duke felt the
loss most keenly. Report says she made a good end.'

'Report speaks true,' said Philippa.

'What of the pestilence? I hope report does not speak
true there. Cheapside is in the thick of town.'

'There have been some cases,' Philippa admitted, 'but
your mother takes every precaution, and Beth is gone
into Lincolnshire with the Lancaster children, so my
mind is at ease regarding her.'

'So you come to bear me company?' There was a
hopeful look on his face, but Philippa was glancing
towards the Duke and Duchess who stood together, as
tall and fair as any of the mythical figures portrayed in

Court masques. John was holding Blanche's hand, his head inclined towards her, his expression one of listening tenderness. For an instant the look on Philippa's face was unguarded and then she said guiltily,

'What did you say?'

'Nothing of importance,' Geoffrey said, and fell to talking of other matters.

(ii)

The crossing had been smoother than she had expected despite the autumn season. Their quarters were cramped but it was possible to walk on the decks without much discomfort, and the huddle of buildings that signified the approach of Calais found Philippa eager to step ashore. She would have liked to travel further in order to revisit her farm, but the campaign plans did not allow for it, and Geoffrey assured her that little would be gained by such a detour.

'The place scarcely pays for itself much less brings profit,' he said. 'When these wars are over then we must see what can be done to improve the land.'

It was fortunate she did not rely on the farm profits for her income. As it was her annuity from John had been doubled in the Queen's Will, and Geoffrey was a generous provider. To return there would only stir an old pain.

Calais Castle which overlooked the harbour would be their lodging until the army had fought its necessary battles. Though not as handsome as the Savoy it was well appointed and evidence of the Duke's affection for his wife was apparent in the arrangements he had made for her comfort. Tapestries had been brought from Flanders and fires blazed in every chamber to withstand the increasing chill of November.

For the first time Philippa was seated at the high table, within glancing distance of the Duke. She had schooled herself not to think of him save as the husband of Blanche, but she could not school herself from stealing quick looks at him from time to time. He was nearing thirty and at the height of his vigour and beauty. Beauty was the correct word to employ, she reflected, watching the play of the firelight on his strong features. The flames imparted a reddish glow to his blond hair and the ruby on his hand glowed with a fire of its own, seeming to contain the energy that spilled out of him.

'You are not eating, my love.' His voice chidingly anxious, was directed towards his wife.

'I have not much appetite,' Blanche apologised. 'The sea journey stole my appetite and your departure will take it quite away.'

'It will be a week before we leave,' he said, covering her hand with his own, and at once exclaiming, 'Blanche, your skin feels exceedingly hot!'

'It is my old guest, the feverish headache,' she said quickly, but from where she sat Philippa could discern the flush on Blanche's usually pale cheeks.

'We shall have the physician look at you,' John began, but she shook her head, saying in a fretful manner quite unlike her usual calm gentleness,

'Why be forever fussing? I am not a leaf to be blown away by the wind. Take care of your war and leave me to fret about my own health.'

The rest of the dialogue was drowned by the musicians who had begun to play, but the expression on the Duke's face was one of the most lively alarm.

Philippa crumbled the bread at her trencher and found a prayer leaping into her mind. 'Dear God and Our Lady, let it not be the plague.'

'It is perchance a little fever that ails the Duchess,' Geoffrey said in a low voice as they rose from the table.

'She was ever more delicate than her appearance suggests.'

Philippa nodded, slipping from his side to her accustomed place near the Duchess where she was ready to wait upon her.

'The music plays out of tune,' Blanche said abruptly. 'It makes my head ache.'

'We will have the physician,' John said, but she twisted away from him, saying,

'It is but a fever, no more. Let me be, John. Go and fight your war and let me be!'

She had left the Hall before anyone could prevent her and the Duke, checking the music, rapidly followed.

'She is certainly not herself,' Philippa said in alarm.

'I will seek out the physician,' Geoffrey answered and left the Hall as rapidly as the Duke.

'Mistress Chaucer?' One of the attendant soldiers had entered and was detaining her, his face white under his helmet. 'They are saying there is plague in the port, that some of the men who came with us are showing the first symptoms. Must I tell the Duke?'

'I fancy that he already guesses,' Philippa said, moving towards the staircase which led to the royal apartment.

The physician was already there, bent over the Duchess who lay moaning irritably on her bed, her long fair hair straggling loose from its filet. John was there too, pacing restlessly, his fists clenched impotently. Sickness was something he couldn't fight with weapons or words, and the recent death of his mother had rocked his security.

'You had better go to your own quarters,' he said curtly as his eyes fell on Philippa. 'You have not had the pestilence. Until we can be certain what ails the Duchess it is not wise to risk contagion.'

Philippa would have argued, but he had stepped to the bedside and was questioning the physician eagerly, his anxiety a palpable thing coiling in the room. She turned and went quietly away, taking a seat in the antechamber.

Hours stretched into days. She ate without tasting what was on the plate before her, lay down fully dressed to sleep, sat on the stool in the antechamber while in the room beyond the Duchess fell from restless fever into a stupor.

'It is the more deadly variety of the disease,' Geoffrey told her at one point. 'If she had the boils then they might be lanced and the poisons released, but the evil humours have turned inwards. There is nothing anyone can do but wait.'

He looked haggard, his voice shaking. Philippa, noticing, thought it strange that he should have felt a devotion to Blanche comparable to her own for the Duke. They were joined by a mutual and forbidden loving. But she loved the Duchess too, she reminded herself fiercely. Blanche of Lancaster was a very great lady and, like truly great ladies, had the art of talking to her inferiors as if they were her friends, of being unselfishly interested in their concerns.

A priest hastened past them, his head bowed over the Host. Sliding to her knees Philippa crossed herself, hearing from within the loud and tortured cry of a new-made widower.

'Her body will be cered in lead and taken back to England for burial,' the Duke told his assembled household.

It was only hours since the bell had tolled, twenty-eight tolls – one for each year of Blanche's life. John was in full command of himself, his mouth compressed, his voice level. If he had wept it had been in private and quickly over for his eyes were bright and dry now. Around him there were stifled sobs and groans. Blanche had been a gentle mistress to others besides Philippa.

'The list of those returning will be posted on the main gate,' John was continuing in the hard, flat tone. 'The rest will prepare to march by the end of the week.'

The campaign then would go on. This was his defence against grief. When a man is fighting he has no leisure to weep. Or perhaps he intended to fling himself recklessly into danger, not caring how soon he joined his late wife. Thinking of that possibility Philippa's heart swelled with pain and pity. She wanted to run to him, holding him tightly against hurt, but he had not once glanced in her direction. For him she could only be a reminder of his unfaithfulness to the wife he had truly loved.

'We are to join with the Prince of Wales and Prince Edmund,' Geoffrey told her when they had been dismissed along with everybody else. 'There is a rumour that the Prince of Wales is sick '

'Plague?' She whispered the word in horror.

'Dropsy like Her Grace. He is not yet forty, but the rumour is that he finds it difficult to sit a horse any longer.'

'There is so much sadness in the world,' she burst out. 'Why so?'

'It is the human condition,' he said, 'as are the joys we know when the sadness is gone. The world is the finer for having contained such a lady.'

'You cannot match your grief to the Duke's,' she said, piqued. 'To her you probably meant nothing at all.'

She had not meant to say anything so wounding. She had meant to tell him that she did understand his devotion to her, that she had felt something of the same, but the words came out despite her resolve and hung, harsh and ugly, on the air.

'Jealousy is not an emotion that becomes you, Philippa,' Geoffrey said.

He spoke more coldly than he had ever spoken to her before, and her feeling of guilt vanished.

'Your infatuation for Blanche of Lancaster was eminently fitting, I suppose?' she snapped.

'Another ugly word. The Duchess was as far above me as the stars. Less a woman than a symbol of all that is bright and flawless. Cannot you understand that?'

Philippa bit her lip. Part of her knew exactly what was his meaning; another part of her rejected it angrily.

'Men talk a deal about ideal women,' she said crossly. 'I would call their feelings by a grosser name.'

'I will not ask you to pronounce it,' he said, 'for I'm sure you know it well.'

It was the first time they had quarrelled, the first time she had ever expressed impatience with his worship. She wished she could wipe away the conversation, sympathise with the sorrow he felt, but she was too sorrowful herself. She could think only of John, engaged now in planning the march into Gascony, holding his grief and guilt inside himself and not even allowing himself to accept her condolences.

'We must not part in anger,' Geoffrey said. 'This death makes us say what best remains unsaid. We are not angry with each other. We are only railing at death itself.'

But his words came too late. In his grief for Blanche she saw magnified her grief for the Duke. Turning away she said, hard and bitterly,

'That is too clever for a mere wife to understand. You had best write a poem about it.'

Eight

(i)

As they moved into Lincolnshire the landscape became flatter as if some giant hand had smoothed it out. The roads scarcely curved as they dug deeply into fields that gleamed with water, stretches of marsh where tall reeds stood sentinel, windmills turning their sails lazily on the horizon. Here and there clusters of huts built on stilts rose like storks out of the water. Philippa looked at them with interest, wondering if Geoffrey, newly gone into the Netherlands, was looking at a similar scene.

The brief and bitter campaign was over and the princes had come home again, but Geoffrey had been sent to the Low Countries to begin negotiations for a trade treaty. Her husband was becoming an important man, a fact she acknowledged with mixed feelings since it was good to know that he was achieving his ambitions but meant that they were separated again, with the breach between them no less unhealed for not being mentioned.

Plague still blew foetid over the land, but with the New Year the number of deaths was diminishing. In Cheapside she had found her mother-in-law in her usual excellent health, preoccupied with her daughter Kate's latest pregnancy. Her sharp and kindly eyes had flicked over Philippa's figure and unspoken had been the comment, 'Beth is now three years old and has no siblings.'

She had stayed only a few days in London and set out on her journey to visit Katherine on the day the princes returned to London. Something in her shrank from seeing John or of attending the delayed funeral of the Duchess. It was better to be absent, to fix her mind on her child. There had been no word from Katherine and no news generally meant good news.

'Yonder lies the Swynford estate,' one of her escorts said.

Philippa craned her neck in the direction he was pointing and frowned.

'Are you sure?' she queried. 'It looks very small.'

The house ahead looked not only small but mean, no wall surrounding it to divide it from the yard where a few tattered chickens squarked and scratched. She had envisaged a park at least.

'I brought the little maid here, Mistress Chaucer,' he reminded her. 'They do say that Sir Hugh wastes his money and takes no heed to his land.'

'That will do,' Philippa said sharply and rode on, closing her ears against further gossip. Sir Hugh had been absent on campaign for much of the time but surely her sister had set things to rights.

Nobody came to greet them in response to the man's vigorous 'Halloo' save a slatternly girl who wound her hands in a grubby apron while she volunteered the information that the mistress and the little ones were all gone to Lincoln.

'To which house? For what purpose?' Philippa asked.

The girl thought that my Lady Swynford had gone to the Duchess's house.

'Then we must ride on into Lincoln, I suppose,' Philippa said, suppressing her irritation, which arose as much from hearing her sister called Lady as from the neglected state of her home.

'I know the house of the Duchess – God rest her soul,' the escort said. 'It is no more than an hour's ride.'

The temptation to dismount and investigate the state of her sister's housekeeping for herself was almost overwhelming, but the sun was beginning to fall down the sky, so she nodded and turned her horse to ride away.

The landscape changed as they approached the city, the flatness broken up into little hills that dipped and rose modestly as if they feared to reveal their steepness. She hoped there would be refreshments ready at the end of the journey. The inns where they had lodged during the long ride from London had been comfortless, with hosts who served one reluctantly, fearful that the customers on whom they depended for their livelihood had brought the plague with them.

'The castle stands outside the city,' her escort said, pointing to a hollow green with trees. 'Bolingbroke they call it.'

He was proud of his knowledge but she was irritated again by his implication of her being merely the sister of Sir Hugh Swynford's wife with no idea of how the nobility lived. It was on the tip of her tongue to inform him that she was the one who had been demoiselle to the Duchess but she checked it and rode on down the slope into the wood.

The trees were not as thick as they appeared from above, their evergreen still frosted, the grass beneath rimed. The bridle-path was wide and there were pockets of mellow sunshine between the gnarled trunks.

The two who had ridden with her from London loosened the knives in their belts, for though there were few travellers in this season there were always outlaws and beggars to prey upon those who ventured far from home.

A rustling from a nearby thicket stopped them in their tracks. So far the journey had been tedious but uneventful, and the prospect of being attacked and robbed so near its end most unwelcome.

The rustling ceased abruptly and an instant later a dishevelled figure burst through a gap in the thicket, laughing and gasping.

'*Pax! Pax vobiscum*, I pray you,' the newcomer called and sat down on a tussock of grass, as what looked like a crowd of begrimed dwarfs surrounded her, one of them swinging down from a low branch of a nearby oak.

'Katherine!' Philippa's voice vibrated with outrage.

Katherine gaped up at the mounted party with such foolish stupefaction on her face that her sister feared for a moment she had actually lost her wits. Then she scrambled up, brushing off the dwarfs who resolved themselves into five children of varying sizes.

'Philippa? Oh, but you ought to have sent word that you were coming and then we would have been decently attired and on our best behaviour!' Her voice was a mixture of pleasure and chagrin, her cheeks flushing as ruddy as her unbound hair.

'What,' Philippa asked faintly, 'is going on? Why are you running about like a – a wanton?'

'We were playing a game,' Katherine said, biting her lip to prevent her laughter. 'I am the French and the children are the English.'

For the first time Philippa recognised her own child in the grubby little girl with tangled brown hair who peered up at her shyly, thumb in mouth.

'Beth?' Her eyes flew accusingly to Katherine again.

'We are very close to the castle,' the latter said quickly. 'If you would like to dismount we can walk there together.'

'Thank you, sister, but I believe I will ride on,' Philippa said with chilly dignity. 'We can talk when we are tidied. I assume there will be someone to open the doors?'

'The butler is on duty, I believe,' Katherine said vaguely. 'Children, let us run back home now for the war is over and it is time for supper.'

She waved her hand with a lamentable lack of shame and loped off, ankles showing beneath her kirtle, her hair still streaming free.

'Ride on,' Philippa said sharply, checking the grins of her escorts.

(ii)

It had been a relief to find the castle well appointed and the butler a stately gentleman who had received her with due ceremony and bidden two neat maidservants conduct her to a bedchamber where a fire burned brightly and clean linen was put on the bed while she was sponging her hands and face in the warm water a kitchen lad brought up.

Evidently Katherine's presence here did not denote some kind of official charge. Philippa was heartily glad of it, for she would never have permitted herself to give an adverse report on her sister's conduct. Yet even if she was merely visiting her behaviour was quite unsuitable for a wedded lady in her mid-twenties.

She arranged her veil over her braided hair and went down into the hall where Katherine, looking somewhat tidier, waited to embrace her.

'You ought to have sent word,' she repeated. 'How did you find out I was staying here?'

'I went to the Swynford house. Katherine, the whole estate looks terribly run down. Have you no steward to oversee it while your husband is away?'

'The serfs are not easy to control,' Katherine said, putting her arm about her as they went to the table. 'Many of them died when the plague broke out, and even under normal conditions the land is often flooded and hard to work. I have no great fondness for the place, I can tell you. So when the governess of the

Lancaster children died – just after we received the sad news about the Duchess, God rest her sweet soul – I decided to come over. The little ones were in sad case, weeping for mother and governess, and several of the other servants ill, though it proved not to be plague but a case of bad oysters – anyway I felt it my duty to stay.'

'It was a kindly action,' Philippa acknowledged, 'but surely running around in the woods is not the way to show respect to the memory of the Duchess?'

'The two older girls were miserable enough to sink into a decline,' Katherine said. 'I don't believe their mother would expect them to fall ill with grieving. They have brightened up wonderfully since I came. And what do you think of your Beth? She is the prettiest thing.'

The children, also washed and combed, were trooping in and Philippa, somewhat mollified by her sister's remarks, looked eagerly at the small brown-haired girl. Her first thought was the thankful one that this miniature replica of herself had nothing in her of her half-sisters and brother. Philippa and Elizabeth of Lancaster were pale versions of their late mother and three-year-old Henry was a handsome child with his father's hair darkened to auburn.

Her own Beth was looking at her shyly, not certain if this was her mother. Philippa longed to throw her arms about the little girl, but the servants were present and she contented herself with drawing the child to her and kissing her on the cheek.

'Tell me about France,' Katherine said in a low voice as they began to eat. 'I was so very sorry to hear of the death of the Duchess. She invited me here on a number of occasions when she came and she was always so gracious. The Duke must be devastated.'

'You use the right word,' Philippa said sombrely.

'He came once when I was visiting,' Katherine said. 'He did not even notice that anyone else was in the room. The love between them was a beautiful thing to see.'

She did not mean to wound, but Philippa could not restrain herself from saying,

'I wish you knew the same happiness with your husband, but your letter breathed discontent.'

'Hugh means well,' Katherine said. 'I cannot complain of his ill-treatment or neglect, but he is so dull, Philippa. He has no interest in the land and he cares nothing for the welfare of those who work it. It is a relief to me when he goes on campaign.'

'That is a most undutiful remark to make,' Philippa said, shocked.

'You asked me why I was discontented,' Katherine said. 'So I speak frankly to you. You and Master Chaucer are happy together, so you cannot understand how it feels to be tied to a man for whom one has neither affection nor respect.'

Philippa hastily took a sip of her wine. Her sister's words had not only shocked but saddened her. Despite the coolness between herself and Geoffrey the basic fabric of their friendship was not even ripped. There was both affection and respect between them and she wished for her sister something comparable.

'You cannot remain here at Bolingbroke indefinitely,' she said at last, seeking to turn the conversation into safer channels. 'Your own house lacks a mistress.'

Katherine sighed, her eyes moving slowly round the raftered hall. Implicit in her gaze were the words, 'But I prefer the luxury of this.'

'The Duke will make provision for his children,' she said at last, 'and when I am sure they are all right I will go back to Swynford Manor and try to bring some order into it. Oh, but you are fortunate to be either at Court or at Cheapside with no domestic duties to plague you.'

Philippa was silent. Not even to her sister could she confide her longing for a house of her own where she was absolute mistress. With both the Queen and the Duchess gone her Court duties were at an end and there was nothing to replace them.

'The Duke's children are hardly your responsibility,' she argued. 'The responsibility that should concern you is your own house. Sir Hugh will not be pleased if he returns to chaos.'

'He will not even notice,' Katherine said, making a small grimace. 'Oh, sister, you have not yet seen my son! He has eight teeth already and can say several words. And he can stand alone though he is not yet one.'

'You must take care lest he gets bandy legs,' Philippa said, relieved that the conversation could take a domestic turn. Something in the way her younger sister had ensconced herself at Bolinbroke disturbed her very much.

The meal concluded, Katherine swept her off to the nursery where Philippa could admire the sleeping Tom. She was able to give a full measure of praise since he was a pretty child unlike his older sister, Blanchette, who had inherited her father's dark, plain countenance.

A bedchamber had been prepared for her use, and she stretched out thankfully on the feather pallet, glad that the hours of jolting in the saddle were over. In a few days, when she had persuaded Katherine to return to her own home, she would mount up again and take Beth back to Cheapside. The one fact that was abundantly clear was that under her sister's influence the child would grow up to be a hoyden.

(iii)

'Now the house begins to look decent,' Philippa said with satisfaction, rubbing the small of her aching back.

It had taken a week of hard scrubbing and washing to remove the accumulated layers of dirt that a too indulgent mistress had permitted. The serfs on the small estate were lazy and insolent, taking advantage of Hugh's absence and Katherine's kindness to do as little work as possible. There was no doubt that her sister was popular but there was also no doubt that she commanded small respect. She let work slide while she played with her children or dreamed of a more exciting life at Court.

'It all looks very fine,' she said now. 'The servants deserve a holiday.'

'For doing tasks they ought to have done in the first place? Sister, you must keep firmer control,' Philippa said, exasperated. 'You and I ought not to have been forced into doing any of the work ourselves in order to set the example. They should obey your word.'

'You have worked harder than any of us,' Katherine said placatingly. 'I am truly grateful.'

'Only try to keep them up to the mark when I have gone,' Philippa said.

'Must you go so soon?' Katherine asked. 'I hoped we might spend some of our leisure together. And I shall miss Beth. She is quite like my own child.'

Philippa's lips tightened imperceptibly. Beth had greeted her prettily enough but at the first opportunity she had gone back to her aunt, climbing on Katherine's knee and demanding a story. She was affectionate and Philippa was thankful that she hadn't fretted during her absence, but she felt a pang all the same. In future she resolved to spend more time with her daughter. Perhaps when Geoffrey returned from the Netherlands he would lease a small house where his wife could live.

'Someone riding in,' Katherine said, shading her eyes with her hand.

They stood in the low-raftered hall with both doors open to speed the drying of the recently washed floor, and the solitary rider was a lone figure against the grey sky.

'It is Chubb, Hugh's squire,' Katherine said as he

cantered into the yard and dismounted. 'I suppose he brings word of Hugh's return.'

The squire, seeing them, pulled off his hat and paused to scrape his boots against the step.

'Lady Swynford.' He paused, cleared his throat, and began again. 'Lady Swynford, I bring sad news. I wish it were not so. I have ridden slowly the better to delay –'

'Delay won't turn bad news into good,' Philippa said impatiently. 'What news do you bear?'

'Sir Hugh is – he died of the flux almost a month ago,' the young man said. 'It was in France, my Lady. He stayed behind with others who were sick but he grew worse. I was with him until the end and I made what arrangements were necessary for the burial. It grieves me very much to have to give you such tidings for he was a fine master.'

Katherine's clear pale skin had paled further and her eyes were huge. For an instant Philippa feared that she would faint but she merely drew a quivering breath and said, 'I will have food and drink brought for you, and we will speak of this later. It has been a long ride for you.'

'I wish it had been longer,' Chubb said. 'He talked so much of coming home to you and his children. He was a brave knight, my Lady, and he deserved a better end.'

'Endings are endings however they come,' Katherine said. Her voice still shook but her eyes were dry. Her long fingers twisted in her apron.

'You had best sit down, sister,' Philippa said, worried by Katherine's calm.

'I will walk a while,' the other said and stepped past them into the yard, her pace increasing as she went.

'I will have refreshments brought,' Philippa said, staring after her. 'She is badly shaken, I fear.'

'Poor lady.' Chubb sighed. 'She must have looked forward so greatly to the homecoming.'

Philippa, ringing the bell for one of the maidservants,

said nothing. Katherine's feelings were not the concern of a squire, but she had certainly seemed very shocked. Perhaps she had felt more affection for her lumpish husband than she realised.

Having given her orders, Philippa excused herself and followed across the yard into the low-lying meadows beyond. A few minutes' brisk walking brought her up to Katherine who stood at a gate, looking out to the horizon.

'Sister?' She stopped, her hand half outstretched.

'I never wished him dead,' Katherine said, not turning her head. 'Oh, I never loved him, though he fell in love with me and often told me so, but I could feel nothing for him save a mild tolerance. He was so dreadfully dull, Philippa. He could talk of nothing but the campaigns in which he intended to fight. I did try to make the estate pleasant for him. I really did try in the beginning, but he took no interest. He used the farm profits to gamble with and he was harsh with the serfs. He had no imagination and never saw them as human beings at all. Oh, it shocks you that I could say such things at this moment, but I'll not weep and wail and be a hypocrite. I never loved him, but I never wished him harm.'

'There will be details to arrange, lawyers to see,' Philippa said. 'You would be wise to keep what you have just said between the two of us.'

'Yes, of course.' Katherine turned, giving her a faint smile. 'I have always been able to talk with you as if I were talking with myself. I promised myself that when he came home this time it would be different. I would make an effort to respond to him, to give him the love a wife should feel for her husband. I was full of the most excellent intentions.'

'I'm sure you made him happier than you realise,' Philippa said gently.

'I don't think I ever made him happy at all save when

I had the children,' Katherine said. 'Oh, little Tom will be Sir Thomas Swynford now, for the title is hereditary. One year old and a Sir!'

She put her hands to her mouth, half laughing, half sobbing, her eyes filling at last with tears.

'We must send for the priest and have Masses offered for his soul,' Philippa said, trying to avert a possible attack of hysteria. 'And the servants must wear black armbands.'

'I cannot spend the rest of my life here,' Katherine said suddenly. 'I shall wither like a dead leaf and crumble into dust if I am trapped here with no prospect of release. I don't think that I can ever bear such a life.'

'You must give yourself time for mourning,' Philippa said sensibly. 'A noble widow is not likely to remain without suitors for very long. Geoffrey will certainly do what he can when he —'

'For heaven's sake, Philippa,' Katherine interrupted vehemently. 'I said I didn't want to stay here for the rest of my life. I didn't say I wanted to jump into wedlock again. I have been tied into marriage these four years. Now I want to be free. Why must I be linked up again?'

Philippa chided herself for tactlessness. She had meant to comfort, but Katherine's face had flushed with annoyance.

'Perhaps there will be a place for you at Court if that can be managed,' she temporised.

'I'd not be a burden on you or Master Chaucer,' Katherine said more quietly. 'You are my only relatives now apart from my babes. There will not, I fear, be much money. Poor Hugh never managed his income well.'

'Like father,' Philippa said wryly and reached up to hug the younger woman. 'Don't fret about the future until it arrives on your doorstep,' she advised. 'The lawyers will be able to tell you exactly how much value can be placed upon the land. It will be Tom's heritage.'

'And Blanchette will have to find a husband as I did,' Katherine said. 'Wouldn't it be marvellous if women could be independent without having to take husbands unless they really desired them?'

'That is a shocking notion,' Philippa said severely. 'Women are not created to live alone. You wouldn't be without your children, would you?'

'That was the best thing that ever came out of my marriage,' Katherine said.

She spoke, Philippa thought, with irritation, as if being titled and in possession of an estate were worth nothing.

The mourning for Sir Hugh Swynford was conventional if not heartfelt. The servants and the serfs accepted the news of his death with an indifference that proved he had been a harsh taskmaster. The priest, dragged from the side of his common-law wife to offer Masses, had a decided hint of ale on his breath, and only Chubb seemed genuinely to grieve, but he had seen Sir Hugh at the occupation he most enjoyed.

To Philippa's relief Katherine conducted herself with a dignity that concealed her paucity of emotion. With her red hair tucked beneath a whimple and her slim figure shrouded in weeds, her vitality was muted. The little ones, seeing this new grave mother in unfamiliar black, fell silent and wide-eyed.

She had done everything she could to help and now she must return to London. As she folded her clothes and hunted for Beth's clean kirtle, she privately acknowledged a sense of release. The estate was isolated, marooned in the midst of low, marshy land, with only the constantly moving arms of the windmills against the sky to provide variety. No doubt when spring came there would be beauty in the emerging flowers but the complete absence of society, the flat dull faces of the serfs as they went unwillingly about their tasks, the slothful priest must have cast down even

Katherine's high spirits. It was small blame to her that she had gone to the castle and frolicked with the children to help them forget their grief over the death of their mother. Buckling the straps of the saddle-bag, Philippa vowed to speak to Geoffrey about her sister as soon as possible. If a steward could be appointed to take charge of the Swynford estate then Katherine might well be given a post at Court where she would be in a better position to make a more favourable second marriage.

'I shall miss you,' Katherine said wistfully as they embraced.

'As I shall miss you,' Philippa rejoined. 'Will you write and let me know what the lawyers say?'

She would have preferred to stay on herself until the legal matters were resolved since her sister was unlikely to have much knowledge of affairs, but Katherine had assured her that she would manage very well, and somewhat reluctantly Philippa had made her preparations to ride south-east again.

'I shall write a long letter,' Katherine promised, 'and tell you everything that I am told myself. I fear Tom's heritage won't be very rich. But he can be a knight like his father. I go to Bolingbroke next week to tell the Duke's children that my own babes have also lost a parent. They will be sorry for it but glad to see me again.'

She was undoubtedly telling the truth, Philippa thought, mounting up and reaching to take Beth on the saddle before her. It hadn't escaped her notice that despite her sister's rather slovenly ways and her lack of discipline over her servants when Katherine entered a room there were always smiles of welcome. Even Beth, seated in the crook of her arm, was craning her neck to take a last, tearful look at her aunt.

Nine

(i)

It was exciting to be at Court again, even though it was Alice Perrers who had issued the invitation. Alice was on the crest of the wave now. Acknowledged mistress of the ageing and widowed King it would be foolish, as Geoffrey pointed out, to insult her.

'And you cannot deny that you would enjoy a taste of noble society again,' he said. 'My mother is only too happy to have Beth and it is only for a week or two.'

Another consideration had been Geoffrey's own trip to Italy which began in December, a bad season of the year for travelling, but if trade links were to be strengthened with Padua it was important that negotiations should be embarked upon as quickly as possible.

'I shall enjoy my own travels the more if I know you are also well entertained,' he assured her.

It was one of his nicest traits, that he should concern himself with her pleasure when most husbands merely assumed their wives needed only the domestic round to keep them happy. And Beth wouldn't suffer. She and Dame Agnes got along together as only an elderly woman and a small girl just on five can.

So Geoffrey had departed for Italy and Philippa had kissed Beth and Dame Agnes and set out for Windsor which had been marked as the venue for the Yuletide festivities.

The royal family had shrunk since she had first come to Court. The Queen had died as had the Duchess Blanche and the Duchess Elizabeth, and the slant-eyed retarded boy born to the Prince and Princess of Wales had also died but was little regretted since there was still tiny Prince Richard to inherit the throne when his grandfather died.

And surely that couldn't be very far off, Philippa thought, making her curtsy before the grey-bearded figure who peered at her uncertainly before turning to Alice who sat, all velvet and gems, at his side.

'Do I know this lady?' he enquired.

'Of course you do, Sire,' Alice said encouragingly. 'She is Master Chaucer's wife. You have sent him into Italy to begin the trade negotiations.'

'Ah, yes, it is Mistress Philippa.' A veined, liver-spotted hand was extended. 'I remember you very well now, Mistress. But do you not live in Lincolnshire?'

'That is my sister, Lady Swynford, Your Grace,' Philippa said.

'Well, you are very welcome anyway,' the King said vaguely and beamed at Alice.

'Have you heard from your sister recently?' Alice asked. There was a faint graciousness in her tone that irked Philippa. It was as if she were trying to ape the manner of a queen when she was only the old King's fancy-woman. Yet she looked very splendid with the velvet of her gown as near crimson as possible and her black hair looped up at each side of her narrow, clever face.

'She is at Bolingbroke,' Philippa said. 'Milord of Lancaster sent word that he wished her to remain with his children.'

The letter from Katherine had startled her. Carefully spelled (her sister must have been doing some belated studying) it informed her that the Duke had sent his butler to request her at the children's desire to stay for the moment at Bolingbroke until he had leisure to decide what to do about his motherless family.

Well, they were motherless no longer, Philippa reflected as she curtsied again, being careful to turn towards the King and not to Alice. John of Gaunt had taken a second wife, for purely political reasons marrying Constantia of Castille, daughter of King Pedro. The sixteen-year-old Infanta brought with her a large dowry and the opportunity of a future throne. Philippa wondered if she had also brought beauty, charm or affection.

'Surely it is Mistress Chaucer?'

The plump lady whose expression was too cheerful for the trailing black weeds she wore had taken her hand as if they were old friends. Though the figure had thickened and the golden hair was due more to art than nature Princess Joan had retained her apple-blossom complexion and pretty smile.

'Madam.' Philippa began to curtsy before the widow of the Prince of Wales but the other shook her head, drawing her aside into one of the minute antechambers that fringed the Presence Chamber.

'I heard you had been invited to spend Yuletide here,' she said. 'It is so many years since we met. You were only a girl and now you are wed with a little girl of your own. Time has dealt very gently with you. But then you cannot be thirty yet.'

'Almost,' Philippa said ruefully.

'I am forty-five,' Joan said mournfully. 'Isn't it too terrible? My poor Edward is forever assuring me that I do not look it, but I take care never to let him see me without my paint on.'

'I was so grieved to hear of his illness,' Philippa said sincerely, 'and of the death of your son.'

Tears rushed into Joan's eyes and she squeezed Philippa's hand before saying, 'He was not quite right in the head, you know. Very sweet, but he would not have lived to grow up. And so we must look upon it as a blessing. But Edward should have survived into old age. It is the lung fever as it was with Lionel. Two such splendid men.'

'Your son Prince Richard must be a comfort to you,' Philippa said.

Joan brightened but looked faintly doubtful.

'Well, he is not yet four,' she said, 'but he is a pet, a perfect pet. He will make a lovely monarch one day. Not too soon, I pray, for he is but little yet.'

'His Grace seems to be in good health,' Philippa said politely.

'In body,' Joan nodded, 'but in mind I fear he is often somewhat confused. Mistress Alice takes advantage of that, of course. She accepts jewels from him, then shows them to him when he has forgotten them and asks him if he will buy them for her. Of course he always gives her the money which she promptly squirrels away. Very vulgar!'

Philippa murmured something, but could not help reflecting that it was prudent of Mistress Perrers to think about a future when she would no longer have the protection of the King.

'Have you a post at Court now?' Joan was enquiring.

'No, Madam, I am here only for a brief visit,' Philippa said. 'I spend most of my time in my mother-in-law's house now. My husband is often abroad on the King's business.'

'And quite a coming man,' Joan approved. 'It is a pity that he is not more often here to entertain us all with his verses.'

'Diplomacy brings in a better income,' Philippa said frankly.

'Has he finished his poem about the Duchess yet?' Joan asked, lowering her ample frame to a stool and reaching for a bunch of sugared grapes.

'The Duchess?' Philippa looked puzzled.

'His tribute to Gaunt's late wife. It is rumoured that it will be one of the most beautiful tributes to a lady ever penned.'

Would it indeed? At that moment Philippa forgot her own affection for the deceased Blanche and remembered only that Geoffrey had idolised her.

'My husband writes many verses,' she said stiffly. 'We don't often discuss them.'

Joan smiled, her eyes kind. She was more interested now in the grapes she was popping into her rosy mouth, savouring each one with voluptuous pleasure. No matter that she was old and plump. Joan had a charm that only mellowed with the years.

Blanche had possessed charm too, a delicate, remote charm that had held two men captive. My husband and my lover, Philippa thought, and realised that it was five years since she had thought of John of Gaunt in that fashion, but now she felt threatened by a stupid poem written about a lady whom Geoffrey had adored as if she had been one of the statues of a saint in church.

She dropped a curtsy and slipped away, seeking the narrow slip of room that had been allotted to her. It was a compliment that she should have been given a bedchamber to herself, but she suspected that it had been paid more to Geoffrey's increasing importance than to herself. She had passed the demoiselles' quarters on her way and heard them giggling and prinking as they prepared themselves for the evening. Young girls with silly dreams in their heads of white knights who would carry them off.

For this evening she would wear one of the three new gowns she had bought. Of tawny brown, the girdle of blue silk to match her veil, it was flattering to her hair and eyes. After a few moments' consideration she pinned the flower brooch that John had given her to the neck. The pearl was Constantia now, she supposed, and presents were her right. He had been a generous husband to Blanche. He would be a generous husband to his Spanish Infanta.

She thrust her thoughts aside and went down to the hall, finding an inconspicuous seat among the lesser ladies. One or two, recognising her, smiled a greeting; someone else enquired after Geoffrey's health.

The King was already seated, his grey head inclined towards Alice who occupied a chair at his side. For all the world as if she were the Queen, Philippa thought indignantly. The throne on which Queen Philippa had been used to sit had been removed but Mistress Perrers leaned so far sideways that her head was under the royal canopy as often as not.

The King's younger sons, Edmund and Thomas, were there, the former looking like his late brother Lionel, Thomas now a thin, dark youth who still looked as if he had strayed into the royal family by mistake. At the other side of the King the Princess Joan was picking at her food as if her appetite was of the smallest, her eyes resolutely averted from Alice.

This still being Advent the dishes were of fish and cheese, meat being forbidden until the day of Christ's Nativity. Not until midnight on the eve of Yuletide would the purple be stripped from the altar and statues of the churches and kissing-rings hung over doors and windows.

From outside trumpets sounded thin and shrill. The herald, craning his neck to see, called loudly,

'Make way for His Grace John, Duke of Lancaster, and Her Grace Constantia, Duchess of Lancaster!'

She had not expected them to be here. For an instant her heart leapt with excitement, and then she willed it into calmness again. They were both here. John had brought his new Spanish bride to spend Yuletide with his family.

Constantia was not beautiful. Philippa saw that at once and felt foolishly relieved. The new Duchess was very small and thin, her skin sallow, her black eyes narrow under a stiff lace cap that made her look top-heavy. She had a certain dignity, but none of the gentle grace that had made Blanche such a charming woman.

The Duke towered over his wife, broad-shouldered and long-legged, his fair hair touched with auburn in the light of the blazing fires. He was shrugging off his heavily furred cloak, tossing it to a page, mounting the dais, kneeling for his father's embrace, kissing Joan, clapping his brothers on the back, smiling at Alice. With his coming something vital and gay entered the company. It was as if Advent was rushing to an end. The musicians struck up a cheerful tune and John's voice rose above the hum of conversation.

'I have elected myself as Lord of Misrule for this season, Your Grace. This must be a happy time with past sadness laid aside, don't you agree?'

There was applause and laughter. Philippa, putting the palms of her hands together, saw that under her robes the stomach of the new Duchess was already swollen.

(ii)

The purple had been stripped from the altar and there were kissing-rings over the doors and windows. The sweet, sexless voices of the choristers had echoed the angels in that field of long ago. A long line of poor people had received as much meat as they could hold on the points of their knives and a measure of ale. Mummers, wonderfully masked and horned, had acted a play and there had been a joust in which only two knights suffered broken limbs. John of Gaunt had been an energetic Lord of Misrule, forever thinking up new pursuits to amuse the revellers, coaxing his stiff foreign wife into playing snapdragon, teasing Alice as if he approved of her having pushed her way into his dead mother's place.

He had greeted Philippa with a kind courtesy that failed to single her out from the other ladies, his voice warm while his eyes seemed to look past her in search of someone else.

'It is a shame that Geoffrey had to set off at this time,' he said. 'A journey across the Alps in winter is no picnic feast, but I've no doubt that he will tell us about it in his inimitable manner when he returns.'

Philippa nodded obediently, wondering for the tenth time what other people saw in her pleasant, ordinary husband that she missed.

'I hope to send for my children soon,' he went on. 'Your sister has been staying with them at Bolingbroke and from what my daughters write to me she is greatly loved by them. I intend to offer her the post of governess to them. Do you think she will accept?'

It was on the tip of Philippa's tongue to warn him that her sister would prove to be about a page ahead of her pupils but she refrained. To spoil Katherine's chance of making extra income and of leaving the isolated estate where she had never been happy would have been unkind. Instead she answered meekly,

'Katherine will be delighted, sir. The Swynford estate does not offer her much variety of scene or pleasures.'

'Sir Hugh was somewhat improvident, I fear.' He shook his head, then looked at her with more attention. 'And you are well and contented?' he asked abruptly. 'You and Beth?'

He had not mentioned his daughter before. Philippa felt a glancing pain at her heart and smiled brightly as she replied,

'Beth is with my mother-in-law, my lord. She is a very pretty little girl, very loving.'

'Geoffrey is fond of her?' There was a trace of anxiety in his voice.

'He regards her as his own child, as does everyone else,' she said levelly, wanting suddenly to hurt him.

'I am glad of it,' he said, but there was a flash of pain in his eyes. He would have liked to acknowledge Beth, she guessed, as he acknowledged his daughter by Marie St Hilaire, but that child had been born before his first marriage. To admit his paternity of Beth would be to admit that he had been unfaithful to the wife he had adored. He had bowed then and walked away, calling to his brother Edmund to help him plan the evening's entertainment.

Tonight Philippa was wearing the second of the three new gowns. It was of lemon velvet, with fur trimming the long sleeves and scooped neckline. Her face was round and smooth between the loops of brown hair and she was pleased with her reflection. She looked younger than her years and the slight plumpness of her small figure was becoming.

There were joints of meat on the trestle tables now and confections spun out of sugar to represent angels and shepherds. There was also wine, rich and red from Gascony. She helped herself to a beakerful and tore with her small white teeth at a wing of chicken.

In the centre of the hall some tumblers were performing with leaps and somersaults that threatened at times to land them in the middle of the pies and jellies. The King was laughing heartily, his fingers paddling in Alice's bodice. Smoke from the fires swirled up in the draught blackening the gold-painted cornices. Behind the stool on which she sat two dogs argued over a bone.

Perhaps it was the wine which she had drunk rather too fast, but a great wave of sadness broke over her. Everybody was having a good time and so many had died – the Queen, the two gentle Duchesses, the Prince

of Wales and his sad, retarded little son, Prince Lionel
who had barely lived long enough to take a second wife.
Geoffrey was on his way to Italy over high, cold
mountains where one false step could mean death and
Beth didn't know who her true father was. A large tear
splashed off the end of her nose into the beaker of wine.
If she stayed here any longer someone would notice her
distress. She could feel more tears gathering behind her
lowered lids, preparing to slide down her cheeks.

Under cover of the noise and laughter she slipped
from her place and hurried through a nearby door. The
swathes of holly mocked her unexpected loneliness. For
a moment she stood, wiping the back of her hand
childishly across her wet eyelids. There was no reason
for her to be unhappy, she told herself, but the
unhappiness was there like a cold, dead weight on her
heart.

Someone might pass by and see her. She hastily began
walking down the corridor towards the tiny chapel
where prayers were sometimes said when the weather
made it difficult for old or infirm members of the
household to make their way to St George's Chapel.

The stone-ribbed vault with its painted Madonna was
empty as she had expected, only the Sanctuary Lamp
and a few candles providing illumination. There were
no kissing-bunches here, nothing to remind one of
Yuletide when everybody was supposed to be happy. A
step sounded on the stone behind her and the Duke's
low voice echoed hollowly in the stone walled space,
rippling along her nerves.

'Something troubles you, Philippa.'

It was not a question. The pain in her was soothed by
the knowledge that he had seen her leave the hall and
been concerned enough to follow.

'I was alone with the whole Court present,' she said
slowly. 'Does that sound stupid?'

He shook his head.

'I have been alone since Blanche died,' he said simply. 'On campaign, in council, trying to read or write or listen to music –'

'But you are wed again,' she broke in.

'In Constantia's bed I am more alone than anywhere else,' he said flatly. 'I married her so that one day I might be King of Castille. She dislikes marriage, I think, but she has been taught that a wife must submit. She submits with the look of a martyr on her face, and her chief joy in bearing a child is that for many months she need not submit again.'

'She is not like the Lady Blanche,' Philippa said. 'She was always gracious and good. She had no spite or sulkiness in her.'

'You served her and so remember.' John took her hands, exclaiming a moment later, 'But you are freezing cold! What will Geoffrey say if his wife will be found iced to death in the midst of the Yuletide festivities?'

'He will probably write a poem about it,' she said and giggled suddenly, her eyes sparkling as the tears in them dried into diamonds.

'With me as the villain who saw it happen and kept on my cloak. Let's remedy that.'

He had pulled off his cloak and was wrapping it about her shoulders, his hand smoothing aside her veil. Above her his eyes were tender and mocking, seeing her again clear and once desired but seeing her without the sting of guilt.

'You are very kind,' she said, embarrassed by his steady regard.

'I am very selfish,' he answered. 'For too long I have clung to my grief, neglecting my children because I dreaded seeing their mother in their faces, telling myself that all the love in me was dried up when she died and I had nothing left to give any other woman.'

'You have much to give any woman,' she said in a low voice.

'Constantia would not agree. She will not have Blanche's name mentioned. Can you imagine anything more foolish than to be jealous of a dead woman?'

Philippa, her chin snuggled into the fur of the cloak, shook her head, thinking that for all his magnificence the great John of Gaunt knew little of the dark places of women.

'You are so pretty,' he said, and touched her cheek with a ringed finger. 'I had allowed myself to forget how pretty you were. Is Beth like you?'

'The image,' she told him.

'Then she will be a sweet woman. I have wished to acknowledge her as mine, but that would lay a burden on her and shame Geoffrey. Also I like to think that you and I have a secret that we can share.'

'The past is dead. You said so yourself.'

'But you and I were not buried with Blanche.' He took her hands again, drawing her close, his expression inexorable and tender. 'Of all the ladies I know I feel most at ease with you. You loved Blanche and you know how it is possible for me to have loved you too. You are a wise and discreet woman, Philippa Pan.'

Her old nickname given her by Prince Lionel's fragile Elizabeth. Everything in her shivered towards him though she remained silent and motionless.

'I hoped that you might be here for Yuletide,' he said. 'I have been weeping inside for a long time, Philippa, and I believe you have been weeping too. I saw you tonight abruptly leave your place and in that moment I wanted to tell you that I knew exactly how you felt, that laughter and merriment are nothing when we are alone in a crowd. So I followed you. Are you angry with me that I married you to Chaucer? He is a good husband to you, is he not?'

'We have been good friends for many years.'

She wished he would not talk of Geoffrey who at this moment might be sliding and slithering in deep mountain snow. At this moment she didn't want to be reminded of Geoffrey who had accepted Beth as his own, and wrote poems that other people said were wonderful.

'I have often thought that we were bound together, the four of us,' he said thoughtfully. 'You and I and Blanche and Geoffrey, like the ends of a love-knot that nobody else in the world can untie. And now that Blanche is gone the three of us hold the memory of her. Are you warmer now?'

Not warm but hot. Waves of heat chased through her and her cheeks were pink, her heart hammering.

'You are so pretty,' he said again and scooped her up suddenly, as he had long ago on the evening he had ridden masked into the great hall.

At the last moment something in her wanted to protest that the game had gone too far, but his mouth covered hers and the words were lost before they could be uttered.

Ten

(i)

She had not meant to stay so long at Windsor. A week or two and then she would be home had been her promise to Dame Agnes. But the Court lingered until Yuletide had become New Year and Candlemas lay just around the corner.

'We must be circumspect,' John had warned her. 'Constantia is full of jealous fears and fancies. She doesn't love me but she fears that another might. It is part of her condition, I believe, and I would not be unkind to her.'

So in public they held aloof, he escorting the thin dark bride, she seated demurely among the lesser ladies. Only when the last tapers had been extinguished did she retire to her slip of a chamber and wait there for the occasions when he could come to her. They were not frequent. Once a whole week went by without her catching more than a glimpse of him, tall and golden with his two brothers. But when he did come then the waiting was forgotten in the joy of his closeness. She had forgotten his skill as a lover, the ease with which he caused her to open out to him as if she were a bud and he the sun.

'I have a surprise for you,' he told her one night.

They lay in the sleepy aftermath of loving, her hair unbound, his silvered by moonlight.

'A pleasant one?' She nuzzled his neck.

'I have sent for my children,' he said.

'Oh?' Philippa wondered what especial pleasure lay for her in that.

'Your little sister is coming with them. It will be good to see her again, won't it?'

'Katherine coming to Court?' Philippa sat up and looked down at him. 'Oh, my lord, it is years since she was in society. She will feel sadly out of it.'

'Since I appointed her as governess I could hardly send word that she was to stay behind,' he said mildly. 'Are you not pleased?'

'Yes, of course. It is only that – you and I,' she hesitated.

'She will not share your bedchamber,' he said. 'Nothing will change between you and me.'

'But it has to change.' Her voice was small and sad. 'Geoffrey returns in May. I cannot see you after that, not alone.'

'That's true.' He was silent for a space.

'I would not have Geoffrey find out,' she said. 'It would shame him.'

'How could it possibly shame him to have his wife loved by a king's son?' John asked. He sounded puzzled.

'To be a cuckold,' she began, but he laughed, pulling her down again.

'Geoffrey is my friend as I am his patron. He married you partly as a favour to me, knowing you carried my child. What's changed?'

She wanted to explain that she and Geoffrey had not been married before, but he was kissing her again and the thought was muddled in her mind.

'We have until May,' John said, raising his head, tracing the round curve of her breast with his forefinger. 'Afterwards something can be worked out.'

His arrogance had an innocence about it that disarmed criticism. Philippa steeled herself to say,

'When Geoffrey comes back you and I must not meet

again save in public, my lord. He is too good a husband
to be openly betrayed.'

She had chosen the wrong word. Even in the
moonlight she could see the dark flush on his face, and
hear the ominous rumble in his voice.

'Since when was my love betrayal? My affection for
Geoffrey has been constant. My love for you never
alters that.'

'The betrayal is mine,' she said hastily. 'I sin against
my wedding vows.'

'Sins of the flesh are generally excused in heaven,'
John said comfortably, his temper subsiding. 'We will
make confession before we die. And if you want our
loving to cease while Geoffrey is at home, then I'll
agree.'

Wisely she held her tongue, but even as she
responded to his loving she promised herself that by the
time Geoffrey came she would be in Cheapside, a
dutiful wife. The Duke would be disappointed, but
though he was sincere in his protestations of love she
knew that the quality of his loving was a fragile thing,
having nothing to do with the adoration with which he
had regarded his wife. She doubted if he would ever
love any woman with his entire heart again. Meanwhile
she had until May. That for the moment was sufficient.

A few days later a cavalcade of Lancaster children
streamed through the gates, with an escort of outriders.
The Duke ran to greet them as if he were a schoolboy
again himself. Philippa, standing with a group of other
ladies, pulled her mantle close and drew herself to her
fullest height. Katherine, she thought wryly, wouldn't
have shrunk.

Neither had she grown dignified. Philippa blenched
as the tall, slim figure slid from the saddle of her mare
and called cheerfully,

'Here we are, children, and your father comes to meet
us.'

Her hair was straggling loose from under the brim of her hood and her pale skin was flushed by the wind. There was mud on the border of her cloak and a hole in the heel of her stocking, but the Duke was laughing, seeming not to care for the lack of protocol.

'So you have brought my family to me, Lady Swynford?' he was exclaiming. 'Surely the size of it has grown since I was last at Bolingbroke!'

'These are my own two,' Katherine said as they were lifted from the swaying litter. 'This is Blanchette and this is Tom. I could not bear to leave them in Lincolnshire.'

'You are a devoted mother, I see.' He looked approvingly from her to his own three. 'Also a very excellent governess. My children look well and happy, and I thank you for that.'

It must pain him to see his daughters, both pale copies of his dead wife, Philippa thought, and winced when Katherine said,

'My Lady Philippa grows more like the sweet Duchess every day.'

He seemed not to mind her reference however, merely nodding as he embraced the two solemn little girls, and swinging Henry up to his shoulder.

'It is so good to see you again, sister,' Katherine was saying as she bent to kiss Philippa.

'You look well,' Philippa said, feeling awkward for her sister's untidy state. The other didn't appear to notice that her gown was soiled, but answered,

'You look so pretty. Is that a new gown? Geoffrey must be a generous husband. Did you bring Beth to Court? Oh, it is so good to be out of that dreadfully flat county. I swear that there were times when I felt as if I could see clear to the end of the world with no people in between. Am I to have a room near the children's quarters? What kind of Yuletide did you have? We had a dull one, I can tell you.'

Several who stood near by were smiling. Philippa's cheeks were burning with humiliation. Dear Mother of God, but Katherine was behaving like a hobbledehoy. She would not keep her post as governess for very long. John of Gaunt was one of the most dignified of men save in his most intimate moments. He would not countenance his children being under the influence of one so gauche.

'We must make Candlemas more agreeable for you,' John was saying, lingering to speak to Katherine.

'Oh, for the moment it is sufficient to be at Court,' Katherine said. 'But you will not keep your children at Windsor, will you? You have a splendid palace of your own, the Savoy, which I am sure they would like more.'

'I bow to your judgement,' John said gravely.

His blue eyes were glinting with laughter.

'Then if you will excuse me,' Katherine said, gathering the children up as if they were so many chickens, 'I shall get some of the travel grime cleaned off them before they make their bows to His Grace. Philippa, shall we sit and gossip later?'

'You must pardon my sister,' Philippa said nervously as the tall figure glided away. 'She has been trapped on a small manor for so long that she has grown rusty in courtesy.'

'She is certainly an original,' he said, still gazing after Katherine. 'Why didn't you tell me how amusing your sister was?'

'I was not aware –' Philippa began, but he was walking away from her, raising his voice banteringly,

'Do not steal away my children yet, Lady Swynford. Let me show them where you are all to lodge.'

(ii)

The Duke had decided to return to the Savoy with his children and their new governess. He had avoided the palace since the death of his first wife for it bore the stamp of her personality more strongly than any other of his properties, but now abruptly he had resolved to settle his family there. His new wife and her coming child would remain in his quarters at Westminster where he would visit them often.

'It will be wonderful to be so near to Cheapside,' Katherine said. 'We will exchange many calls, you and I. When Geoffrey returns it will be less lonely for you.'

It would not have been lonely had Katherine stayed in Lincolnshire, Philippa thought with resentment. It was not the younger woman's fault. Katherine had no idea that before her arrival Philippa's nights had not always been spent by herself. Innocently she made a point of coming every evening to bear her sister company after the children had gone to bed, and by the time she returned to her own quarters it was past the hour when John usually came.

'I never see you now,' she found opportunity to whisper to him as they stood near during a masque.

'It is a little difficult to arrange with your sister here,' he murmured back. 'I would not have you embarrassed by her knowledge.'

He was right, of course. It would not have increased Katherine's respect for either of them to discover that they were lovers, but she couldn't help contrasting his behaviour with that of his father who flaunted the clever-faced Alice like a jewel.

Candlemas had come and gone and the royal party was breaking up, the old King going back to Westminster where he would make pretence of ruling and buy more gems for Mistress Perrers, Princess Joan to Oatlands where her small son, Richard, was, and the Duke to the Savoy.

Philippa had been nearly two months absent and was guiltily conscious that she ought to relieve her mother-in-law of the responsibility of Beth. It was foolish to outstay her welcome when she had no official duties and John no longer came to her chamber. She had hoped he would remain behind for a day or two after Katherine and the children had departed, but when he had settled them at the Savoy he would join his wife for a brief spell.

She was pleased and flattered when Joan sought her out to say goodbye.

'I hope that you will visit me one day, Philippa,' the plump and charming princess said, taking her hand. 'It is often lonely to be a widow. I miss Edward quite dreadfully sometimes.'

'Surely you will be often at Court, Madam?' Philippa said. The King was extremely fond of his daughter-in-law, she knew.

Joan frowned, pouting slightly.

'I am not anxious to spend too long away from my son,' she said, 'and I am reluctant to bring him often into the company of Alice Perrers. She is a vulgar person, flaunting her power over His Grace, seeming not to mind that the whole world knows her for his leman.'

Philippa hid a smile, recalling the scandals that had reverberated about the Princess Joan's head years before when it was discovered that she had married two gentlemen at the same time. Her thought must have been reflected in her face because Joan said,

'I may not always have behaved strictly correctly but I never flaunted myself. Alice has no taste, no sense of how a gentlewoman acts. She has climbed high and she will fall as far. Now you are a great contrast, always so discreet and polite.'

'Madam?' Philippa looked at her.

'You must remember that I am cousin to the Plantagenets,' the older lady said. 'I know them from childhood. John is the best of them, a man of honour and kindliness, but a prince who will never forget what is due to his rank. He will not openly shame his wife even if there is no affection between them. He must appreciate the discretion of your own public conduct.'

'He has spoken of me?' Philippa said faintly.

'With the greatest respect and affection,' Joan assured her. 'And only to me. John and I have always confided in each other. Are you going to tell him about the coming child?'

'But I am not –' Philippa stopped short, symptoms she had been trying to ignore rushing into her mind.

'I am not often wrong,' Joan said. 'Having borne six myself I am familiar with all the signs. Perhaps it is your husband's babe? Is that possible?'

'Just barely possible, my Lady.'

'Then there will be no scandal,' Joan said. 'But you ought to tell John. He will want to do everything he possibly can.'

'Perhaps it is not so,' Philippa said, but Joan shook her head, the laughter lines deepening around her brilliant green eyes.

'I am not often wrong about these matters,' she said. 'Had I not been born a princess I declare that I might have become a midwife. I wish you well, my dear.'

She was a kind-hearted lady, with a gift for friendship, but she didn't really understand, Philippa thought. To her love was a light and laughing thing. She had never known the dark places of the spirit.

Nevertheless the Duke must be told. The problem was how and when, since in the bustle of departure there was small opportunity for private conversations.

The thought of not telling him lingered in her mind, but that would be wrong. He would want to do what lay

in his power for the coming babe. In her own mind
Philippa was quite certain that it was his. In five years of
marriage to Geoffrey she had not quickened, and
having lain with John again she was now pregnant. She
wondered if anyone else had been as sharp-eyed as the
Princess Joan, but concluded that was unlikely. At the
Court she was an insignificant figure, invited more out
of kindness than out of any merits of her own.

Not until the evening after supper was there an
opportunity for her to approach him. It was the last
occasion on which the family would be all together for
some time and the smaller children had been permitted
to stay up and eat in the great hall. There seemed to be a
great number of them, their fresh faces contrasting with
the grey hair of the King and Alice's painted features.
From where she sat Philippa let her gaze run over them.
Lionel's ten-year-old daughter Elizabeth had all the
fragility of her dead mother and none of the good
humour of her dead father. She sat with pursed mouth,
ignoring her Gaunt cousins. John's daughters, Philippa
and another Elizabeth, were pale, colourless little girls,
their faces demure. But his son, Henry, had character in
his square, high-coloured little face and energy in his
stocky frame. Philippa noticed with amusement that he
had a jewelled dagger stuck proudly in his belt. A
warrior already.

These children sat at the High Table, but from their
fidgeting it was clear they would have preferred to be
sitting at the lower table where the two Swynford
children were with their mother. Philippa's eyes moved
to Katherine and she stifled a sigh.

Katherine was wearing what was clearly her best
gown, a robe of pale green trimmed with grey fur, but
her red tresses were escaping from beneath the green
cap she wore and her freckles were as numerous as they
had been in childhood though Philippa had advised her
time and time again to rub them daily with lemon juice.

Even her manners were countrified. Instead of taking tiny bites and wiping her mouth after each one in the approved fashion she was holding a wing of duck in her hands and biting it, her tongue catching the juices and her eyes glinting with enjoyment. It was manifestly unjust that she could eat like a trooper and remain as thin as a willow.

'There must be dancing tonight,' the King said loudly. He was looking more alert than usual, his eyes darting among his courtiers. 'Tomorrow we return to Westminster and to work, so tonight there must be dancing.'

It was a superfluous order since every night there was dancing, but there were murmurs of approval and Alice said promptly.

'Sire, we would all be very dull if you did not think of ways to entertain us.'

'Ah, you should have seen me when I was young,' he answered. 'I could leap higher than any youth in the Court and tire out a dozen partners in one evening.'

'Then I am glad that I was not then born,' Alice retorted, 'for I'll swear that you have more energy than I have now.'

It was arrant flattery but he beamed, leaning to pat her hand. Philippa looked away, unwilling to see the King whom she had respected behaving like a senile fool. However he was still monarch and as he had ordered dancing then dancing there was. Philippa watched John lead his stiff Spanish wife into the cleared space, his head politely inclined to her black one, her face an expressionless mask as usual. It was hard to realise that she was already carrying his child. Philippa wondered if even in bed she remained frozen. John had never told her any details. Though he had no love for this wife he was too gallant to talk about her disparagingly.

'Isn't it exciting to see all the great people enjoying themselves?' Katherine demanded. She had left her place and sat down by her sister, spreading her wide green skirts. From anyone else the comment might have been construed as sarcasm, but Katherine meant exactly what she said. Her grey eyes were as wide as a child's and her smile was guileless.

'Tomorrow you go to the Savoy. You will find a very grand place there too,' Philippa told her. 'I hope it will not make you even more dissatisfied with the Swynford estate.'

'You never had to live on it,' Katherine said darkly. 'The Duke has engaged a steward to oversee it now so that it may yet show a profit for my Tom to inherit.'

The youngest children had been hustled off by their respective nurses, and only the three pale grand-daughters of the King remained, seated together.

'You are fortunate to have property,' Philippa chided.

John had danced with his wife and escorted her back to her place. Now he was leading his sister-in-law, Princess Joan, on to the floor, shaking his head at her voluble protests that she was too old and fat and he ought to find a younger partner. Joan was still light on her feet despite her weight and from the laughter that issued it was plain that her partner was enjoying himself.

'I do wish someone would ask me to dance,' Katherine said.

'We are neither of us truly of the nobility,' Philippa reminded her.

'No indeed,' Katherine agreed without taking offence. 'Oh, poor father may have been Herald Guienne but he never made any money in his life, and neither did Hugh. Had they not been born what they were they never would have got on at all. I believe that your Geoffrey will do better than either.'

To be reminded of the absent Geoffrey at the moment when she was waiting for a chance to confide to John that she was carrying his child was irritating. Philippa said sharply,

'You must learn to speak with rather less freedom, sister. Your husband was a brave man who died on campaign.'

'Of dysentery,' Katherine interposed, choking back a giggle. 'Oh, I do know it must have been dreadful for him and I'm sure I never wished him a moment's harm, but there is nothing very heroic about getting dysentery. And he was terribly boring, you know. He had nothing to talk about save his fighting.'

The dance was ending. John stood with the Princess Joan, his head raised as he glanced about the huge chamber. He was clearly seeking another partner. Philippa held her breath, but he turned away and was bowing before Alice.

'That is a handsome man,' Katherine said, nodding in his direction. 'I remembered him as comely but he is better than I remembered. Isn't it strange that his new wife doesn't love him? He is very starved of love, I think.'

It was on the tip of her sister's tongue to reply indignantly, 'Indeed he is not.'

'He loved the Duchess Blanche very deeply,' she heard herself say.

'His grief will grow gentler if he is encouraged to talk about her,' Katherine said. 'Her memory ought to be kept alive. His children gain much comfort from recalling the things they used to do with her. Oh, but Mistress Alice will not dance. She prefers to sit with the King.'

'Shameless,' Philippa murmured.

'Oh, but she loves him well,' Katherine replied immediately. 'She will not wish to dance with anyone else.'

'Alice Perrers loves the jewels that His Grace bestows upon her,' Philippa demurred. 'You believe that all the world is as well intentioned as yourself.'

'Most people are,' her sister answered tranquilly, and began to rise when her name was spoken loudly.

'After dealing with my family you deserve a dance if

you can endure having your toes trodden upon,' John was saying. It was he who had called her and he strode now across the floor towards her with one hand held out.

'I was hoping that someone would ask me to dance,' Katherine exclaimed, 'but I didn't expect to find myself so fortunate in my partner.'

'You have not danced with me yet,' he said. 'I am not the most graceful of men.'

'You said that in the hope of coaxing a compliment from me,' Katherine retorted, 'but I shall reserve judgement, my lord.'

Her manner and words were too familiar, Philippa thought unhappily. One must never forget the rank of those who condescended, but John was smiling.

'Your sister is refreshingly honest,' he said to Philippa as he led the other away.

They danced well together with no treading upon toes that Philippa could see. Once she heard him laugh at some remark that Katherine passed and the vow she had made to tell him of her situation wavered. On this last evening at Windsor he wouldn't thank her for the news that he was to be a father again.

Eleven

(i)

Geoffrey drew a deep breath and pursed his lips in a soundless whistle.

'It seems,' he said genially, 'that I left you in bud before I crossed the Alps.'

'The babe is due at the beginning of August,' Philippa told him. It was almost true, the child being more likely to arrive at the end of the month but there was no point in putting questions into her husband's mind.

The decision to say nothing to the Duke had cost her some tears. John was fond of children, and would have looked at her more tenderly had he known she was carrying his, but the time for telling him had slipped by. Better for him to remain in ignorance.

'This is a happy gift for my homecoming,' Geoffrey said, kissing her. 'I began to think that Beth would be our only child.'

It was a measure of his goodness that he treated Beth as if she were his own. Indeed in the roundness of her face and the stockiness of her frame she had begun to resemble him as much as Philippa. There was no trace in her of the Plantagenet gold.

'Did the mission go well?' She judged it wiser to keep away from the subject of the coming child as much as possible.

'Well enough. I believe trade will certainly improve. The land of Italy is so beautiful, Philippa. I wish I could take you to see it. The colour of the stones – they are mellow gold with a sheen on them like the oil that comes from the olive presses in Tuscany.'

'Were the inns where you stayed clean?' she interrupted.

It was a perfectly sensible question for an affectionate wife to ask, but for some reason he looked disappointed.

'They were very clean,' was all he said, and shortly afterwards went off to Westminster to give his report to the King.

She had hoped that Geoffrey would begin to consider the possibility of buying or leasing a house of their own but he seemed content for them to stay in Cheapside. Indeed Philippa and Dame Agnes were firm friends since both could make a conversation on the merits of white thread over blue or the spices to add to a broiled fish, but it would have been pleasant to have had her own kitchen where she could instruct the maids and a garden where she might grow flowers. Dame Agnes considered flowers to be a waste of time unless they were edible.

In July the Duchess Constantia was delivered of a girl. 'A tiny dark little thing like her mother,' Katherine said on one of her rare visits. 'I have not seen her but the Duke declares she will be a pretty girl. He always regards his own children as surpassing all others.'

There was a smiling indulgence in her tone that made Philippa look at her more closely. Katherine was wearing a new gown of figured silk with a narrow sash binding the high waist. The low neckline revealed a deep cleft between high, pointed breasts. There was a new and disturbingly voluptuous quality in her smile.

'Have you given any thought to taking a second husband?' Philippa asked abruptly.

'A great deal,' Katherine said, 'and I am resolved never to marry again save for love.'

'That's a ridiculous statement,' Philippa said coldly.

'Probably.' Katherine smiled again. 'Nevertheless I am resolved upon it. Sister, did it never strike you as even more ridiculous that while younglings are expected to sigh for love they are expected to wed where often there is no love at all?'

'Marriage is a practical affair.'

'Then let us be practical by all means,' Katherine said obligingly. 'I am a widow with two children and a small estate now being administered on my behalf by a most efficient steward. I have comfortable apartments in a luxurious palace where I take care of children who have grown very dear to me. Why should I marry for the sake of wearing a ring on my finger and handing all my property over to my husband?'

'You should be forcibly wed,' said Geoffrey overhearing, 'because in your single state you are a temptation to every bachelor and every married man with eyes in his head.'

'Do you include yourself among those gentlemen?' she challenged.

'Alas, but I have a pretty little wife who keeps my gaze fixed only upon her,' he replied.

'You need not make it sound like a penance,' Philippa said crossly. 'And little is good when I am as large as a house.'

'I love every acre,' he assured her, and would have kissed her but she turned her head away, feeling pettish for no reason.

When Katherine had gone, stepping lightly up to her horse which was held by a servant wearing the Lancaster livery, Geoffrey came back into the room and sat down, chin on his hand as he stared into the fire.

'Your sister is growing into a beauty,' he said.

'Growing into? She is twenty-seven years old and finished her growing ages ago,' Philippa said.

'I spoke metaphorically. You were trying to persuade her to marry again?'

'A woman requires the protection of a husband,' Philippa said.

'Not if she has other protection,' he said.

'What other protection?' Philippa shifted awkwardly in her chair and looked at him.

'Rumour has it that the Duke has cast a favourable eye upon her,' Geoffrey said. No need to specify the name of the Duke. Her heart gave an uncomfortable flutter and her cheeks paled.

'Rumour generally wears a lying face,' she said.

'Rumour goes further and whispers that she is already with child by him.'

It was not possible, of course. John would not turn from one sister to the other. It was very possible. John was the King's son, a royal Plantagenet, and the Plantagenets took what they wanted wherever they willed.

'If that is so,' she said in a small, cold voice, 'then she must certainly be quickly wed. The Duke will tire of her.'

Unspoken were the words 'as he did of me' but they hung heavy in the air. Geoffrey rose and laid his hand on her shoulder for a moment, and went away without asking any questions.

It was not possible, she repeated to herself. At Windsor he had rediscovered his passion for herself. But that had been in the winter, and in the months since Katherine had been at the Savoy. Katherine with her freckled white skin and hearty eating habits and the silver-grey glance of her eyes. It was not her sister's fault. Katherine had no idea that there had ever been anything between herself and the Duke. He had been more discreet in their affair but if rumour whispered now then he had ceased to care about the reputation of his mistress and Katherine was to be pitied. She was certainly to be pitied, Philippa repeated to herself.

(ii)

Her prayers must have been answered for the child was born a couple of weeks earlier than she had calculated though, by the date she had given, it was late, but Dame Agnes knew of several women who had endured eleven-month pregnancies.

'And the babes so large their poor mothers were in agony,' she said, swaddling the new babe with loving, grandmotherly hands. 'This little mite is small for all that he was slow in coming. What will you name him?'

'Tamkin,' Philippa told her.

Propped on pillows she was luxuriating in the new lightness of her body. The birth had been swift and easy for all that she was full thirty and had not borne a child for nearly six years.

'He does not resemble anyone I can bring to mind in the family,' Dame Agnes said, peering at the tiny face. 'Very fair skin and his eyes quite a bright blue.'

'Babies always have blue eyes,' Philippa said.

'But not usually so brilliant.' The older woman peered more closely. 'I don't know but what they will remain blue. You and Geoffrey both have brown eyes.'

'My sister's eyes are grey.'

'Then it's likely a mixture.' Dame Agnes laid down the baby and gave her daughter-in-law an affectionate look.

'Tamkin Chaucer,' Philippa said, exchanging smiles. 'It has a nice ring to it.'

'As does Beth,' Dame Agnes reminded her. 'We must take care not to make too much of the little one at her expense. Children can be jealous.'

'I was never jealous of Katherine,' Philippa said. 'When she was born I wanted her for my own. She was more fun than the doll I had.'

A wild, scrawny, naughty little sister with a smile like sweetness itself. Their childhood had been punctuated by her shrill cries of 'Philippa, wait for me.'

'She always followed where I had been,' Philippa said and choked back a sudden sob.

'Too much excitement,' Dame Agnes said. 'I'll brew a tisane.' Bustling from the room she frowned silence upon Geoffrey who was just entering.

'Are you feeling better?' Ill at ease in a sickroom he shuffled his feet like a schoolboy.

'I was never ill,' Philippa said with an excellent imitation of her usual briskness. 'I am of the opinion that childbirth is natural and that women make too much fuss about it.'

'Don't tell your friends or they will lose their power to make their husbands feel guilty,' he advised laughingly.

'I have been wondering why Katherine hasn't been to see me,' Philippa said. 'You sent word to the Savoy?'

To her surprise he flushed slightly and turned to look down into the cradle.

'Is something wrong?' She spoke sharply, guilt raking her.

'Katherine isn't at the Savoy,' he said.

'Not there? Has she been dismissed?'

'She returned to Swynford Manor,' Geoffrey said, still fiddling with the cradle covers.

'To Lincolnshire – without telling us? Geoffrey, why?'

'Rumour was speaking truth,' he said. 'She is with child by the Duke. I had it from Alice Perrers.'

'Who would greatly have relished telling you!'

'You do her an injustice,' he said mildly. 'She is not spiteful. She wished me to hear it from a friend so that I could break it to you.'

'Break it gently, you mean?' Philippa's voice had risen. 'What need to do so? What else did Mistress Alice have to say?'

'Beth's parentage is not entirely a secret in close royal circles.'

'I'll not have it known,' she warned.

'Nothing will be said,' he assured her. 'It is only that the Duke told his father and now –'

'–and now the King slobbers family secrets in Alice's ear,' Philippa cried, her cheeks flaming. 'I'll not be shamed or have Beth hurt.'

'Mistress Alice feared that you might still have some love for the Duke and so be upset when you learned about Katherine,' he said. 'I told her that you and I were happy together and that you were more likely to wish joy to him and your sister than complain.'

'Heavens, yes, though I wish they had shown more discretion,' she said brightly. 'With him it is but a midsummer madness, but it may hurt Katherine's chances unless she finds a second husband quickly.'

'Apparently she has made it known that she doesn't wish to marry again.'

'She cannot mean to bear the child out of wedlock! The Duke will not allow it. He will find her a good man as he did for me.'

'John of Gaunt has left for Castille where his future kingdom is in some disarray,' he told her. 'He will not return to England until after the child is born. Oh, he knows about it, but Alice told me that he will respect Katherine's wishes and not force her to anything. He will acknowledge the child as his own.'

'That isn't fair!' Philippa sat bolt upright, her eyes flashing. 'He has never acknowledged Beth.'

'But you yourself wished for discretion,' Geoffrey reminded her.

'And the Duchess Blanche was alive. He would have ridden over the whole world before he would have caused her pain.'

'He has no love for his new wife, that's sure,' Geoffrey said. 'Their little girl is to be named Catalina, which by an unfortunate irony is Spanish for Katherine, though the choice was Constantia's. Philippa, does it hurt you, this affair between your sister and the Duke?'

'It displeases me,' she said with an appearance of frankness, 'but it doesn't hurt me. How could it?'

For an instant the fear that Alice might have noticed more than she had told Geoffrey made her hands tremble, but he merely smiled, his expression lightening.

'We have a good, solid marriage, my dear,' he said. 'I wish your sister were as fortunate, for the life of a royal mistress is beset with pitfalls.'

'Perhaps it is over between them, and she will stay in Lincolnshire now?'

'It's their affair.' Geoffrey rose, casting another glance towards the baby. 'I have my own family to attend. A sweet daughter and a handsome son – he will improve in looks, won't he?'

Tension dissolving she burst into laughter, but when he had gone she was surprised to find herself crying.

John's passion for her was spent and would never be revived. He could not have told her more clearly than by taking Katherine as his mistress. But he could not care so well for Katherine since he left her unwed to bear his child. And Philippa had her own private revenge. John had no idea that Tamkin was his son. If it remained up to Philippa he never would have any idea.

She was on her feet again within a week of the birth though Dame Agnes clucked her tongue over the dangers of birth fever, dropped wombs and burst veins. Philippa, however, felt fitter than she had ever felt. Her mirror showed her a glowing skin and a plump figure, eyes sparkling brown in their frame of neatly braided brown hair.

Geoffrey was bound for Italy again in the New Year of thirteen seventy-three.

'To Genoa,' he told Philippa. 'It may be a year before I return, so if you wished to come with me no objections would be raised.'

For a moment she permitted herself to toy with the

dream of travelling in a strange and exotic land and then common sense took over.

'Use your head, Geoffrey,' she protested. 'I am still nursing Tamkin so how could I leave him? Or are you suggesting that I cross the Alps in midwinter with a babe at my breast?'

'Something might have been arranged,' he said.

'I'll not trust Tamkin to a pesky wetnurse,' she said, crossly to hide her sudden wistful longing for a change. 'And even if I did Beth is too young to travel. My place is with the children.'

He said nothing more and when she looked in on him an hour later he was engaged in polishing his long poem in praise of Duchess Blanche, reciting the words aloud as he worked on them. Philippa withdrew without disturbing him, her lips thinning. Even after years the gentle Blanche remained his ideal for all females. If she were in love with him she would begin to feel pain. As it was she felt only relief that her days of loving were over.

Katherine's boy was born in the spring, three months after Geoffrey had set out for Genoa. She announced the news to Philippa in one of her infrequent letters, more distinguished for what was left out than for any information that was imparted.

'My dear Philippa,

'Excuse my long silence but I did not know how best to write to you. You must feel shame on my account that I lay with the Duke, but I do beg you to try to forgive my imprudence. When one loves prudence becomes a falsehood. I did not think he returned my affection but he told me that he did so. Last month I had his son. I will name him John after his father, and pray he grows up into as fine a man. I believe that my lord will be glad.

'I do beg you again not to judge me too harshly. I was never as good and obedient as you even when I was a child. Love is my only excuse. Please write to me and tell me how you and your children do. Whatever has chanced I am always

'Your loving sister

'Katherine'.

She wrote back coolly, sending her best wishes to the babe and to her sister's Swynford children. It was useless to try to express her feelings about Katherine herself. She was not sure what they were. Sometimes a picture of Katherine in her green gown rising to dance with the Duke tormented her thoughts. Her unconventional ways and long silver-grey eyes had bewitched him as surely as if she had used the black arts. At other times she recalled how Katherine had tried to behave as a lady, watching the others at Court, remembering to make a curtsy of the right depth, innocently believing the world was full of goodness. Had she suspected Beth's parentage for a moment she would never have looked twice at the Duke. If she learned of it now she would be heartbroken to have caused her sister such pain. It was a weapon that Philippa was determined never to use. Meanwhile the year turned from spring to summer, and then it was autumn again and Geoffrey was coming home. So was the Duke of Lancaster. Philippa tried not to think of that.

Twelve

(i)

The Duke had not come into London on his return to England, but had gone directly to his castle of Bolingbroke where his children by his first wife were. He would spend Yuletide there, Geoffrey informed her, and seemed not to realise that his words gave her a jolt of pain as sharp as it was unexpected. What possible difference could it make to her where he went or what he did? The affair between them was over, had really been over before Beth's birth. The conception of Tamkin had been the result of a brief resumption of the desire he had once felt for her, over almost as quickly as it had begun. As had his affair with Katherine.

'I am glad to be home again,' Geoffrey said on that first evening, settled in the best chair with his mother and youthful stepfather hanging on his descriptions of Italy, his wife sewing in the corner, and the two children tucked up in their cribs in the room above.

'But it is not your home,' Philippa heard herself say.

She had not meant to say anything at all, but the complacency of his tone irritated her. Geoffrey gave her a surprised look but Dame Agnes unexpectedly sided with her.

'Philippa is right,' she said. 'After all the work you have done for His Grace you ought to be granted a Grace and Favour residence. Not that it will please me to lose you, but every woman deserves to be mistress of her own household.'

'I was not complaining,' Philippa said quickly.

'You were speaking frankly and echoing my own thoughts.' Dame Agnes gave her daughter-in-law an affectionate glance. She had never ceased to be thankful that her son had chosen such a sensible wife. Knight's daughter though she was Philippa was easy in any company, a loving mother and a faithful wife. When Dame Agnes reflected that he might have wed the younger Roet who had borne a bastard to the Duke of Lancaster earlier in the year she breathed a sigh of relief.

'You should speak to the King,' she repeated.

'That won't be for many months yet. I am bidden to Windsor for the St George's Day Celebrations,' Geoffrey said. 'Until then I am free to follow my own concerns.'

'Which means your nose will be buried in some book or other.' Torn between pride and exasperation his mother sniffed.

'The Book of the Duchess is finished,' Geoffrey said eagerly, ignoring the sniff, 'and I am now polishing a new long work, "The Book of the Lion". It is adapted from the French and will read well in public, I believe.'

His mother and wife exchanged speaking glances, while his stepfather said, with that faint air of diffidence that characterised all his utterances,

'I would be most happy to hear part of it when you feel so inclined.'

'You have more important matters to occupy you than listening to verses,' Dame Agnes said. 'We must plan for Yuletide. Since nobody is bidden to Court it will be a modest family celebration.'

Planning for Yuletide would fill up all the moments when Philippa found herself dreaming into space, her mind quite blank. Once John had filled all the blank spaces. Now there was nothing. Geoffrey was not sufficient. She admitted the fact sadly to herself. She had prayed that when he came home the comfortable friendship they shared might be transmuted into something more, but it hadn't happened. Geoffrey made love to her in exactly the same way as he had always made love, with charm and gentleness but without ever touching the innermost core of her. During the day he visited his friends in the city, of whom he had a great many, or worked on the poem for St George's Day, or played with the children. He was too indulgent with them, she considered. Beth who was almost seven was going through a difficult time with her front teeth loosening and her back ones often aching, and Geoffrey tried to alleviate the pain by spoiling her, while Tamkin had quickly learned that he had only to roar for Geoffrey to pick him up. She had hoped for an ally in Dame Agnes but the older woman spoiled them in a way she would never have spoiled her own children. So it was left to Philippa to take a sobbing Beth to the toothpuller and firmly turn away when Tamkin demanded attention he didn't need.

Yet in the end Yuletide proved more enjoyable than she had expected. The goose was cooked to perfection; the waits sang as sweetly as ever; Geoffrey bought her a furred cloak with a hood that was both warm and flattering; and no word came from Lincolnshire.

They were both invited to Windsor for the celebrations in April. The prospect of going to Court again was both painful and pleasing. John would be there with his Spanish wife, and she would have the chance to see him and convince herself that all her feelings for him had faded. The midsummer madness that had swept away two sisters was over. She told herself that firmly as the frosts gave place to teeming rain and then the first rays of the April sun broke through the clouds.

'And do not forget,' Dame Agnes warned, 'that you have no house. Remind His Grace of the excellence of your work.'

'You would do better to remind Alice Perrers,' Philippa said to him later. 'They say it is she who dictates policy.'

'And probably more ably than the King,' Geoffrey said. 'His senility is well advanced, though he is only sixty-two.'

'You said that as if it wasn't old,' Philippa remarked. 'Isn't it strange? I was thinking only the other day that people I would have considered elderly a few years ago now seem scarcely in middle age.'

'That's because we are approaching middle age rapidly ourselves,' he told her. 'Our point of view has shifted.'

The observation made her thoughtful. At thirty-two she could no longer consider herself young, but she was not sure if she welcomed the calmer years. When she thought now of John her pulses no longer raced. The passions of youth had cooled but something in her regretted their passing.

They travelled to Windsor on the eve of the festival. It was only a day's journey but a sense of expectancy lightened her spirits. Beth and the hastily weaned Tamkin had been left with Dame Agnes; the pack-ponies carried a number of bags filled with new clothes she intended to wear; Geoffrey took pains to enliven the way with jokes and anecdotes; she was no longer in love with the Duke and would be able to greet him calmly when they met.

What startled her somewhat as they rode into the forecourt was the respect with which Geoffrey was greeted by the butler who came personally to escort them to the room allotted to them, a much finer chamber than the tiny one she had been given when she came here alone.

When they entered the great hall she was further surprised to hear their names called by the herald, a distinction usually reserved only for the nobility.

'I didn't know you were grown so important,' she muttered to Geoffrey as they made their way to the High Table where the King sat, Alice at his side, beneath the canopy.

'Alice likes the cut of my doublet,' he muttered back and bowed solemnly as King Edward leaned to shake a finger at him.

'You do not come often enough to our Court, Master Chaucer,' he admonished. 'Alice will scold you later but for now you are most welcome.'

'Also your wife,' Alice said in an audible whisper.

'Also your wife,' the King said obediently. 'One of the Roet girls, were you not?'

'Philippa, Your Grace.'

'Ah yes, 'tis the other one John bedded,' the King said and nodded them away graciously. Only those within earshot could have heard the exchange, but Philippa's cheeks were burning as she walked with Geoffrey to the places assigned to them at a lower table. She was only thankful that the Duke of Lancaster had not yet arrived. It was as the Duke she was resolved to think of him in future. As for Katherine – while she could not in conscience blame her sister she felt humiliated that the proud name of Roet should be associated with a tawdry affair that was obviously common gossip throughout the Court.

As the meal with its numerous highly spiced courses progressed she grew calmer. She was fortunate in having been respectably married, something that Katherine must surely envy as she struggled to bring up her three children alone at Swynford Manor. She would write to her, perhaps even suggest to Geoffrey that they might pay a visit.

That night when Geoffrey drew her closer she responded with something that could have been mistaken for passion save that she knew the difference. But he seemed not to notice and, long after he snored gently at her side, she lay wakeful forgiving her sister.

'The sun always shines on St George's Day,' Geoffrey remarked the next morning.

'Surely not?' Philippa, tying a ribbon on her sleeve, glanced at him.

'I was speaking in metaphors, dear.'

'Oh.' Philippa who was not quite certain what a metaphor was, smiled vaguely. Geoffrey looked quite handsome today, she considered. The small beard he had recently grown lengthened his round features and his knee-length robe disguised his rather stocky legs. He still had all his hair and his teeth, and though he lacked height his carriage had dignity. All in all he was an attractive partner.

The celebrations would begin with a procession of Garter Knights to the chapel for High Mass. Then would come the midday collation and the jousting. Geoffrey was to recite his poem during the meal. He was clutching a sheaf of papers though she suspected that he knew it off by heart.

Those who were not part of the Order founded by the King in his days of vigour crowded into what space remained in the chapel, where they could by dint of craning their necks watch the solemn procession as it wound into the aisle.

'The last gasp of chivalry,' Geoffrey murmured as the trumpets blared.

Philippa made an indeterminate noise. She wished that sometimes her husband would talk sense but perhaps that was asking too much of a poet.

She tensed suddenly as the King, with Alice Perrers at his side, came slowly into view. Geoffrey had been correct. Edward of England was a palsied shadow of the young monarch who had married Philippa of Hainault for love. Stooped and grey, he shuffled along with his mistress clinging possessively to his arm. A murmur swept the congregation as a litter was carried past. On it the Prince of Wales, feeble and coughing, reclined. Princess Joan, for whose sake it was whispered the Order had been created, walked at the side of the litter, her painted lips bravely smiling. It was a long time since her dying husband had appeared in public and her gallantry dared any to comment on his wasted frame. And behind them strode the Duke of Lancaster, his height and vitality in cruel contrast to his father's and his elder brother's condition. He walked alone, his fair head slightly bent, his thoughts evidently far off. His younger brothers, Edmund and Thomas, followed, with the other Garter Knights bunched behind them. But Philippa, her eyes now lowered to her Missal, saw only John of Gaunt.

She had hoped that the long absence would have diminished him. It had not. He looked exactly as she recalled him with no trace of the hard-fought campaigns, the loveless marriage.

The Mass passed in a blur. She knelt, stood, crossed herself, murmured Amen, knelt again, and came out at last into the fresh spring morning.

'My dear, will you excuse me? I must speak with the Master of Ceremonies regarding the recitation,' Geoffrey was saying.

She nodded, smiled, walked with the crowds towards the group of decorated pavilions where the collation was to be served. Beyond them the lists were being prepared for the jousting that would follow. The royal party had already taken their seats in the main pavilion. She hesitated for an instant, unsure of where to go, and then Geoffrey was at her side again.

'We have the honour of dining in the main pavilion,' he said. 'You will be near enough to hear the poem very clearly.'

'That will be pleasant,' she said and felt a pang of guilt at the surprise on his face. Poor Geoffrey! In future she must pay more attention to his scribblings.

But even when she was seated and the trumpets had sounded and the chatter died away and Geoffrey was reciting his translation of the Book of the Lion in his strong, melodious voice it was impossible to concentrate. She could see John – the Duke – out of the corner of her eye, sunlight striking through a flap in the striped canvas. His head was haloed in gold.

Then he raised his head and looked straight at her. For an instant she held her breath, fearful of a rebuff. Then he rose from his seat with a murmured excuse and threaded his way between the tables to where she sat, her hands clasped tightly in her lap.

'Philippa.' His voice was low, pitched so as not to interrupt the recitation. 'This is a very great pleasure. Will you walk with me for a few moments?'

It was the moment to shake her head, to indicate that she was listening to the poem. She rose obediently and went without a glance behind her through the opening nearest to them.

A large crowd had gathered in the open air to hear the poem and it was several moments before they were free of the crowd and strolling towards the castle whose battlements dominated the skyline.

'You look splendid, Philippa.' He had paused and was looking down at her. 'A little extra weight suits you.'

'Thank you, my Lord.' She tried to speak calmly but her voice shook.

'We are very wicked to miss the recitation,' he said ruefully. 'However I shall enjoy it more when I can read it alone in tranquillity. Poetry is best savoured by a winter fire with a goblet of malmsey at one's elbow. Geoffrey looks well too, does he not? I wish I could say as much for my poor brother, but I would not care to hazard a guess as to which of them will outlive the other. Now you look astonishingly young. You have heard my news?'

She had heard nothing. Even now she had to pull her

attention back from the consciousness of his physical presence to an awareness of what he was actually saying.

'Katherine was delivered of a premature son last week,' he said.

For a moment she thought she had misheard his words. John had been born more than a year before. He was already standing by now, or so Katherine had written in a brief letter that Philippa had been too disgusted to answer.

'We were in great fear for his small size for the first day or two,' he was continuing. 'I am assured by the physician however that he will thrive. We shall name him Harry.'

'My sister has borne another child?' She had found her voice. 'She has borne you another son?'

'Now I have two Harries,' he said. 'Henry was very flattered to have his new brother named for him.'

'You have been at Swynford Manor?' Her face was blank with shock.

'At Bolingbroke. I rode like the wind to be with Katherine again. I wish I could have stayed with her longer than a week but I had to visit my wife and daughter at Scarborough.'

'You made good use of your week,' she said.

'I am surprised that Katherine didn't write and tell you. I fear she still regards the penning of a letter as a task to be delayed.'

'You and Katherine.'

'We did not mean the affair to continue,' he said. 'While I was absent I resolved that it must end, but the instant my ship landed I took horse and rode hell for leather into Lincolnshire. The poor girl was trying to cope with everything at her late husband's place, so I bore her and Johnny to Bolingbroke where my other children welcomed them. One week and then I had to pay attention to my sad Spanish Duchess who has not improved with keeping. No, I must be fair to the poor woman. She never wanted to be wed and she declares that Catalina will be the last child she will bear. I stayed with her for several months, and then I returned to Bolingbroke. The babe came early with scarcely any swaddling ready.'

'How inconvenient.'

'Katherine laughed. She always makes light of small domestic mishaps. Philippa, I wish I could thank you adequately for having such a sister. You know, I had moments when I was truly torn between the pair of you. Small Philippa and tall Katherine. So different and yet both so sweet in your ways. You and I will always be friends, I think. You have a good husband in Geoffrey and that sets my mind at rest.'

'While Katherine has no husband,' Philippa said dully.

'She has refused to consider the notion. She will live retired as my mistress rather than bed with another man. I have never told her about us. What we shared was the blossom, very fragrant but fleeting. With Katherine I have found again the love I believed that I could never feel again after Blanche died. And she is like another Blanche with the children. I seem to be the one who is founding a new dynasty, don't I? Seven younglings. Eight if you count Marie St Hilaire, who is by the bye going to become a nun.'

'Nine,' Philippa said.

'Eight. How is it that ladies can never cou –?'

'Marie St Hilaire, the three that Duchess Blanche bore, Catalina, Katherine's two, and my two,' she said levelly. 'Beth and Tamkin. Tamkin is your son too but you were too busy bedding my sister to notice I was pregnant too. Nine, John.'

(ii)

'You should have told me,' Geoffrey said.

His poem had been so well received that the King, prompted by Alice, had granted him a flask of wine every day for the rest of his life, but the flush of pleasure on his face was gone now and his eyes were haggard with reproach.

'What use would it have been?' she asked bitterly. 'My sister had cast her glance upon the Duke. There was no opportunity to tell him. And I wished to keep it from you.'

'But you are telling me now.' His voice was thin. 'You are telling me that while I was absent on the King's business you were leaping into bed again with John of Gaunt. You are telling me that Tamkin is not my son as Beth was not my daughter.'

She bit her lip to stop tears escaping. She had decided that honesty was the fabric upon which the tapestry of their relationship was stitched. Geoffrey had never reproached her about Beth. She wanted his forgiveness about Tamkin too. She wanted no shadows of secrecy over their friendship.

'You could not bear it, could you?' His face had hardened. 'You could not bear it that I am fêted at Court, honoured for those verses you have always declared to be a waste of time. You could not endure to see me fast friends with the Duke. You had to speak out in pretence of honesty to spoil everything.'

'Would you rather have remained in ignorance?' she flashed.

'Yes, a thousand times rather,' he said. 'Tamkin was my son, Philippa. You have deprived me of the knowledge of that. You have tried to sow enmity between myself and John. And you have done it because you are jealous of your sister. You could not have made it clearer that you wed me only out of necessity, that the last few years have meant nothing to you.'

She wanted to cry out that it wasn't as he thought, that though temper had led her to reveal the truth to the Duke she had realised even as she spoke that it was wiser to tell the truth. Now she wondered miserably if she had made a mistake. Perhaps men preferred to live with an illusion that their wives were always faithful and that their friends never betrayed them.

'I did not beg the Duke to take me into his bed,' she said, her mouth ugly with the effort to keep from crying.

'He did not force you into it either. John of Gaunt has never forced a woman in his life,' Geoffrey said.

How quick these men were to defend one another, to lay the blame for their lusts on the wiles of women. He did not blame his patron for the betrayal. He blamed his wife. She read it in the coldness of his glance and the complaining tone of his voice.

'What are you going to do?' she asked nervously.

She had imagined that she knew her husband through and through, that after some initial hurt he would appreciate the courage of her decision to confess, but now she was no longer sure.

'My lord agrees with me there must be no scandal, no thread of gossip to hurt Beth or the babe,' he said. 'We will keep this among the three of us. It is unlikely that you will often be at Court in the future.'

'I did not intend,' she ventured, 'to make you think less of the Duke.'

'The Duke's greatest weakness has always been his fondness for the ladies,' Geoffrey said. 'I have always known and accepted that. I was even flattered that he should have loved you before we wed and asked me to be father to Beth. But I never conceived of a situation when you would give in to him again when you were my wife. It seems I was mistaken.'

Staring at him she thought with sudden bitter comprehension that his attitude to women was derived from the adoration he had felt for the Duchess. Blanche would have cut out her heart before she played her husband false. Geoffrey expected no less from Philippa.

'The Duke cares nothing for me,' she said at last. 'It is over. It was over, I think, even before Tamkin was conceived.'

'He has been most generous,' Geoffrey said. 'He has offered me the lease on a large house over Aldgate. It is well furnished and in his gift. You will have no cause to grumble about not having a home of your own in future.'

'A large house?' she said uncertainly.

'Very large.' His tone was dry and there was a twist to his mouth. 'You will have servants to match your Roet heritage, my dear. I have been offered the post of Controller of Customs for the port of London. That too is within his gift.'

'Your poem must have been excellent.' She gave him a desperate little smile, but he shook his head.

'Good enough for a flask of wine every day,' he told her, 'but the mansion at Aldgate and the new post come to me as compensation, I believe. He has been very generous.'

He sounded sincere. John of Gaunt was still the patron who could wipe out his guilt with a gift.

'He made only one condition,' Geoffrey continued. 'Your sister is never to be told about any of this. The Duke loves her, he told me, as once he loved his first wife. She loves him too, so well that she has refused marriage for his sake and will live in sin.'

Philippa sat down abruptly, folding her hands tightly to stop their shaking. So there was no blame for Katherine who was prepared to live in open adultery with John of Gaunt. There was no blame for John who had seduced two sisters. There was blame only for her because she wasn't a saint like Blanche. In a moment she would scream all her disgust out. But she sat very still, clenching her hands.

Thirteen

(i)

Sometimes, when the house was still, Philippa walked slowly from room to room, pausing in each handsomely decorated chamber to gaze round at the dark furniture, the embroidered hangings, the cups and dishes of copper and silver. In the library there were sixty books which Geoffrey read from cover to cover over and over again. Philippa preferred the solar where she spent much of her time at her loom. Drawing the coloured threads into neat patterns was a soothing occupation. In the winter the room caught the sunshine; in the summer she was sometimes forced to move out of the rays that browned the skin and made one look like a peasant. She took pains over her appearance, proud of her white complexion, the glossiness of her brown hair. There were lines at the corners of her eyes and mouth and her figure was plumper than she wished, but she looked younger than her thirty-four years.

Her favourite part of the house was the enormous kitchen at the back. The rush-strewn flagstones, the gleaming marble sinks and glowing stoves with their bake-ovens, the strings of herbs, apples and onions that hung from the rafters, the salted vats of meat and game, the long tables with their wooden surfaces scrubbed clean satisfied her more than any library could have done. Geoffrey often teased her that she was a frustrated maidservant.

When she thought of her husband the frown lines on
her brow deepened slightly. The relationship between
them could best be described as a guarded friendliness.
He was genuinely busy from morning to night with the
customs duties that Philippa didn't pretend to understand; he was often absent on business for the Court; he
devoted much of his time to writing and reading. When
he was at home he was amiable and pleasant, but he
seldom came to her bed. The habit of sleeping separate
had grown upon them. If he came home late as he often
did he slept in the spare room to avoid waking her, and
this had gradually become his main place of repose,
cluttered with the books and papers on which he was
constantly working. There was a letter from Katherine
to inform them of the birth of her third son by the
Duke.

'I have decided to name him Thomas,' she had
written in her slanting hand. 'He looks like his father
already. My lord will be pleased to have a Thomas.'

Reading the letter, Philippa had thought wryly, 'But
he has a Thomas already though you are not aware of
it.'

Tamkin at four was a miniature John of Gaunt,
fair-haired and blue-eyed. It was a mercy that Dame
Agnes had never met the Duke save on the one occasion
when she had been too flustered to take close note of his
appearance. As it was she often looked with a puzzled
expression on her face, doubtless trying to recall some
relative he resembled. As he grew older the likeness
would become more marked.

There were no such problems with Beth. Nine-year-
old Beth was Philippa all over again. She was never
happier than when she was allowed to help the cook
with the making of pies or preserves; her sewing was as
neat as Philippa's and she had as little real interest in
books. Geoffrey adored her, constantly showing her off
to visitors, declaring that the best man in the world

wouldn't be good enough for a suitor. Towards Tamkin his attitude was subtly different. Ever since he had learned the boy was not his own he had behaved towards him with a kind of wary affection as if he feared the small child might suddenly turn and deny him.

Philippa sighed, and turning her thoughts to pleasanter matters, opened the side door and stepped out into the long walled garden that ran behind the house, its orchard and maze giving one the illusion of being in the depths of the country. Here it was possible to sit or stroll, letting the cares of everyday life slip away. Geoffrey had his books. Philippa had her apple, pear and quince trees, her bushes jewelled with scarlet, purple and black, the borders of white stock that were perfumed only after dusk.

It was a warm afternoon with a breeze to mitigate the heat. She lifted her face to the blue sky, half closing her eyes against its intensity. The scent of mint drifted to her.

Footsteps on the path caused her to turn, shielding her eyes against the dancing motes of gold as the tall figure in brilliant blue and silver approached.

'Your servant said you were out here,' the Duke said.

Her first emotion was to feel a rush of indignation. For two years he had not come near, and she had firmly locked the door on the times they had spent together. It had not even pained her much to read Katherine's letters about her children. Now, without warning or apology, he had arrived in her sanctuary.

'My Lord Duke.' She found her voice and curtsied formally. 'I didn't know we were to have the honour of your company.'

'I did not know it myself until I realised that I would be passing near by,' he said.

'Geoffrey is not here. He is at Cheapside, visiting his mother.'

'Will you give him a message from me?'

'He will be home before the evening.'

'Unfortunately I cannot wait. My brother is sinking and I must be at his side.'

'I'm sorry.' The words were inadequate. Her mind returned to the procession of the Garter Knights two years before with Edward, Prince of Wales, borne on a litter.

'I feel,' he said, 'as if he actually died a long time ago and only now are we bidden to the funeral. When we were boys he was the bravest and handsomest of us all. His long illness has drained us all.'

'I am sorry for the Princess Joan,' said Philippa.

As long as they continued to talk of mutual acquaintances she felt safe.

'Joan has been a devoted wife,' he said, 'but for her too it will be a blessed release. She and I are to be named as joint guardians of Prince Richard. My father's increasing infirmity makes it certain that my nephew will succeed before very long.'

'Then he will have wise councillors.'

'I wish others felt as you do!' he exclaimed. 'The Commons wait like hyenas to tear us as soon as poor Edward is finally gone. They intend to bring charges against those who have been his most loyal friends. Mistress Alice –'

'Mistress Perrers.' Philippa's face had hardened slightly. The clever, grasping mistress of the ageing King had never struck her as admirable in any way.

'My brother Edward has stood her friend for years,' John said. 'He appreciates that our father's affection for her has prolonged his life. So she is greedy and not of noble blood, but she has made him forget his grief over our mother's death. When Edward is gone they mean to drive her away.'

'Surely she has a champion in you?' Philippa said, her voice edged with sarcasm.

'Oh, have you not heard? There is a rumour that I

mean to depose my nephew and seize the throne for myself the moment my father and elder brother are gone,' he said. 'There is even a rumour that I am base-born, that my father is not the King but a Flemish porter with whom my mother had an unlawful relationship.'

'That is the silliest rumour I ever heard!' Philippa cried robustly.

'I wish the mob had more sense,' he said ruefully. 'The trouble is that such rumours are hard to scotch once they are begun. My parents were deeply in love from the first day they met and my mother never looked at another man, but that is forgotten by those who want to drag down the power of the throne to the level of a footstool. They threaten to impeach me – when they have thought of some charges.'

'It is serious then?' Her face was clouded with anxiety as she looked up at him.

'The Commons will be thrown a bone to content them,' he said, 'but they will not be gnawing on me. However I want Geoffrey at my side in the months to come. He is respected by the mob because he is known for the moderation of his views and he bears no taint of treason in his nature. And I have no doubt that he will make a fine poem out of it all.'

'I will tell him,' she promised.

'You look well,' he said abruptly. 'Contented.'

'I am very contented,' she said steadily. 'Is that surprising? I have a kind husband, a very fine house with servants to look to my needs, a life out of the public eye.'

'You don't mention your children.'

'They are both well. I didn't think that news of them would interest you particularly.'

'I have always been interested in all my children,' he reproached.

'But mine you have promised not to acknowledge openly. It is better so.'

'They are still of my blood,' he insisted. 'Philippa, I am

fond of Geoffrey, too fond of him to let the world know
that his son is my son, but both of them are mine.'

'Only by accident of birth.'

'You have not told them? No, of course not. It was
agreed between us. Katherine would break her heart if
she ever discovered that you and I –'

'Katherine may keep her peace of mind,' Philippa
broke in. 'There is nothing between us now, and what
there was never meant much.'

'To me it did,' he said. 'I have never bedded a woman
for whom I felt nothing. Even for my present wife I feel
a kind of tender pity. She is far from home and dislikes
England so much. Marie St Hilaire died some months
ago and I felt grief for that. Our daughter, Marie, has
entered a convent and will devote her life to prayer. For
my legitimate children I have high ambitions. Philippa
and Elizabeth will marry well; Henry is created Earl of
Bolingbroke; for Catalina there will be Castille.'

'I wish them all well,' she said tonelessly.

'Katherine has given me a third son,' he said.

'If that was your true reason for visiting me,' she said
crisply, 'you are late. My sister has written to me and I
have conveyed my good wishes.'

'They are all three pretty children,' he said. 'They are
to be surnamed Beaufort. She is a splendid mother,
splendid in every way. Philippa, will you let me have
Tamkin?'

'No!' She took a step away from him, her eyes
snapping.

'To be reared in one of my castles for knighthood.
Our relationship need not be known.'

'Beth and Tamkin are mine – mine and Geoffrey's,'
she said. 'You will not acknowledge them as your own
and with that I agreed. I will not shame Geoffrey and
you wish to keep my sister in ignorance. You have given
up any rights over them you might have claimed. Beth
and Tamkin both stay with me. To rear him as a knight

indeed! He is four years old, my lord. He is still in petticoats and you talk of knighthood. No, John.'

'If they ever need anything you will tell me?'

'Geoffrey will give them anything they need,' she said inexorably. 'My lord, you cannot change what has been or mitigate what you and I both did. Had you not better hurry to your brother now? You said he was sinking.'

'My respects to you, Mistress.'

He bowed and walked away while she stared after him angrily. The children were hers – hers and Geoffrey's. Under no circumstances would she ever relinquish them.

(ii)

The Commons had had its bone. Alice Perrers had been banished from the Court, the old King forced to send away the woman who had warmed his bed since his queen's last illness. Edward had wept when they had told him that the woman he loved had been lining her purse and the purses of her friends since she had first climbed into his favour.

'The instant the Prince of Wales was in his grave she lost her best protector,' Geoffrey told Philippa. 'John of Gaunt must defend his own position as guardian of Prince Richard. His Grace could do nothing. Her loss will shorten his life, but they never think of that. They are calling this the Good Parliament. 'Tis time they held a Bad one.'

So Alice Perrers was stripped of her influence. She had flaunted herself as mistress of the King and now must sink back into the obscurity whence she had clawed her way. For the moment the Commons were satisfied with that. The Duke of Lancaster had ridden with his henchmen to the Parliament and challenged any to prove that he harboured even one thought of treason. None had answered him.

'The slur on his birth was answered without words,' Geoffrey said. 'Nobility is not something that can be denied. He is Plantagenet in stature and feature through and through.'

His admiration for his patron was undiminished. Men clung together in a secret brotherhood that was more powerful than any love they had for women.

'Is it bad to be base-born?' Beth asked.

She had been quietly plying her needle by the window and they had not even realised that she was listening.

'It is better not to be,' Geoffrey said shortly.

'Are my cousins in Lincolnshire base-born?' Beth persisted.

Philippa and Geoffrey exchanged glances.

'Your Swynford cousins, Blanchette and Tom, are not,' he said. 'Their father was a brave knight who died when they were babes.'

'I meant my Beaufort cousins,' Beth said. 'I heard that their father is the Duke of Lancaster who already has a wife. Does that mean they are base-born?'

'You ought not to listen to gossip,' Philippa said crossly. 'As you are not likely to have much to do with your Beaufort cousins then their place in society is not your concern.'

Beth flushed and bent over her sewing again. For the moment she was silenced. Philippa drew a small sigh of relief and was grateful when Geoffrey began to talk about his next mission.

'We have hopes of arranging a marriage between Prince Richard and the Princess Marie of France. Such an alliance would go far to healing the bitterness caused by past conflicts.'

'Are you using the royal "we" or speaking on behalf of the Council?' Philippa enquired.

She had no wish to undermine Geoffrey's confidence, but there were times when he became a trifle pompous.

'The Duke is good enough to take me into his confidence about much that is discussed in Council,' Geoffrey said, somewhat huffily. 'I am reputed as a man who can smooth the way to many a negotiation.'

'The Prince is only a little boy,' Beth put in.

'Royal weddings take no account of age, sweetheart.' Geoffrey looked amused.

'I am glad that I am not royal then,' said Beth, 'for I don't intend to be married until I am old, at least twenty.'

God forbid she should ever learn any different, thought Philippa, and glancing at Geoffrey saw that the same thought was in his mind.

The marriage negotiations came to nothing. Before Yuletide Geoffrey had returned, looking as near despondent as his stocky frame and cheerful features would allow.

'The French don't trust my Lord of Lancaster,' he told Philippa. 'The slanders about his only waiting until the King dies before he murders his nephew and seizes the throne for himself have wormed their way into the minds of the French Court. They will not send their princess to a country where treason is in the air. All my arguments were of no use.'

'They didn't believe you?'

'They know that I would scarcely speak against my patron. However, I have the rough draft of a magnificent new poem, which I shall call the Parliament of Fowls. Those with country accents may pronounce it as Fools.' He chuckled, brightening up.

Which meant he would spend the next several evenings closeted in the library scribbling away. It kept him from getting under her feet, Philippa reflected, but he ought to take more exercise. He had begun to put on weight which, being only of average height, he could ill afford.

Yuletide was gone before she had realised it and with the New Year Geoffrey was gone again too, on another attempt to persuade the French to send their princess to marry Richard. He would remain away, he informed her in a letter, longer than he had planned, travelling on into Italy to renew some old acquaintanceships. He sent his love to the children and to her. Philippa read the missive with irritation. One day her clever husband might realise that she sometimes grew weary of having only the children and an occasional visit from old Dame Agnes to vary the monotony of her life. Then she scolded herself for being so discontented. There were districts of London where the poor fought over crusts of bread and slept huddled together in alleyways for warmth.

In June the tolling of the bells informed the citizens that King Edward the Third had died, sinking into a final melancholy after the banishment of his adored Alice. He had been a good king, people said, save for these latter years when he had grown a mite foolish. Now his grandson, Prince Richard, was the monarch, the only surviving son of Prince Edward whom they were beginning to call the Black Prince, remembering him in his youth and vigour in his suit of gleaming black armour, son of the Princess Joan whose matrimonial adventures had amused and scandalised the Court years before.

Geoffrey would still be in Italy when the coronation took place but two invitations to the ceremony in the Abbey arrived in Aldgate. Philippa decided to take Beth with her. Had matters been different she might have had the right to sit among the royal children. As it was she could have a taste of the pageantry.

Of the two of them it was Philippa who felt the more excited as they took their seats. From where they sat it was impossible to see the high altar but they would have an excellent view of the procession as it entered and departed. Getting into their places had been more difficult than she had anticipated since the crowds swarmed about the doors, and the two servants she had brought as escort had to lay about them with their clubs before she could show her tickets and be shown to the modest places set aside for her and Beth.

She could enjoy herself without any fear of embarrassment since Katherine had written to say that her health was still delicate after Thomas's birth and that she would stay at Bolingbroke. Otherwise, Philippa thought, she would have come brazen-faced to attend.

Trumpets sounding, the clatter of hooves and rattle of harness in the square outside, a roar from the crowd. Her heart began to beat faster and the palms of her hands were damp. The long line of heralds was snaking into the carpeted aisle between the columns.

'You must remember,' she whispered to Beth, 'that your grandfather was Herald Guienne and had he lived he would have walked here too.'

'And your grandfather was the late king but that I can never tell you.'

Archbishops and Bishops in crimson, scarlet and gold mingled with knights in full plumage, with ladies whose trains swept the ground. As the royal family paced by, Philippa caught her breath, seeing herself as a child first come to Court and believing that a handsome knight would carry her away. Now she saw them through older eyes, but their glitter still dazzled her.

Their Graces had had many children, but there were fewer descendants of that happy marriage than might have been expected. The pale daughter of Prince Lionel paced by, followed by her Lancaster cousins. Philippa and Elizabeth walked with their five-year-old half-sister, Catalina, who looked dark and foreign amid the brightness. Behind them Henry of Bolingbroke, a tall lad of ten, walked alone, as fair and wide-shouldered as his father's kin.

The Princess Joan was escorted by her younger brothers-in-law, Edmund and Thomas, her unwieldy bulk forgotten when one saw the sweetness of her smile. For her this must be a wonderful day, to see her son crowned and anointed. Yet as she paced slowly she took the time to glance from side to side, bowing her greetings. Philippa received a bow and a wave from a fat, beringed hand before Joan passed on.

More knights, jostling together, and then the Duke and Duchess of Lancaster, she tiny and sharp-featured in silver tissue, he magnificent in the blue that was paler than his eyes, his cloak spreading out like a fan as he walked, jewels sparkling and blazing from his proud blond head to the tips of his velvet shoes. Those who accused him of coveting the crown for himself perhaps realised what a splendid king he would make.

He looked to neither left nor right but kept his head high. At his side, despite her silver tissue and the rubies that glowed on her veil, the Duchess Constantia looked dull. Philippa closed her eyes briefly, fighting back a surge of longing that came unawares to ruffle her composure. What had been between them was over and done. That his daughter sat in the Abbey and watched him not knowing the relationship they shared meant nothing. Beth was a tranquil and happy child whose official father was well respected. John of Gaunt had laid claim to eight of his children. Beth and Tamkin were hers.

A long sigh, like a ripple of wind, stirred the incense-laden air. The King was walking alone between the serried ranks of guests and spectators.

Philippa, opening her eyes and sighing with the rest, saw a tall child with delicate features and hair of red-gold surmounted by a simple coronet. His tunic and hose were of white satin, his train of purple edged with miniver, embroidered with the lilies of France and the leopards of England. He was a beautiful boy, his grey eyes raised to the high arches for an instant before he lowered his lids and walked on steadily.

King Richard the Second, born in his father's province of Aquitaine, reared by his gentle mother, tutored by Sir Simon Burley, one of the shyest and sweetest of men, hardly ever glimpsed outside the confines of the country palaces where he had spent his enchanted childhood. It was no wonder that the spectators heaved a sentimental sigh. The long ceremony was beginning. Philippa eased her feet out of her new shoes, wishing she had put comfort before vanity. Beth was wrapped up in the sound of the chanting and singing, in the occasional flurry of activity glimpsed from their inconspicuous places.

Another ripple stirred the congregation. Philippa sat up straighter, craning her neck to try to see, hearing the whisper as it travelled backwards through the echoing spaces of the great Abbey.

'The crown slipped from the cushion as the Archbishop reached out for it. The crown almost fell.'

There were those who would make an omen of that, Philippa thought.

Fourteen

(i)

The Parliament of Fowls had consolidated Geoffrey's reputation as a poet. Now he could rank himself with Gower and Usk, could be sure of a warm welcome at any noble house. His work as a government official had also brought him recognition and considerable wealth. For a man not yet forty he had risen high. But he wore his celebrity lightly, not giving himself airs. He moved easily between the Court and Cheapside.

The three years of the new reign had been difficult ones. The marriage negotiations with France had broken down and there had been another campaign which had to be paid for with higher taxes. Two bad harvests had sent food prices spiralling and pamphlets were frequently posted on the city gates, blaming John of Gaunt, the uncrowned ruler, for the misery of the masses. Philippa tried to ignore them when she went out but she fretted sometimes about the Duke. He had become one of the most hated men in the country which was manifestly unfair since he did not run the Privy Council single-handed, but his retainers swaggered through the streets, knocking people out of the way with their clubs to make space for the proud figure riding on his richly caparisoned steed, his blue eyes surveying the scattering figures with indifference.

She had not expected to meet him again. Geoffrey never took her with him to Court, and from Katherine at Bolingbroke there came only an occasional letter. She had just had another child, named Joan after the King's mother. Philippa sent cold congratulations.

In August Tamkin was eight. He was a tall child, his fair hair and bright blue eyes reminding her of John every time she looked at him. Geoffrey was reminded too. Though he was an indulgent father Philippa guessed that he had never been able to put the pain of that old betrayal out of his mind. She wondered if that accounted for his indulgence. Had Tamkin been his true son then he would have felt no scruples about correcting him from time to time, but he held back, in his gentleness the knowledge that this child was the son of a Duke.

Philippa was thinking of that as she vainly tried to persuade Tamkin to put his toys into the cupboard where they belonged.

'You must spend an hour at your hornbook or you will never learn to read properly.'

'I don't like learning,' Tamkin said. 'I'm going to be a hunter when I'm grown. Hunters don't need to read.'

'But gentlemen do,' she argued weakly.

'Ladies don't.' He shifted his ground. 'You don't read books.'

'I know how to read, and you are not a lady. Now where are you going?'

'To read my book,' Tamkin said virtuously, half-way to the door.

'When you have put your toys away.' Philippa held her temper in check, wondering why Beth had been so tractable when her brother could be so difficult.

Tamkin thrust out his lower lip and glared at her. A shadow filled the doorway behind him and a masculine voice said, smoothly and firmly,

'Put your toys away now without any more nonsense.'

Tamkin had whirled round. For a moment blue eyes stared up into blue eyes. Then the small boy went meekly to pick up the wooden sword, the bits of plaster fort and the miniature bow and arrow.

'My Lord Duke.' Philippa rose, dropping into an automatic curtsy, thinking wildly, 'Why does he walk into my home as if he had the right?'

'Are you a duke?' Tamkin picked up the last of his playthings and looked into the blue eyes again.

'This is the Duke of Lancaster,' Philippa said.

Your father, and when you stand together anyone in the world can see it.

Tamkin, impressed, attempted a very creditable bow. John was looking down at him, the grim set of his mouth touched with humour.

'And you are Master Thomas Chaucer, are you not?' he said.

'Did you hear of me before?' Tamkin asked, wide-eyed.

'Oh, your father is a famous man,' John said. Philippa wondered if the double meaning was intentional.

'Take your toys to the cupboard and then get your book,' she broke in.

Tamkin looked as if he was considering argument but a swift upward glance at the Duke's face evidently convinced him. He went out meekly and John closed the door.

'My servants ought to have announced you,' Philippa said.

'When I visit friends I sometimes prefer informality.'

'Your visits are few and far between,' she said crisply.

'Affairs of state keep me occupied. May I sit down?'

He had always had the power to fluster her. She hastily indicated the best high-backed chair and moved to pour him a goblet of wine.

'So, Philippa?' He drank some of the wine and lifted his head, smiling at her. 'You have not begun to show the years yet. You have raised a fine boy, though from what I heard as I came in he has a will of his own. Does Geoffrey not discipline him?'

'He leaves the children to me.' Fearful that that sounded like a criticism she added quickly, 'The truth is that he is so fond of them that he leaves me to do any chastising – not that Beth ever needed any. She is always amenable and industrious. Tamkin can be difficult at times – he dislikes having to study.'

'If he is to amount to anything he must apply himself to his books for part of the day,' said John. 'Does he have practice at riding and tilting? An active lad enjoys such sports.'

'Geoffrey,' she said drily, 'doesn't often tilt these days.'

'The King is growing into a splendid rider and a considerable fencer, but he lacks company.'

'That sounds strange.' Philippa looked at him. 'Surely a king is always surrounded by others?'

'By his mother who flinches if the rain rains on him and his three tedious uncles of whom I count myself as one. He requires lads about him with spirit, who will treat him as a friend as well as their monarch. He is too much with women and councillors.'

He had paused, gazing into his wine, the look on his face thoughtful. Philippa clasped her hands tightly at her waist and said,

'Why did you come today?'

'My eldest son, Henry, is to be married,' he said abruptly.

'Little Harry?' Astonished, she stared at him.

'Little Harry, as you call him, is nearly fourteen,' he said, his smile broadening. 'I am marrying him to Mary de Bohun. She is twelve and will doubtless keep him in order. I am in favour of young marriages. It ensures fidelity.'

'I don't see how,' Philippa said bluntly.

'My own appetites have caused me intense guilt during my life,' he said slowly. 'Before I was seventeen

I'd bedded Marie St Hilaire, God rest her soul, and though Blanche and I were married young and she was the perfect wife, I was not always the perfect husband. With you I forgot the honour I bore her and admitted that it is possible for some men to love more than one woman at the same time, though in different ways. That facet of my nature has often fretted my conscience. I want Henry to be a faithful husband.'

She bit back a tart comment, feeling sorry for the boy who must supply his father's deficiencies in the probity of his own character. John still had his second wife but his conscience was not so tender that it drove him to return to her bed and leave Katherine.

'I am sure that Henry will do you credit,' she said.

'You will come to the wedding? You and Geoffrey? I would like you to be there.'

'Yes, with pleasure,' she answered promptly.

'About Tamkin.'

'What about him?' The smile faded from her face.

'The boy is at an age when he could begin his knightly training. First as page, then as squire, then as knight.'

Philippa was silent as he went on.

'What do you want for the boy? Is he to be made into a scholar like Geoffrey or a tradesman or a knight? His heritage is knightly at the least. From your bloodline also.'

'He is only eight,' she said.

'I don't intend to steal him away from you for ever,' he said lightly. 'My dear, if Geoffrey agrees let me have Tamkin for part of every year at least, I shall establish him at Oatlands which you called home yourself when you were a child. He will have more space than he could ever have here, more freedom to decide which road in life he wants to take. He is my son, Philippa, and were it not causing pain to those whom I love I'd acknowledge him openly tomorrow.'

Perhaps she had been selfish, she thought, thinking

of herself when she ought to have been considering the boy's future.

'If Geoffrey agrees,' she said, knowing that he would, 'then you may send Tamkin to Oatlands. I won't let Beth follow him.'

'If I were to choose the woman who could rear a little girl into a lady I would name you,' he said. 'Beth is safe in your hands and when the time comes we shall match her well.'

There was a feeling of unreality about sitting calmly with him, discussing their two children. Whatever his faults he did his best for those whom he had fathered. And if she allowed him to have Tamkin then in the future there would be occasions when they could meet, as friends with the old hurts mellowed.

'I must leave. I have a council meeting.' He finished his wine and rose, as tall and golden as he always was in her memory.

She would have curtsied but he took her hand and kissed it, cocking an eyebrow as he looked down at her.

'Thank you for lending me Tamkin,' he said. 'I shall have the travel arrangements made when I have talked with Geoffrey. I believe he will abide by our decision. I shall look for you at the wedding.'

Staring after him she wondered if it would be another three years before he walked calmly into her house and set her heart jerking again.

(ii)

Her new gown was of brown and lemon, the sleeves gathered tightly at the wrists, the skirt falling in wide pleats from a high waistline. One of the latest frilled head-dresses covered her coiled plaits of hair and the veil that hung down behind was embroidered with tiny yellow flowers.

'We make a handsome couple,' said Geoffrey, giving his own reflection a satisfied glance.

'You won't be reciting any of your verses today, will you?' she asked suspiciously.

'No, my dear.' She fancied there was a trace of disappointment in his voice.

'The King will be there, won't he? I shall have to make my bow to him.'

'His Grace will certainly attend. I only wish that negotiations for his own marriage had succeeded, but there is time yet. Shall we go, my dear?'

They were to travel on horseback to spare their fine garments from the mud of the streets. As she mounted up Philippa waved her hand towards Beth who stood at a window above. It was a pity no invitation had come for her. Nobody would have traced the Duke in her round features.

Tamkin had left for Oatlands the previous month, looking very small and vulnerable on his pony with two of the Lancaster henchmen to escort him. He had been cheerfully looking forward to what he envisaged as a life full of horses and toy swords where he would learn to be a knight, however, and had trotted off importantly, leaving her to gulp back tears and wish she had asked Geoffrey to make a scholar of him instead.

To ride to the immense palace of the Savoy again was like taking a journey back in time. She could see herself as a young girl arriving to serve the Duchess Blanche. She shot a glance at Geoffrey wondering if the writing of his poem about the Duchess had exorcised the infatuation he had felt for her. His face bore its usual amiable expression so that it was impossible to guess at his deepest sentiments.

Their invitation had been one among hundreds. Any prospect of being presented to the young King Richard faded into the realms of imagination as they jostled their way through the guests. This wedding was designed to display the Lancaster power and wealth, Philippa realised, as her bedazzled eyes fell on new silken hangings, thick waxen candles blazing in their sconces to light the dull winter afternoon, dishes and goblets of crystal and gold, servants clad as grandly as the guests, and on a carved throne near the platform where the bridal pair would stand the figure of a slim boy in white satin whose hair burned more red-gold than the fires at each end of the Great Hall.

'His Grace.' She pulled at Geoffrey's sleeve, her voice rising in excitement.

He smiled back at her but absently, his eyes moving to a group of handsomely robed men who were acknowledging him with waves and bows.

Philippa was in too good a humour to resent his lack of attention. She patted his arm encouragingly with a whispered,

'Why don't you go and talk with your friends? I know my way here.'

He went with no more than a token murmur of protest and she smiled tolerantly, knowing that he was always flattered by the notice of the rich. He seemed not to realise that he was also rich and important now.

The twelve-year-old bride was being escorted in, her face a mixture of pleasure and apprehension. Mary de Bohun was a pretty child, and her bridegroom was looking at her with boyish admiration. Philippa wondered if his father's plan would succeed and he would remain faithful as John had never managed to do. The little bride was looking at him with shy interest so perhaps the match would prove a happy one.

The procession was forming. Those who had no part in the official ceremony were being hustled to the side. When the vows had been exchanged the bridal pair would enter the chapel beyond with other members of the royal family for the Nuptial Mass. Then would come

the banquet and the speeches and songs and the official
bedding which was to be symbolic only until the bride
had reached her thirteenth birthday.

Philippa looked for the Duke and then she saw him,
entering with his two daughters and a fair-haired boy of
about Tamkin's age. For a moment she was puzzled,
trying to place the child. Then her eyes widened as
Prince Henry, momentarily forsaking his bride, called,
'Johnny, come and help me buckle my sword.'

Johnny? The realisation that Katherine's bastard son
was here at his half-brother's wedding struck her like a
blow. And as she stared at the boy a smaller one squirmed
his way under the arms of the adults, piping,

'Let me help.'

'Harry, you're too little,' Henry was declaiming, but
the younger child was already trying to wrest the sword
from Johnny's grasp.

'Lads, this is a wedding, not a fighting practice,' the
Duke said, moving swiftly to pluck them apart. His tone
and face were full of pride, however, as he held them at
arm's length, exclaiming to those about it, 'God grant
they will always be as eager to serve him.'

Katherine's children by the Duke here openly at
Court. Philippa could scarcely believe her eyes. That the
existence of the children was known generally was one
thing, but that he should bring them to a public celebration so blatantly was quite another.

There was no time at that moment to see more for the
ceremony was beginning. She was edged into a corner by
a pillar from where it was difficult to see anything or to
extricate herself when the vows had been exchanged and
the royal party had moved on into the chapel. She saw
that Katherine's two boys trotted in with the rest.

'We are bidden to the banquet, my dear.' Geoffrey had
found his way to her side again.

'Katherine's children are here,' she said.

'Aye, so I saw.' He sounded unperturbed. 'They are

pretty boys.'

'My sister must have no shame to let them be brought into the Duke's Court with the King himself present,' she muttered, but Geoffrey was steering her into the banqueting-area. Their seats were gratifyingly near the High Table and the variety of dishes on the snowy cloths made her mouth water.

Those who had not gone into the chapel were already eating and in the gallery a troupe of minstrels had begun to play. There was no sense in sitting sullen, she decided, and following their example began to heap her trencher.

There was a bustle by the doors, a burst of applause. The wedding party were processing in. The King looking animated, held the hands of the youthful bride and bridegroom. The Duke walked behind them escorting the Princess Joan who was prettier and plumper than ever. No doubt the bride's family were there too but they were completely eclipsed by the Lancaster splendour. The Duchess was not there. Neither the Duke's Spanish wife nor his daughter Catalina had attended the nuptials.

Katherine's boys were not seated at the royal table but at a side table so near to the canopy that Philippa felt her hackles rise. That nobody else seemed to be whispering about them merely confirmed her suspicion that this was not the first time they had been seen in public with their father.

A tall, slender woman with wisps of auburn hair escaping from beneath the hem of her pearl-embroidered veil had entered the banqueting-hall and stood, looking round, her dress so thickly sewn with gold that it was hard to perceive the green silk beneath. Then her face lit up and she glided towards the table at which Geoffrey and Philippa were seated.

'Dearest Philippa, I have looked forward so much to seeing you, and you are here at last, and not changed at all from when we were last together.'

It was seldom that Philippa was completely at a loss for

words but the sudden arrival of her sister left her dumb. She could only gape at this slim, brown-skinned creature who had reached the age of thirty-eight and still looked like a girl of twenty. Katherine had lost her reputation when she became the Duke's acknowledged mistress, had borne six children and was as lovely as if she had remained untouched by human hand.

'Katherine, this is a pleasure.'

Geoffrey had risen and was kissing her hand and cheek. If he felt surprise he masked it well.

'I wanted to come and see you but ever since we arrived there has been so much to arrange,' said Katherine, taking the place Geoffrey had vacated. 'We came from Bolingbroke only three days since after travelling over the worst roads you ever saw in your life. There is so much time for us to catch up, Philippa. You look charming and so contented.' She chattered as gaily as when she had been a child. Now she was indicating her sons.

'Johnny and Harry are so pleased to be at the Savoy. In a year or two they will begin their training as pages. John believes that they may be accepted at Westminster. And Thomas is doing splendidly at school. He intends to take over the management of Swynford Manor as soon as he comes of age.'

'They are handsome boys,' Geoffrey complimented her.

'And my little Tom and my new daughter are equally fine,' Katherine assured them. 'As soon as the weather is warmer they will join us.'

'Do you intend to make a long visit?' Philippa tried to speak pleasantly, but her tongue felt as if it were sticking to the roof of her mouth.

'We are here to stay,' Katherine said.

'Oh, but surely –' Philippa darted a frantic glance at Geoffrey.

'Since the Duke no longer lives with the Duchess

Constantia,' he said, 'he will need a hostess when he entertains.'

'And we are both weary of being hypocrites,' Katherine said. 'John and I have lived as husband and wife for nearly nine years now. We have been faithful each to the other and I have borne him four children. The entire country knows that I am his wife in all save name. And there is so much business that keeps him in London that we scarcely ever see him.'

It was clear now why the Duke had wished to send Tamkin to Oatlands to be reared. Let his beloved Katherine catch one glimpse of him and she would realise whose son he was. She would realise that the Duke had bedded her sister first. Phillppa drew a deep breath, fighting back the cold rage that iced her veins.

'Excuse me, but I must make sure my sons are not stuffing themselves,' Katherine said. 'We will talk later, my sister.'

She rose, gliding away, pausing to smile at her lover's legitimate heir who waved his spoon cheerfully, calling,

'Lady Katherine, when I have danced with my bride I claim a dance with my sweet governess.'

'Governess? He must be well aware she is his father's leman,' Philippa muttered.

'He is fond of her,' Geoffrey said excusingly. 'She made his children forget their sorrow.'

'And provided him with four more to swell the family,' Philippa said.

'Hush, or someone may hear.' He lowered his voice.

'If she flaunts herself and her bastards she must expect gossip,' Philippa said.

'I thought she was a mite nervous, my love,' he said. 'She talked a little fast and kept glancing for your approval.'

'Which she will not have. Geoffrey, she may be content to ignore it but we are Roets, the daughters of Herald Guienne and not jumped up Alices. How can

she come to live openly at the Savoy, exposing her
children to mockery, ousting the Duchess Constantia?
How can she?'

'Perhaps she wishes to be at the Duke's side while he is
being attacked for his management of the government,'
Geoffrey suggested mildly.

'Nonsense, she is merely an embarrassment to him,'
Philippa said.

'He does not reveal his feelings,' said Geoffrey drily,
turning to watch the Duke who had left the High Table
and was bending over his bastards, evidently com-
plimenting them on their behaviour in church. At his
side Katherine was laughing at some jest he had
cracked.

He saw me first, loved me first, bedded me first, got
me first with child. But he did not choose to set me up as
his mistress. He married me off to a man who thinks
only of his books. He had our son sent away lest
Katherine find out the truth now she is in London. My
feelings have never counted for anything with anybody.
The words hammered in her brain and there was no
respite.

(iii)

They were in mourning for Dame Agnes who had died
after what she had insisted was no more than a slight
chill, leaving her property to her third husband,
Bartholomew Chapel.

'I don't grudge him a penny of it,' Geoffrey said
sincerely. 'He made her a happy woman, and we have
plenty. The Duke continues to be generous, yearly
increasing my annuity.'

He paid us off with pensions and the lease of a
mansion house, Philippa thought. Her head had been

full of such thoughts ever since the wedding. Sometimes she felt as if she had a tight chain holding her heart so tightly that it was hard to breathe.

Geoffrey had gone to confer with the lawyers about the probating of his mother's Will. He would be late home and she would sleep alone. She preferred to sleep alone. It was better to fill her dreams with dreams of John's tall, lithe body, his laughing blue eyes, when her stocky, dull husband was not by to furnish cruel comparison.

Katherine had sent word that she intended to visit. As if she were a Duchess, Philippa thought, and wished that she was not still obliged to wear black for Dame Agnes for the colour made her skin look sallow.

Katherine had chosen to wear grey, a tactful shade when visiting a house where the family had been bereaved. A sly choice for the gentle colour made her hair blaze more red. Embracing her, Philippa said,

'You came alone? I hoped you might bring Blanchette. She and Beth are the same age.'

'Blanchette is being difficult.' Katherine's face clouded over. 'She has never accepted my relationship with John. He has treated her with great kindness but she can scarcely bring herself to speak to him politely. The silly girl believes herself in love with Sir Thomas Holland and cannot accept the plain fact that he means to marry elsewhere. Girls of fourteen are much more difficult than boys to rear.'

'My Beth is always amiable,' said Philippa, with her sweetest smile.

'She resembles you, does she not? You and Geoffrey?' Katherine asked the question with a smile.

So we are settling down to a cosy gossip about our children? So be it.

'She resembles me. Why should there be anything of Geoffrey in her?'

'Because he is her father – isn't he?' Katherine hesitated as she asked.

It would be so easy to nod, to smile, to change the subject. The bitterness within held her prisoner, and the words that came were light and deadly.

'My marriage was somewhat rushed, if you recall, but it was not because of poor Geoffrey's lusts. The Duke arranged the match – to spare me shame.'

'John? Oh, but that is so like him,' Katherine said. 'He thinks most highly of Geoffrey and is always so courteous towards ladies. I wish more knew his private face and then they would not blame him for every ill in the land.'

'He wished also to spare his wife pain,' Philippa said.

'The Duchess Blanche? I cannot see how your –' Katherine's voice trailed away as swiftly as the wild-rose colour drained from her cheeks. Her grey eyes were huge and blank, robbed of their silver.

'I am tired of the long deceit and would make an end of it,' said Philippa, or perhaps it was not she who spoke but the creature of bitterness hidden within. 'Katherine, you love John of Gaunt and he behaves as if he returns your loving, but he has no constancy in him. Has he ever told you about Marie St Hilaire?'

Katherine neither spoke nor shook her head. She simply went on staring.

'When he was a lad she bore him a daughter, another Marie who entered a convent not long since. That was small blame to him for he was not wed, but then he wed Blanche of Lancaster. She gave him four children of whom three survived and was the wife other men prayed they might find. He was not faithful to her, Katherine.'

'A lapse,' said Katherine, white-faced.

'Had it been the one,' said Philippa, 'one might forget, but both before and after the death of the Duchess he – Sister, wake up and look at the situation as I have done. Why do you imagine he pays me an annual pension? Why has Tamkin been allowed to live at Oatlands to be reared for knighthood? The Duke fathered both my children and then tossed me aside, as he will toss you aside when he meets someone fairer.'

'Both your children?' Katherine said faintly. 'You and Geoffrey never —?'

'The only children that Geoffrey is capable of bearing are written in rhyme.'

'John is not like that.' Katherine licked her lips. 'He would not take one sister and then another. He would not.'

'If you come with me to Oatlands I shall show you my son who is as like the Duke as are your children.'

'I don't believe you ever lied to me in your life,' said Katherine. 'I wish to God you were lying now, but you have no reason, no reason. I cannot ask him, Philippa. True or false such words would rouse his anger against us both. I have to think. He is in Dover now, trying to raise some taxes. I have to think.'

She had risen and was swaying to the door. Watching her Philippa felt a fierce satisfaction mingled with a shame so deep that she could hardly endure it.

'I have to think,' repeated Katherine, and opened the door, walking through the hall like a sleepwalker.

The main doors opened and closed. Philippa unclenched her hands, seeing scarlet crescents where she had dug her nails into her hands.

From the open doorway Beth said,

'Oh, my lady mother, how could you pretend for so long and keep us from our real father?'

Fifteen

(i)

Guilt had a sharp and bitter taste upon the conscience. Philippa felt as if she had just woken from a dream in which she had been forced to watch, powerless, while a stranger with her name destroyed all the safe familiar things that had held her life together.

Katherine had returned to Lincolnshire with her children. That much a hard-eyed Geoffrey informed her.

'She has not betrayed your part in all this except to me, for she would not have my patron turn from me. She has left word that she intends to go on pilgrimage.'

'Then she no longer loves him,' said Philippa, but that comfort was snatched away.

'She will never stop loving him,' said Geoffrey, 'but she remembers the family loyalty she owes to you and she will not stay with a man who cast aside her sister. She will not be here when he comes home. She will never be here for him again. You did your work well.'

'I did not wish her to be deceived as I was deceived,' said Philippa numbly.

'You were never deceived,' said Geoffrey. 'You went to the Duke's bed knowing the first time that he was married, knowing the second time that you were married. Had you refused he would not have forced you. Milord Lancaster never needed to force a woman. You went of your own free will, my dear, as did

Katherine. But the difference was that he loved her as a man loves a wife. He will not take her desertion lightly. If he ever guesses that you were the one who drove her away he will be ruthless in revenge.'

'Will you tell him?'

'I shall say nothing. Philippa, what possessed you to speak out? After all these years, why did you do such a terrible thing? Was it in the hope that he might turn again to you? He never will.'

'I would not have him,' she smiled sullenly.

'And what of Beth and Tamkin?'

'He need know nothing,' she said quickly. 'Beth overheard. I would she had not, for she takes no pleasure in finding herself granddaughter of a king.'

'You have robbed her of a father and given her nothing in return but the consciousness of her own bastardy.'

'She will not love you less because of this,' she said quickly.

'And she will not love you more.'

'So it is all my fault, as usual.' She began to shred the leaves of the posy she was carrying, each green bit scattering over the skirt of her gown.

'No, not all of it,' said Geoffrey sadly. 'We have all been to blame in our separate ways. I loved you well when I married you. Does that surprise you? I did not agree to marry you merely to oblige my patron, you know. I wanted you for yourself and I was ready to wait until your passion for the Duke had cooled and you turned to me. But you turned to the Duke again instead, and I knew then that I would never win you. Now I no longer wish it.'

'What are you going to do?' she asked almost inaudibly.

'We shall go on as before,' he said. 'I have a great deal of business on hand and my books. I am contented enough. I pray you too will find contentment again.'

His chilly sorrow was more painful to her than a blow.
In a year's time she would be forty, an old woman who in
the midst of an attack of jealous fury had spoiled
everything she held dear.

Beth had fled to Geoffrey, sobbing out her distress at
the revelation of her parentage, and though she had
speedily calmed down and seemed now as usual, Philippa
could tell the girl had been so deeply shocked that she
would not soon recover. She was as industrious and
amiable as ever but the laughter at the back of her eyes
had fled and she spent many evenings in the library with
Geoffrey, listening to him reading his verses to her, as if
she tried to assure him that her affection for him had not
been diminished.

There were rumblings of trouble in the world outside
the mansion at Aldgate. The new poll tax was proving
almost impossible to collect; the recent bad harvests had
impoverished even the richer peasants an the renewal of
the French campaigns was going badly with English ships
set alight in the Channel and the French even daring to
land on the Isle of Wight.

When a group of workmen arrived and began to instal
steel shutters to the lower windows of the house, Philippa, outraged at the mud being trampled over her
mosaic floor, stormed into the library where Geoffrey
was working with Beth, sewing quietly, by the fire.

'If it is not too great a trouble,' she said icily, 'perhaps
you will tell me why my home is suddenly invaded by
artisans.'

'I am increasing the defences in case of trouble,' he said
mildly.

'I haven't noticed any French troops marching
through the city.'

'It is not the French who worry me,' he said. 'The
peasants are gravely discontented and are threatening
rebellion.'

'Down in Kent,' said Philippa scornfully. 'Some crazy

priest is demanding equality for all classes.'

'John Ball. I am glad to find you so well informed on current events.'

'So why must my house be turned upside down because a mad priest stirs up a Kentish rabble?'

'Because it is possible to walk from Kent to London. Because the men of Kent are not alone in their discontent. Because it is better to take precautions than wail about damage later.'

'The peasants would not dare to rise,' she said uncertainly.

'One hopes not.' He gave her a smiling dismissive nod and wrote on steadily.

'Mother, I want to talk with you,' said Beth. She had laid aside her work and her face was serious.

'Later,' Philippa said, but Beth followed her out of the room, catching at her sleeve.

'Now, Mother. I have to talk to you now.'

'About what?' Philippa averted her eyes from two men carrying in a steel shutter. 'What is so important that it cannot wait?'

'I have decided to enter the religious life,' Beth said.

Philippa stared at her for a moment, then said flatly, 'Don't be so utterly ridiculous.'

'It has been in my mind for a long time, Mother.' Beth's round face was earnest. 'Recently the desire has become stronger.'

'You are fourteen years old, a baby. You cannot possibly be serious.'

'I am very serious,' said Beth. 'Mother, ever since I was a little girl I have never dreamed of husbands and babies the way other girls do. I always had the feeling that I wanted something more, something different. Now I understand why.'

'Do you indeed?'

They had reached the solar and Philippa tried to maintain the light sarcasm of her tone, but in her daughter's firm mouth and steady brown eyes she glimpsed something implacable.

'How could I marry any man knowing what I know now?' asked Beth. 'I could not enter into any marriage unless I was honest, and how could I be honest when I was fathered by a man who was not your husband?'

'By John of Gaunt. That makes you an excellent catch.'

'I am not going into a convent because of who I have learned I am,' said Beth. 'That is only the excuse for following the vocation I truly desire.'

'Beth, you are a pretty girl. Any young man will be happy to wed you and not bother his head about your origins,' protested Philippa.

'But I shall not be happy to have any young man,' Beth said steadily. 'I want to be a nun, Mother. I would not be allowed to take my final vows before eighteen, but I can be a novice at Sheppey. You told me once that Aunt Katherine was lodged there and the Sisters were very kind.'

'Your ideas will change as you mature,' said Philippa.

But looking at Beth she feared they would not. Beneath the sweetness and obedience of the girl was a rock of obstinacy.

'Then I shall not take my final vows,' said Beth. 'I know that I won't change though. I won't change but I would like to enter with your blessing.'

'Have you talked to – to Geoffrey?'

'He told me that I must do what makes me happy, but that I must consult with you.'

Philippa bit her lip. Geoffrey had clearly abdicated any responsibility for the girl he had loved as a daughter. She, Philippa, must give the final yea or nay.

'Will you not delay for a year? You are very young,' she said at last.

'I want to enter now,' said Beth. 'Mother, I love you very much and I don't blame you for what happened, but I shall begin to blame you if I stay here much longer. I can't help thinking about you with the Duke, wondering how you could submit to him. I want to leave now, while I still love you. You won't be losing me. There will be visits and I shall be happy.'

'We shall talk further,' said Philippa, but she knew that Beth had won. If the girl was entering a convent to avoid fleshly desires then it would prove cold comfort when she came up against the realities of religious life with its penances and lack of independence. If she had a true vocation then she would be happy. Whatever the result it would be for Beth to choose in the end.

(ii)

In the autumn the men of Kent marched, tramping through the lanes and fields, chanting their slogan of equality,

'When Adam delved and Eve span who was then the gentleman?'

'A revolutionary concept if I ever heard one,' said Geoffrey. 'Very idealistic, but not in the least practical. How can the uneducated mobs hope to legislate for themselves? This is a cry of defiance against the King's ministers, especially John of Gaunt whom the peasants blame for every ill that God or Fortune sends.'

He had come home early from the city, ordering the shutters to be put up at the lower windows and the servants to arm themselves and remain within. The previous week he had taken Beth to the convent, not to Sheppey since travel was hazardous in the present state of affairs, but to Barking. It was a slight consolation to know that she was near and that visits were permitted, but the eagerness with which Beth mounted her horse told Philippa more plainly than words that her child was lost to her.

'Do you really expect there will be trouble?' she asked uneasily.

'There is already trouble,' Geoffrey told her. 'John Ball has an army of thirty thousand and their leader is a man of great personality called Wat Tyler. The King and his Council have taken up residence in the Tower though the King, being young, wishes to meet with the rebels and listen to their demands. If the Duke were here then I would be less worried but he has his army in Yorkshire.'

Philippa hoped silently that the Duke would remain in Yorkshire. The peasants would kill him if they ever caught him. No man in England was more hated, and the old canard about his not being the true son of the late King had been revived with damaging effect since these bitter and starving men were past listening to reason.

'You will not be required to leave the house, will you?' she asked.

'Not if I can avoid it,' he said drily. 'However, my dear, you must not rely solely on me for any hopes of protection. My days of brawling are over. We shall both put our trust in our stout defences and the loyalty of our servants.'

He spoke lightly but there was a hopeful look on his face as if he waited for her to say something. Irritably she said,

'Oh, I would not depend on you for protection, you may be sure. You would be writing a poem even while the mob was breaking into the house.'

But the sounds that reached her from the other side of the river when she ventured out briefly into the orchard sent her indoors again, to snatch up a piece of sewing on which she could fix her frightened thoughts.

There was no cause for alarm, she told herself. She was not responsible for the poverty and wretchedness of the peasants; their anger was turned against the Council and perhaps those who like Geoffrey carried out the wishes of the Council. But the sounds penetrated to where she sat and as darkness fell she looked out of the window and saw flames licking the sky.

'They are setting the city ablaze,' she said, her face whitening.

'I have to go out,' said Geoffrey abruptly.

'Don't be a fool! What can you possibly do?' she demanded.

'I have business the other side of the river.' He put her aside, not roughly but firmly, and went down the stairs.

What business could take him out of the security of Aldgate to where the rioting mob was burning and looting? Philippa repressed an urge to yell after him and sat down by the open window. Geoffrey would please himself, she supposed. Since her conversation with Katherine they had lived in the same house but never been further apart. Perhaps when this riot was over she would find an opportunity to improve matters.

Geoffrey didn't return that night and having dozed in fits and starts Philippa rose and sent two of the servants out to discover what had been happening. They came back with expressions composed of mingled excitement and dread.

'His Grace is riding out to meet with Wat Tyler this morning on Blackheath, to discuss new laws and grant pardon,' one of them said.

'The Princess Joan was caught by the Kentishmen but they let her go. She's in the Tower now with the King and most of the Council. Archbishop Sudbury's been killed and his head stuck on a pole and Sir Simon Burley too. That's why they'll be needing the pardons.'

'Have you seen Master Chaucer?' she asked impatiently.

They shook their heads and one of them said,

'We couldn't find a boat to take us across the river. The Palace of the Savoy is torched.'

'What?' The colour ebbed from her face. 'What are you saying?'

'Whole place was gutted,' the other said, not without a certain relish. 'All the fine furniture and the hangings destroyed and the windows smashed and everything else burned.'

She remembered her first sight of the Duke's magnificent palace, the room she had occupied where he had come to her when he could, the grounds with their trees and carp ponds and tiny gilded summer-house where she had often sat.

'Was anyone hurt?' she heard herself ask.

'Not many were home,' came the reassuring answer.

Thank God for that! Had John been in residence they would have torn him to pieces. She hoped his son Henry and the little Bohun bride were safe in the Tower with the rest of the family.

She dismissed the servants and went through a side door into the garden. If the King was meeting with the rebels then the immediate danger was over. She wished that Geoffrey would come home. But the day wore on and he didn't come. She kept the shutters up at the lower windows and despatched a couple of men to seek him out, but they returned with a garbled tale of Wat Tyler having been killed and of King Richard's galloping across Blackheath towards the rebels, crying, 'I myself will be your leader!'

'That saved the day for they cheered His Grace to the echo and swore they'd trust him to set everything right for them.'

'But did you hear any word of Master Chaucer?' she persisted.

They shook their heads and she dismissed them abruptly, holding in her anxiety. If anything had happened to him – he was past forty, no longer young

and apt to puff and pant a little after any exertion. If he
– when he came back she would make a special effort to
be nice to him.

It was dusk and she had ordered the candles to be
lighted when he came back, swathed in his thick cloak
with his beard uncombed and his eyes red rimmed with
fatigue.

'Is it true the rebels burned down the Savoy?' she
demanded.

She hadn't intended to greet him with that, but the
words spilled out despite her resolve.

'Yes, quite true,' he said. 'The King, God bless him,
prevented massacre by offering to take Tyler's place as
leader and right all the wrongs of which the peasants
complain. It will not happen, of course. Wiser and more
cynical counsels will prevail. Have you any milk?'

'Milk?' Philippa, her hand poised over the wine jug,
looked at him. 'You want milk?'

'For the babe, until we can find a wetnurse.'

He was carefully unfolding himself out of the heavy
cloak, revealing a bundle held in the crook of his arm.

'What the devil are you doing with a baby?' Philippa
said in astonishment.

'The mother died last night,' Geoffrey said. 'She was
very sick and the alarm of the rebellion proved too great
for her.'

'But why did you bring it here?' She went closer,
peering at the tiny screwed-up face.

'The girl, Cecily Champain, was not married. The
boy's grandparents cannot bring it up.'

'But why should you?' Her voice rose into a squeak.

'Lewis is my son,' said Geoffrey.

'That's not poss –'

'It is perfectly possible, my dear. Because neither
Beth nor Tamkin are my true children doesn't mean I
am incapable of fatherhood. Cecily was my one
excursion into unfaithfulness.'

'You are bringing your bastard into this house?' Her hands clenched.

'Didn't you?' he enquired with delicate malice, and left the room, holding the bundle with care.

(iii)

It was foolish of her to come here, but some instinct stronger than reason had drawn her. She told the two servants who had escorted her to wait at a distance and ridden on up to the blackened ruins and overgrown gardens of what had been the most magnificent palace in London. Dismounting she tethered her horse to a post and walked slowly on. After almost a year it was difficult to make out the design of the original building.

She was not alone. Turning a corner she stopped short, knowing now why she had come, her eyes on the man who stood looking up at a wall where blackened carvings still bore traces of gold paint. After a moment he became aware of her presence and turned, his sombre face lighting into a smile that hurt her heart.

'Philippa, would you believe I was thinking about you not long since?' he said. 'How are you?'

'Well, my Lord.' She dipped a curtsy.

'This will be rebuilt,' he said as if she had asked a question. 'This will be the finest palace in London again.'

She wondered if he had learned yet that it was never possible to rebuild when more than stone and wood had been destroyed. Then she saw the darkness at the back of the blue eyes and knew that he had learned hard lessons.

'I came to see,' she said. 'I am leaving London soon.'

'Oh?' He cocked an eyebrow in the way she remembered.

'Geoffrey has been offered a post as Chief Customs Officer at Hythe so we shall spend some years there. It will be a change to be in the country again.'

'I hope he will not be long away. The King needs such men about him.'

They were talking as stiffly as strangers. He seemed to realise it too and said,

'But political appointments are poor subjects for conversation. How are you really, Philippa? I heard that you have a son now.'

'Lewis,' she said briefly. 'He is Geoffrey's son, legally adopted.'

'I heard something of it. And Beth is in the convent at Barking.'

'You sent the community at Barking a very handsome gift,' she said awkwardly.

'Why should I not? I want the best for her, for all my children.'

'Do you –?' She hesitated.

'I have not seen either Katherine or her children since I went to Dover to try to raise the taxes. She went on pilgrimage, I believe. She has the right to her own life.'

'She didn't leave you because she wished it,' Philippa said.

'She has communicated with you?' He gave her a sharp glance.

'I told her that Beth and Tamkin were your children,' she said. 'I told her that we had been lovers. She left because of that, because she believed that I still loved you. She left because of that.'

His revenge would be savage, Geoffrey had said, and for an instant seeing flame leap into his face she quailed, but the rage was gone as soon as glimpsed, and his voice when he next spoke was weary.

'Had she still been at the Savoy she might have been killed. So I owe you her life at least. Perhaps good does come out of evil. You and Geoffrey are still together though.'

'We live in the same house,' she said, as wearily as he.

'Perhaps all will yet go well.' His voice mocked the vain hope of happiness. 'I wish you no hurt, Philippa. I never did.'

'What will you do?' she ventured.

'I am reconciled with Constantia,' he said and his smile was bitter. 'As soon as the King's marriage to Anne of Bohemia has been consummated I shall probably go abroad. I am still King of Castille, you know.'

'Will you retain Tamkin in your service?' she asked.

'Of course. You are generous, Philippa.'

'No,' she said. 'No, John, I was never really generous at all.'

And she walked slowly away without looking back.

Epilogue

The invitation had taken her completely by surprise.
After four years' silence the sight of the letter with the
Lancaster crest on it and the seal of scarlet made her
hands tremble.

'My well beloved Philippa Chaucer,
'It is the pleasure of His Grace King Richard that
you be installed into the Fellowship of Lincoln
Cathedral on the ninth day of February next.
Please indicate your acceptance to this bearer.
'My heartiest good wishes to Geoffrey and your
children,
'Your affectionate friend,
'John, Duke of Lancaster.'

'What on earth does it mean?' she demanded of
Geoffrey.
'A Fellow of Lincoln Cathedral has a vote on the City
Council and a percentage of all profits made by the wool
staple of the city,' he told her. 'It is an honour, my dear.'
A final sop to John's conscience, she thought, or a
sign that he had forgiven her for telling Katherine?
Whatever his reasons she felt apprehensive.
'You will accompany me?' She gave him a pleading
look.
Geoffrey shook his head.
'I have news of my own,' he told her. 'The King

231

wishes me to return to London where I can attend him when necessary at Court. The Queen was so delighted with my work on Troilus and Cressida that she wishes to extend her patronage. As I am too old to rush backwards and forwards between Kent and the capital I have decided to resume my tenancy at Aldgate.'

'But what of me?' There was dismay in her voice. That all this should have been settled without one word to her displayed only too clearly the gulf that yawned between them.

'My dear, your pension makes you financially independent,' he said patiently. 'This house was bought in our joint names. You have every right to continue to live here or to live with me at Aldgate.'

'Which do you want?'

'I wanted a wife,' he said wryly.

'And Lewis? Where is Lewis to go? He regards me as his mother.'

It was odd that the five-year-old Lewis seemed more her child than either Beth or Tamkin. Beth had taken her final vows the previous summer, her round face serene and rosy within its whimple. The Duke had sent a handsome dowry to Barking. Tamkin was in the Duke's service as page and on his rare visits home talked only of horses and archery practice. There had been a difficult interview with him when he had fixed his bright blue eyes on her and asked,

'Am I the Duke's son?'

'Yes.' She had no choice but to give the simple, straightforward answer.

His fair skin had flushed scarlet, and then he had raised his young head, saying with a little quiver in his voice,

'So though I am Tamkin Chaucer I am also Gaunt's bastard. Thank you for telling me.'

'Geoffrey loves you like a son,' she had protested, but his smile had been older than his years.

Since then she noticed he seldom came and when he did he treated Geoffrey as though he were a favourite uncle and avoided saying 'Father'.

But Lewis belonged to both of them. She was surprised at how closely this miniature edition of Geoffrey had twined himself about her heart. He was like his father in his passion for books, and had already told her solemnly that he was going to the university when he was a big boy.

'I shall not deprive you of Lewis,' Geoffrey had said. 'He will begin school soon, but he still needs a mother more than a father. We can come to some amicable arrangement should you choose to remain in Kent.'

They had left the matter there. She would make up her mind later, she decided, when she had endured the trauma of seeing the Duke again.

She had sent her formal acceptance and shortly afterwards begun her journey into the north-east. A mild winter had made the roads easier than usual and in the fields past which she and her escorts rode the sowers were already out, spraying seed as they toiled over their strips of land. She hoped that the harvest would be a plentiful one. In the years since the revolt all the promises the idealistic young king had made had been revoked by his Council and the collar of serfdom bit deeply into the callused necks of many. If this year's harvest was good they would hate John of Gaunt less, she thought, and marvelled that she should still care.

They were to lodge at the Mayor's house, a handsome mansion within walking distance of the elegant cathedral. When the flat countryside with its frieze of windmills came into sight after a week's travelling she heaved a sigh of relief. The inns where they had stayed had not met her standards of cleanliness and the pain in her side was troubling her again.

The pain had been coming and going for months though she rubbed it with coltsfoot ointment, but at forty-four she expected to suffer from the aches of advancing years. Yet she prided herself that she didn't yet look like an elderly person. Her brown hair was sprinkled with grey but she dyed it carefully with henna to restore its richness of shade and the judicious use of paint lessened the crepiness of neck and eyelids. From time to time she also tried to curb her appetite for sweetmeats, but her willpower inevitably faltered. Nevertheless she was still a pretty woman, neat in her travelling-dress and cloak with one of the new-fangled wide head-dresses fixed securely over her veil.

Dismounting at last she dismissed her escorts with a smiling injunction not to drink themselves into a stupor before their return journey – advice she feared would be ignored – and was conducted by the butler to a small but well appointed chamber.

There was warm water to wash in and a maidservant to help her into the gown of pink and brown she had brought with her for the banquet. When she was ready she hesitated and then pinned on the brooch that had been the Duke's gift so long ago. The twigs of gold still supported the tiny flowers with their hearts of diamond, topaz, ruby, garnet and pearl. On the rare occasions she looked at it she was always struck by the way the golden twigs plaited themselves together into a knot.

The banqueting-hall was far smaller than many in which she had supped but it was a superb apartment, the walls panelled in the latest style, two fires blazing, the high table laid with crystal and silver. The hall was crowded and as the herald announced her she felt an old frisson of nervousness. Geoffrey ought to have come with her and not left her to make the long walk to where the Duke waited to receive.

He had aged less than Geoffrey, keeping his figure and thick yellow hair only slightly faded since the day she had first laid eyes on him, and he was magnificently attired, but her eyes swept over him, resting on the

figure at his side. It wasn't possible but there stood her
sister, a tall, slender wand of a woman in a grass-green
gown, her hair flowing from a silver hennin that further
increased her height.

'Welcome, Philippa.' John bent to kiss her cheek,
preventing her from curtsying. 'As ever you look very
pretty. I am delighted that you accepted the Fellowship.'

She could not have uttered a word had her life
depended on it. Fortunately she was spared by
Katherine who stepped forward, embracing her,
exclaiming in her soft voice,

'Oh, Philippa, this is such a day!'

'It certainly appears to be,' said Philippa weakly,
finding her voice.

'John and I are reconciled at last,' said Katherine,
taking Philippa's hand and leading her to the dais. 'He
came to see me and we talked – or the Duke talked and I
listened. Had it not been for what you told me I would
never have fled from the Savoy and I might well have
been killed on the night it was burnt. I went on
pilgrimage, you know, from shrine to shrine, seeking an
answer to so many questions, but there are none. We
each choose to be happy or unhappy, and I cannot
imagine happiness without John. We shall give our
excuses at the Judgement Seat, but if we are condemned
we shall neither of us regret our loving.'

It was obvious that they still loved. The Duke even
while he nodded amiably in Philippa's direction kept his
eyes on Katherine. And Katherine glowed like a girl.
She was past forty but her tanned skin was smooth and
silver threads lay like a patina of frost over her vivid
hair.

'Tell me about your children,' said Philippa, taking a
goblet of wine that waited at her place and sipping it
gratefully.

'All of them? For I count John's children as mine,'
said Katherine laughing. 'His daughter Marie is named

as Prioress of her convent. She is not yet thirty so it is a
great honour. And Philippa and Elizabeth are to be
married. Pippa is to wed King Jao of Portugal and Liz is
to marry Sir John Holland. They are both good
matches. And Henry's wife has a son, named Hal.'

'The Duke is a grandfather then?' If she repeated it
often enough to herself she might begin to credit it.

'As for my own children.' Katherine drew a long
breath. 'Blanchette has taken her vows. I wish she had
chosen marriage but she has a genuine vocation, I think.
Your Beth also entered the religious life.'

'Also against my wishes,' said Philippa wryly.

The two sisters glanced at each other with a rare
accord.

'Thomas is a squire in the service of the King,'
Katherine was continuing. 'He is very like Hugh, poor
mannikin. Johnny is also page with the Court; Harry is
enrolled in a seminary, quite determined on becoming a
priest; Tom is also a page and my Joan is with me. She is
much like the Princess Joan, God rest her sweet soul,
but we are hoping she embarks on fewer husbands.'

And suddenly they were both giggling like girls while
the musicians began to play.

'But what of you?' Katherine's grey eyes were bright
with interest. 'How is Geoffrey?'

'He is recalled to Court,' said Philippa. 'The Queen is
a great admirer of his poetry. He is now planning a
collection of stories set within the framework of a
pilgrimage to Canterbury. I have not actually read any
of it yet, but it will make his reputation.'

'You love your husband very much, don't you?' said
Katherine.

For a moment Philippa hesitated. It was the Duke
whom she loved, she thought in confusion. She had
been snared in his golden net when she was only a girl.
Dazzling, hated John of Gaunt who had loved two
women deeply and several briefly. She thought of

Geoffrey with his chunky frame, his dry humour, the expression of undeclared hope in his eyes when he had given her the choice of staying in Kent or returning to Aldgate. He had wanted a wife, she recalled, and a wife was not a woman who wasted her years in lusting after a man who no longer loved her.

'Oh, we rub along together very comfortably,' she said, and wondered if the house in Aldgate would require much cleaning when she and Lewis went home. When all this high-toned nonsense of Fellowships was over it would be a real treat to inspect her kitchens and work in her herb garden again. And if she found leisure she would ask Geoffrey to read her his latest poem.

Afterword

In 1387, the year after she had been admitted to the Fellowship of Lincoln Cathedral, Philippa Chaucer died. She didn't live to see the triumph of her husband's *Canterbury Tales*. Geoffrey himself didn't live to complete them but died in 1400, retired from his duties at Court.

Of their children Beth died in obscurity as a nun, Tamkin became Constable of Taunton Castle and a wealthy landowner, Lewis took his degree at Oxford and became a courtier.

In 1396, after the death of Duchess Constantia, John of Gaunt finally married his mistress, Katherine, and died three years later. Katherine outlived him by four years. Of the children she bore to the Duke her son Johnny married a granddaughter of Joan of Kent and founded the royal lines of Tudor and Stuart. Her daughter, Joan, became grandmother of Edward IV and Richard III. Her son Harry became a cardinal. Her son Tom took his degree at Oxford and also became a courtier.

John of Gaunt's eldest son by the Duchess Blanche forced the abdication of his cousin Richard II who was imprisoned in Pontefract Castle and there murdered with the connivance of Thomas Swynford, Constable, Katherine's legitimate son by Sir Hugh Swynford.

Henry ascended the throne as King Henry IV and began again the campaigns against France which would culminate in the victory of his son, Prince Hal, at Agincourt.